"Still, I owe you a debt," he said in a whisper. "Tell me, is there really nothing you need?"

The smile on her face faded. Besides a kiss from him? A night in his arms? She'd once thought she could give up her virtue for one night with the unattainable earl. But...she had her pride. She stiffed her posture, remembering painfully that he was not for her to fantasize about anymore. "No."

"Well, if you change your mind, do speak up" he said, seeming to gulp. "You're an attractive young woman. Marriage must be on your mind. If I can ever introduce you to any eligible bachelors, find a way to let me know."

Charlotte closed her eyes, cut to the quick by his seemingly generous offer. It was kind of him, but she couldn't seriously let the man she still secretly loved help her find a husband she might never have feelings for.

HEATHER BOYD

USAT BESTSELLING AUTHOR

SEDUCED IN SECRET

Distinguished Rogues

18

SEDUCED IN SECRET © 2021 by Heather Boyd
ISBN: 978-1-925239-94-2
Editing by Kelli Collins

Chapter One

August 1816
  Hill Street, London

Charlotte Waters complained and cursed—under her breath, of course—but it was no use. They were going to be late because her parents only hurried when it served their interests. Now she was in danger of missing the most important announcement of the season…and her life.

Papa set his hat over his steely gray hair with great ceremony. "Well, I think I'm ready to go out. What of you, Mrs. Waters?"

"I feel I've forgotten something," Mama muttered, looking around and patting her sides.

"You've forgotten nothing, Mama," Charlotte promised, trying not to roll her eyes even as she put an arm behind her mother's back. Mother had once left port without Charlotte, her only daughter, *and* their luggage. She hadn't returned for the luggage—and Charlotte—for close to a month. To say Charlotte was forgotten by her parents most of the time was an understatement. She'd learned to look out for herself the hard way. "We must go."

Mother took a step toward the door, but Father unfortunately didn't.

"I say, Mrs. Waters, did you perchance have time to read the mail this morning?" he asked. "There was a letter sent by the Duke of Falconbridge. I put it by your chair earlier."

"I did indeed see it, Mr. Waters," Mama replied. "It is an intriguing idea to go back and examine what we first saw through the lens of long experience. Our first collaboration was where it all began for us."

"He's described a well-funded venture for a change, too," Papa said with a delighted chuckle and sparkling eyes. "There would be no half measures or hardship when you travel on a peer's unlimited account. Not like the first time, eh? We nearly had to tote our own trunks through the desert that first year."

Charlotte pressed against her mother's side, hoping to move her by sheer body weight alone. Unfortunately, Mama was quite tall and had excellent muscle tone and resisted initially.

But Charlotte persevered and she managed to maneuver her mother out to the top step. "There's not a moment to lose."

"Yes, there is much to be done," her mother assured her, turning to cup Charlotte's cheek. It might have been endearing if Mama's full attention had remained upon Charlotte for longer than a heartbeat. She turned back to Father, who had thankfully followed them outside. "I think it could not come at a better time for us," Mama replied.

Charlotte grabbed both her parents by the hand and towed them down the front steps as fast as she could while they continued their conversation. The carriage had been waiting half an hour already to take them into the heart of London. Charlotte bullied her father to enter the carriage first, and then her mother followed, of course.

Only then did Charlotte settle herself into the carriage and give the order to depart.

If Charlotte left it to her father to provide the coachman with instructions, they might still be sitting before the house for a week while her parents debated which roads to travel to reach their destination. Father did enjoy the sound of his own voice, and Mama loved nothing more than to debate every issue. The only thing they ever agreed about immediately was the importance of their work translating obscure historical texts. Their obsession with the history of far-flung places surpassed their interest in anything nearby.

While her parents continued their conversation about Falconbridge's letter and their work, Charlotte tuned them out and strove to calm her racing heart. This might just be the most terrible day of her life, and her parents had no idea of her anxiety. It was rumored to be the day a most important wedding date was announced, officially, with the calling of the banns for an arranged marriage.

The cream of the *ton* could be in attendance today.

But only one person mattered. A man. And not just any man. The earl Charlotte loved in vain. She wanted one last long look at Lord Hurlston as a bachelor before he took the fatal step toward becoming a married man.

The calling of the banns would make him *officially* unavailable forever.

Although Hurlston could hardly be aware of her existence, Charlotte was determined to be there to support him today. He was not marrying for money or love—well perhaps there was money involved though she'd not been privy to the details. He was doing his duty to please his family in a marriage arranged long before she'd ever met him.

Charlotte railed silently about that, as she always had when she considered his future. It was not fair. No one could love or admire Lord Hurlston more than she did. But she hadn't a chance to prove her worth to him and never could. Lord Hurlston had been betrothed since childhood to a neighboring family's daughter—Elizabeth Mayflower.

A lovely name, and she was reputed to be beautiful, too. Not that Charlotte had seen her yet. Few in society had, in fact. Hurlston had kept his bride in the country for years pending their marriage. But he was a permanent fixture in society and continued to frequent *tonnish* amusements as a carefree bachelor.

But not for long. If the banns were read today, he'd be married in a month. So, today Charlotte must swallow this last bitter draft and then try to put her hopeless admiration for the unattainable man firmly behind her.

First, Charlotte would witness the calling of the banns with a smile on her face. Wish him every happiness if she came close enough to him to speak a few words. She had not been privy to any actual discussions of the wedding, but wallflowers gossiped, which is why she'd known it was vital she attend church today.

She peered out the window, anxious that their carriage stop for nothing. She had to see him…*Winston*. Charlotte had no qualms about admiring him from afar so long as he was not married. It might be her last chance to do so without guilt. He would of course spend the next weeks escorting his bride about Town, hanging on her every word and deed. He might even be so busy that they never spoke again.

To mark the occasion, if it came to pass, she would spend the remainder of this day mourning a love that could never be.

Charlotte swiveled to look at her parents, realizing they'd fallen silent. That only happened when they'd reached an agreement. "What was it about Falconbridge's letter that's so important?"

"My dear daughter, I despair of your flighty mind." Her father set his lips into a disapproving line. "You were told that Falconbridge has offered to fund our next expedition."

"Yes, in two years' time," she replied. The discussion about another trip to Africa had begun before their return to London and had raged between her restless parents every day since.

"No. Sooner than that. Funds have been committed for a voyage before winter sets in. No point wasting our time here in London when we could be doing something worthwhile."

Charlotte gaped at them, shocked. "But you promised to stay in London until I am married!"

Mama clucked her tongue. "Do not be shrill. Your father's work is important."

Charlotte braced herself into the seat. "And my life is not?"

At the start of the season, her parents had grudgingly promised to remain in London until she wed. Two consecutive seasons she'd been promised. Another expedition meant giving up on her dream to have a home and security, packing up her possessions, saying farewell to friends, and leaving Hurlston behind, too. Not that he'd notice her absence. But she would feel his, and everyone else's.

Charlotte might have enjoyed travel when she was younger, without knowing what she'd missed out on. Now she was keen to find herself a husband and start a family. She had dreamed all her life of having a place to call home. Somewhere that she'd stay longer than a few months. To have the same friends year after year and have a loving husband to kiss and talk to.

One glance at her parents' closed-off faces and tight lips told her all she needed to know. She could argue till she was blue in the face, scream until her throat was hurt, cry until she had no more tears to shed…but they'd made up their minds to go now rather than wait for her to marry.

They were taking Charlotte with them whether she liked it or not.

She feared they'd never want to return to England, and where would that leave her? Stranded in some faraway port, a spinster firmly on the shelf—her memory of ballrooms and dinner parties and dancing slowly fading.

Her parents had never been comfortable in England. Conforming to society's strict rules and expectations of engaging in conversation irritated them, but it pleased Charlotte very much. They thought nothing of dragging her into wilderness filled with dangerous creatures with sharp teeth. The only danger here was a rogue with ruin on his mind.

And none had considered Charlotte for that yet.

She let out a frustrated sigh. "Let me stay behind. Please. It would cost very little for room and board for me here."

Mother sighed, but it was Father who spoke to end the discussion. "Enough, daughter. Your place is with us."

Charlotte desperately wanted a settled life in England. She'd never have that if she let her parents drag her from pillar to post.

St. George's church suddenly came into view, and the sight of its tall spires darkened her heart even further. She could never have a life with Lord Hurlston as her husband—she'd always known that—but thanks to her parents' selfish obsession, she might be denied any life in England at all.

Charlotte wet her lips, trying to wipe the sadness from her heart. She usually enjoyed going out to mingle with society. But her parents' news was a double blow to her usual optimism.

She climbed out of the carriage ahead of her parents and waited, tapping her foot for them to join her on the steps. Her one consolation in coming to a place of worship was that here, they would not speak of shrunken heads and slaughtered monkeys wrapped in leaves roasting on fire pit coals at their feet. That sort of heathen cookery left most hostesses gasping for breath or fainting clean away. Was it any wonder invitations of late had been few and far between?

Here at church, the *ton* was always on display and on their best behavior and so were her parents. There might be a stern-faced matron or two seated beside a young gentleman looking green about the gills–unhappy to be going about in public so early in the day. But it was the place to observe families larger than her own. Everyone smiled and flattered at a ball. Here at church, not so much.

In church, her parents would be blessedly silent, and leave Charlotte to her newfound misery for at least half an hour.

The service had already started as they hurried to find any pew with room for three.

Charlotte looked eagerly for Hurlston's familiar face before she lowered herself to the hard bench. He was sitting in his usual pew, his eyes downcast to a book of prayer. Although the distance between them was great, she easily imagined his long dark lashes lying thick upon his cheeks and his fingers stroking the leather binding of his tome as they often did. His aristocratic nose was perfectly formed, his lips just the right shape. He was clever, too, and he'd a lovely voice for readings, which she'd shivered all the way through one glorious night in the company of mutual acquaintances.

He was a superb dancer as well. The movement of his long-muscled limbs had been a source of unending fascination from Charlotte's spot sitting among the wallflowers. Hurlston was a man built to inspire a lady to swoon. How lucky his past lovers must have been to deserve his intimate attention in their beds.

Charlotte was lucky to have danced with him a few times over the last season. A mutual friend convinced him to do it, of course, but dear God it had been glorious to be in his arms at last.

A smile suddenly curved his lips, and he glanced directly at a woman to his right. Charlotte didn't recognize the lady, but she feared the woman was his intended bride—Elizabeth.

Charlotte lowered her gaze to her hymn book quickly, fighting the ever-present sadness that came with thoughts of him tying the knot to another. Hurlston could never know that she admired him, but then, every lady in society did as well. They all knew that he was long-engaged to marry his Elizabeth.

The vicar paused and then delivered the news to the congregation—announcing the impending marriage of Lord Hurlston and Elizabeth Mayflower with a great deal of pleasure. The couple turned toward everyone and nodded their thanks when applause broke out.

For the first time, Charlotte could see her competition clearly.

So beautiful, his future bride. His Elizabeth—a perfect woman with long flaxen hair, styled in ringlets around a pale face. Eyes demurely downcast but for the occasional flash of green as she looked at Hurlston. The woman was without any flaw that Charlotte could detect from this distance. She forced a smile, but her soul felt like withering at the unflattering comparison to her own well-rounded measurements.

Charlotte set her hands to her churning belly and steeled herself to survive this loss with as much grace as possible. She'd never really had a chance to compete with someone like that for Lord Hurlston's affections. Why had she ever hoped he'd realize his mistake? A wallflower and a nobody with eccentric parents would make a poor wife for a popular earl.

Charlotte let the rest of the sermon flow over her without really hearing it. There was no comfort in religion. When the service came to an end, everyone stood. Charlotte delayed, wanting to wait until as late as possible to raise her face.

As the prospective bride and groom progressed down the aisle accepting congratulations, beams of sunlight struck their heads, and the sight caused many to sigh out loud. Hurlston would be a happily married man. It simply couldn't be any other way.

Hurlston passed her by without so much as a sideways glance and disappeared out the door. Charlotte brushed her cheek, discovering it wet with tears she'd not realized she'd been crying the whole time. She prayed no one noticed her distress, or if they did never asked her about it.

"Well, that's that then," she muttered to herself finally and stood at last.

This time, she did not need to urge her parents toward the

door. They seemed in quite a rush to return home, in fact. Charlotte dragged her feet, unable to feel any enthusiasm for home or the future. No one tried to delay her on the way out either. Why would they? She was just a wallflower. One of many unfortunate fixtures at balls and parties, invited to make up the numbers but rarely sought out. Like a lamp or a potted palm disguising an ugly corner.

On the street, standing out front of the church, was Aurora Hillcrest and the former Eugenia Hillcrest, now Mrs. Berringer. She wanted to go to them, but they were all gathered about Hurlston, being introduced to his intended bride.

Charlotte was about to suggest to her parents that they should move closer to her friends when Lord Hurlston's laugh suddenly rang out, firm and delighted.

She cringed at the sound. How could she seek to join her friends when they were likely talking about the rightness of his match right now?

He was so happy today, and she was heartbroken. It was better that nobody realized it. Charlotte walked away from him, following her parents. "Lovely sermon," she said as she caught up to them.

Lord Hurlston's large carriage appeared before the steps of the church, and he helped his bride and aged mother to enter. He joined them swiftly and, once seated, looked out the window at everyone. For one fleeting moment, their gazes met and held…and then he was driven off.

Mother nudged her. "Now that your father and I have finally agreed on a date for our departure we can begin to make our preparations."

She glanced at them, startled. "When did you decide that?"

"Just now. Were you not listening again? We leave August the twenty-fifth."

No, she had not been listening at all. She'd been too busy catching a last glimpse of her true love leave her behind. Charlotte did a quick calculation in her head. "But that's barely three weeks away! How am I to find a husband in three weeks?"

Mother clucked her tongue. "You've had five months with not a single suitor asking for your hand."

Charlotte glanced around hastily to make sure no one had heard that remark from her mother. "But I want to be married."

"Then you have three weeks to find a husband, and if you do not wed in that time, too, I expect you to come with us— without a single word of complaint," Father demanded.

"But—"

"Time and tide, daughter. Time and tide."

Charlotte might have rolled her eyes if not for the panic that assailed her. She had three weeks to find and marry a husband.

Impossible.

Chapter Two

"Thank you all for being here with us tonight as we begin our journey toward matrimony," Winston Bell, Earl of Hurlston and future husband, said, looking around the dining table of his Hanover Square townhouse where his family and friends lingered at the end of a long meal. He glanced down at Elizabeth and took her hand in his. "I think you can all agree, I'm a fortunate fellow to have found someone so special to join my family."

"Meant for each other since the cradle," Mr. Mayflower told everyone in a booming voice, his hands folded over his full belly. The man was undeniably happy, and it showed in every word he'd uttered since the dinner party started a few hours ago.

"Never mind that," Winston called, attempting to shut him up. He was trying to find the right words to express his appreciation for Elizabeth and the future they'd share together.

"We all know you're one smug bastard today, Hurlston," Scarsdale called out. "Just leave it at that, would you?"

Winston laughed. Perhaps he'd said enough already. Elizabeth's cheeks were already red from embarrassment again. "I suppose there will be other dinners where I can extol the virtues of my future bride."

Mother rose and whispered to him, "I think it time we ladies left the gentlemen to their port and cigars. Certain gentlemen are forgetting their manners."

Winston nodded. "As you prefer."

"Ladies, if you would follow me." Mother drew Elizabeth away from him. "Tea is waiting in the drawing room."

However, Winston needed to speak to Elizabeth tonight. Since Mr. Mayflower seemed distracted finally by conversation, it was the perfect time to slip away with his daughter. He drew his brother aside. "Peter, if you could stand in for me a moment."

"Of course."

Winston went out to the hall and found Elizabeth had waited for him there. "Come with me," he urged, directing her toward his study, where they could be alone. He shut them in and then went to his desk immediately. "I think you will find my offer acceptable," he murmured as he handed a sheaf of papers to his future bride. "The original marriage contract was not fair to you. Your father was grossly shortsighted."

"Father only cared about the connection to a great family, not my needs." Elizabeth took the papers from his hand and turned away to read their new bargain by candlelight.

Their betrothal agreement could not be altered, but another contract with Elizabeth could still be made. Winston thought he had been more than fair in improving upon the terms of their marriage contract. Ten thousand pounds for Elizabeth, exclusive use of a property in Bath, and a new traveling carriage for her use alone—to be delivered after their marriage.

The original marriage contract their fathers had signed granted Elizabeth a title, but very little else beyond responsibilities. Now, with his long-overdue correction, Elizabeth would have money of her own upon their marriage, a consideration he'd heard brides rarely got after a marriage contract had been signed more than a decade ago.

Winston wanted to be a good husband. Fair and generous with his wife. Their marriage was arranged, but he would always consider her needs. "Your father arranged the best match he could make for you at the time."

"So did yours," she murmured, eyes flashing with irritation.

"Yes, but a lot has changed since then," Winston murmured, hoping they would not descend into another squabble. The terms of the marriage contract had been a constant point of irritation between them for years now. Upon their marriage, Winston would become heir to Elizabeth's ancestral home and all the land surrounding it, since Mayflower had no male heir to inherit. An increase of one hundred acres of good farming pasture to his own family holdings of seven hundred.

"It's insufferable how he's already strutting around telling everyone he'll be related to the Earl of Hurlston," she complained.

"It will be the truth," Winston replied, but a sour taste was building in his mouth. Despite their long association, Winston did not particularly care for Elizabeth's father's habit of trading off their connection. Harold Mayflower was a pompous windbag at times too. Right now, he was probably extolling the virtues of the Hurlston estates as if they were his own. They had little in common but Elizabeth and for the sake of peace between the families, Winston overlooked a great many of Mr. Mayflower's outrageous boasts. Thankfully after the wedding, Winston still had reason to be in London more than the countryside.

In less than a month, before winter set in, Winston and Elizabeth would be man and wife at last. "Our marriage will make him happy."

"I suppose it must," she murmured, and then whipped around his desk to sign the papers.

Winston studied his wife-to-be from a distance. Locks pale and perfectly curled, skin without a blemish. There was a timelessness to her beauty few could match. And yet, he felt not the least bit moved by her. He supposed desire out of the bedchamber was largely unnecessary in an arranged match like his.

"When can I expect the funds?"

"Five thousand pounds will be available the day we wed. All you need to do is present that document to my banker, and the money will be yours to do with as you please. I care not what you spend it on."

"Five thousand?" She shook the papers at him. "This promises ten! You tricked me, just like your father did mine."

He held up both hands. Elizabeth was clearly still tired after her journey to London, and when she was tired, she often over-reacted to the slightest thing. It had been a long day, after all and he assumed she'd not read every word of the document. "As we discussed before, the balance is yours upon the safe arrival of my heir. My father did this with my mother, although his generosity was not as large as mine."

"Only two sons lived. You and Peter." Elizabeth shook her head, jaw clenched. "One hundred pounds apiece was all *she* got."

"Yes, and don't forget his enduring fidelity and love into the bargain." He sighed. "The hundred pounds was a mere token payment. Symbolic for them. But he lavished her with gifts all through the years of their marriage, too, I assure you. He used to say Mother was the real treasure in their marriage anyway. Just as you will be mine. You may run up bills all over town if you like before the wedding and I'll settle them without question."

Elizabeth stood abruptly from the desk. "I will be glad to see Bath again."

Winston winced. "There is the matter of my heir to discuss."

Her eyes widened. "So soon?"

Winston fidgeted. He must share Elizabeth's bed to get his heir and neither of them were getting any younger. "I would have liked to talk about intimacy between us before the banns were read, but there was little opportunity for so personal a discussion the way your father hovers about."

She looked at him with an alarmed expression.

"For heaven's sake, don't think I'm about to pounce on you after all these years." He raked his fingers through his hair. "I want to discuss the getting of children. How we proceed etcetera when we wed. Please sit down so we can discuss this quietly."

He gestured her to a chair, and he sat beside her, uncomfortable. "I would never force myself upon you," he vowed. "Your wishes are important and nothing else needs to change between us."

She looked away, and he could see a blush brightening her cheeks to a deep shade of red.

"It is something we must do," he reminded her. "Soon after we wed."

She bobbed her head several times, agreeing silently with his suggestion.

He extended his hand to her, asking her to put her trust in him. Eventually she did, but he found her fingers cold. "It will be awkward, I know. We've known each other all our lives."

"Yes."

"But we'll muddle through this, just as we did our first kiss." He leaned toward her, smiling at the memory. "Now *that* was awkward, wasn't it?"

She stiffened. "I was terrified my father would find you with me and proclaim me wanton."

"I was eager and didn't consider the harm I could do to your reputation back then." Their relationship had never been physical. He'd kissed her hand many times at Christmas and on her birthday, and one time, managed to claim her lips in a long kiss. But it had felt odd, and she'd rebuffed his attempts to get her alone ever since. Now they were on the cusp of marriage, she didn't have to worry about her father catching them together and kissing. "The days of maintaining strict propriety are soon to be behind us," he promised.

She shrugged. "Some worries never leave a lady."

"True. But I vowed last month when I came to you, I would never give you any cause for concern."

Winston had gone to her to offer a way out of the marriage, if that had been her heart's desire, but was given assurances that becoming his countess was what she truly wanted.

So now it was time to get on with the rest of their life together. Now they could kiss anytime they had a chance. It might make sharing a bed on their wedding night easier if they became more familiar with each other beforehand.

He had started to lean in to kiss her cheek when Elizabeth suddenly stood. "It's been a long day and there are guests waiting for us, I'm sure. Your mother will be wondering where I am."

"I told her I wanted to speak to you alone tonight and she thought it a fine idea," he advised, a bit disappointed she moved so fast to stand. "Run along if you must. I'll return to the gentlemen and we'll join you ladies shortly."

"Very well," she murmured, before sweeping from the room.

When he was sure she was gone far enough away not to hear him, Winston let out a loud groan. Discussions with Elizabeth about bedding her had made him unusually tense. He hurried to pour himself a drink and decided to sit at his desk for a moment to collect his thoughts before he rejoined the others.

The thought of marriage filled him with a mixture of excitement and utter dread. It wasn't that he didn't like Elizabeth. He admired her, knew her past and nature as well as his own. But he didn't love her.

Despite that, their bargain, the money, and freedom he promised her, would go a long way toward smoothing over any future irritation between them. Her father had been quite strict with her spending over the years, and she'd come to resent him for his tightfisted ways.

Winston shuffled the papers, glad to have one more matter out of the way. He put them in the desk drawer to deal with first thing tomorrow morning. His solicitor thought him mad to waste money on a wife when he hadn't needed to.

He heard a step at the door. "Is she gone?"

"I thought you had agreed to take my place, brother?"

"Mayflower's taken over the proceedings again so I came to see what you were up to."

"As you can see," he murmured, "there is always so much to do."

Lord Peter Bell, Winston's younger brother by ten years, scowled. "Always working. You're no fun anymore."

Winston shook his head. He was the eldest and his days of larking off with friends was behind him now. "I'm doing my duty, of course."

"Duty?" he scoffed. "Is that all you can think about? Even tonight?"

"It is important," he promised. "Especially tonight."

Marriage was a serious business.

"You should be out there drinking with your friends, not letting Mayflower rule the roost."

"I'll rejoin everyone in a moment."

He locked the drawer and hid the key in its usual place and discreetly studied his brother. Peter Bell was rounder where Winston was lean. Peter loved to drink and enjoyed good food in excess. Darker of hair than Winston, and he kept it long just to irk their mother, too. Peter smiled constantly, loved to tease, but could hardly sit still for long enough to learn. He'd make a terrible earl with responsibilities.

Winston was more bookish and had inherited his father's title in the last two years, though he tried to find ways to cope with the added pressure. He rode every day for exercise and to clear his head, visited Gentleman Jackson's once a week to box to maintain a trim figure and vent any frustrations that darkened his mood. He enjoyed London society, found great pleasure in watching the games others played out in their love lives, and he adored his family…Mother, even his rascal of a brother —even if he was too busy to *play* the way Peter still expected him too.

Life would be quite dull without his brother constantly reminding him not to become obsessed with increasing the family fortune. "What are you really doing here?"

"Is it wrong I should want to spend time with my brother?"

"You've been avoiding me for weeks," Winston reminded him. "Since I wouldn't buy you that phaeton you fancied."

Peter suddenly sat down, hands dangling between his knees. "Do you feel different? Panicked? Now you're about to be leg-shackled? I can cover for you while you make an escape. Perhaps flee to the continent."

"No."

Peter had always made it clear he had a low opinion of arranged marriages, especially Winston's to Elizabeth. He'd thought the notion of them together was absurd and said so often.

Peter hooked one leg over the arm of the chair and then the second joined the first. "How's the mood of your future bride when you talked to her alone tonight? Was she a proper young lady or was she braver than usual and let you make love to her?"

Winston smiled tightly, pretending amusement at the question rather than reveal the awkwardness he felt. "Her mood tonight, or any other night, is really none of your business, and I will remind you one final time to be respectful toward her."

Peter laughed softly. "I suppose now she's almost family, I'd better do the pretty by her or risk being sent to my room without supper."

Winston scowled. "I'd prefer you offer no false affection to my future bride. She's nearly your sister."

Peter's smile dropped away. "I never asked for a sister."

Winston grimaced. Peter had never liked Elizabeth. The pair never warmed to each other despite all the years spent rubbing shoulders. They were neighbors and it had been impossible for them to avoid each other. "You'd have been burdened with a sister no matter whom I married," he said quietly.

"It could have been anyone but her," Peter complained, bursting to his feet. "There's still time to wriggle out of the obligation or even run from it. You don't love her."

"Enough." He squared his shoulders, angry that even now, Peter would still not accept the way things must be, tonight of all nights. "Go. Find something to amuse yourself rather than bothering me with your own doubts. But I don't want to learn you spent more than your allowance before your birthday arrives. I told you, I won't pay any debts beyond that sum no matter what."

"Tight fist," Peter muttered under his breath and then offered a false smile. "I'll make myself scarce and leave you to enjoy what little freedom you have left."

"I will be busy tomorrow," Winston murmured. He intended to spend the morning with his future wife. "I'll see you at dinner. I've a full schedule tomorrow. What will you do with your day?"

"I've no idea. Something fun and energetic. Unplanned. Spontaneous. Do you remember what that was like? To do something completely unpredictable. To just go out alone because you could."

"Good night, brother," he replied, ignoring the jibe that he'd become set in his ways. "Try not to start a riot before dawn."

Winston stood and pulled down his waistcoat and watched his brother go with a heavy heart. Peter always could say just the right thing to get under his skin, but Winston was definitely too old for chasing him through the house and turning him upside down, as he had when Peter was a child. Though he might do that with his own son one day soon.

That thought cheered him momentarily.

But nervousness filled him at the idea of bedding his bride. Marriage and women were the great unknown for him still.

Winston strolled back out to the hall to where his friends remained drinking and smoking his cigars and joined in with the conversation.

He had a good life. Even if it was not the grand unpredictable adventure Peter craved.

Chapter Three

Charlotte covered her mouth and screamed.

She felt foolish, but her friends Aurora and Eugenia had assured her that venting her frustrations out loud would do her nerves a world of good. She collected herself when it was over and glanced around guiltily, hoping no one important had been nearby to hear her outburst.

Society, she was resigned to see, moved on without the slightest interest in what she'd been doing.

"Does that help at all, dearest?" Aurora Hillcrest asked, her face full of concern and hope.

Charlotte lowered her hands from her mouth slowly. "Yes, and that was so unlike me, I may have to do it again someday soon."

Aurora laughed softly. "No one heard or noticed."

"You were not even terribly loud," Mrs. Eugenia Berringer promised with a soft laugh of her own. "Now down to business."

Charlotte truly had the best friends. They had answered her panicked message last night, suggested meeting first thing so they could talk privately away from prying ears, and likely disapproval. Although they promised her all would be well if she expressed her pent-up panic to begin feeling calm, the anxiety remained.

She was worried. "I *need* to take control of my own life and stop waiting for fate to deliver me the perfect husband. He does not exist."

Eugenia pulled a face. "There's still hope you could marry for love though."

"I would like to believe that, but the facts are staring me in the face. My parents demand I marry or go with them. I have exactly three weeks to achieve that end. It's time I stopped waiting for a handsome prince to save me. I'll probably have to save myself, and him, too!"

"With only three weeks for a courtship, you will most likely have to marry by special license."

Charlotte hadn't the luxury of time to waste on a proper courtship. She needed a husband now. "I have my own funds to pay for a special license if my potential husband is hesitant to put up the blunt for it, but how is one arranged?"

"Thaddeus would be happy to explain that, if and when you take him into your confidence," Eugenia suggested. "He's had first-hand experience with the process of applying for us when we married. We might see him this morning, too. He left early to go riding with the duke."

"Oh." Charlotte spun about as horses thundered past on Rotten Row, peering at each rider in turn. She hadn't planned on revealing her desperate situation beyond her closest friends. But Eugenia was married now, and she suspected she and Mr. Berringer kept few secrets from each other. She might as well confide in him, too, she supposed. He'd always been kind to her. "Right, I will speak to him about this, though later when I need to. And, so, all I need now is the name of potential spouses."

"Well, we've already ruled out Pinner and Brandestock and a few others. Why not Lord Sullivan? He's still unwed," Aurora noted as they strolled a little farther under the watchful eye of the *ton*.

Charlotte twirled her parasol behind her head and considered the man mentioned. He was an earl and a gentleman. She could do worse but… "Lord Sullivan is nice enough, I suppose, but I don't think I'm what he's looking for in a wife. We've danced, but I've never noticed him looking at me with anything more than polite regard before."

"No one else seems to think they're what he's looking for either," Aurora grumbled. "He's worth considering anyway. At a pinch."

Eugenia sighed. "Few know the kind of spouse they need, really."

Charlotte grinned. "You made the right choice in Mr. Berringer, Eugenia. It's easy to see you are both happily wed."

"I am," Eugenia agreed. "But let's not be distracted from our mission. Today, tomorrow, and for however many days hence, our focus is on finding you a good man to marry."

"Thank you." Charlotte heaved a heavy sigh. If only her parents had ever had as much interest in her future as her friends did, she'd have been married long ago.

Aurora grinned. "Tell us what sort of man you really dream of, Charlotte. And no half-truths, my dear."

Charlotte folded her parasol when they moved under a trees and used it as a walking stick, stabbing the point into the ground. She would never tell the truth to anyone but her closest of friends. But she would always have to keep her feelings for Lord Hurlston to herself. There was no point mentioning him now. "Tall, but not so tall that it's awkward to kiss him."

"I'm glad to see you've thought of the essentials," Eugenia murmured with a delighted grin.

She laughed. "It's your fault if you think that's too brazen a consideration."

"Not brazen at all. This is a man you're going to kiss for the rest of your life. Should you have a sore neck for the whole of it?"

They all laughed together.

"I'd rather not. I want to kiss my husband on occasion."

"Was your heart set on marrying a lord?"

Her mind immediately turned to a certain unavailable earl. "No."

"What about someone less important but still prominent? A barrister or even a well-to-do banker would ensure a very comfortable life here in England."

"I am interested in anyone who will take me on at this point. I can hardly be particular, can I? I'm not seeking a love match. There's no time to dither and hope love will magically appear before my parents' departure date—"

Eugenia stopped her. "Charlotte, it will be a colder alliance than what we'd hoped for you. Are you sure there's no other way for you to stay?"

"No. They were quite clear." She steeled herself. "I'm sure I don't want to spend six months in a leaky boat, only to face years of living rough with only the barest of civilization about me," she replied firmly. "Marriage was always my first choice for my life. A home and family. Children playing at my feet during a long English winter and a kind husband eager to talk to me and kiss me. Companion or governess were second and third options, but my parents won't hear of either."

Aurora hugged Charlotte tightly to her side. "I wouldn't dream of letting you go for a governess if it can be avoided. Being a lady's companion is not without difficulties, though either, I must warn you. You would likely face lecherous scoundrels without honorable intentions in that role. I did. A husband is what you must have indeed."

Eugenia bit her lip. "Marriage is forever. But making a bad match might be worse than Charlotte's current future. The man she chooses to marry needs to be worthy of her, too, let's not forget. She'll have to live with him for the rest of her life. And don't forget she must welcome him into her bed if there are to be children."

Charlotte's cheeks warmed. She'd coped with crawling insects in her bed, snakes in her boots and leaking roofs for years at a time. Being afraid all the time was unpleasant. An English husband she hardly knew and didn't love might just be far easier on her nerves, especially if he was kind and the settling-down sort.

"Do you know I've spent three-quarters of my life living away from England? Every time we've returned, I have had to make new friends all over again because everyone I know had moved on with their lives while I was gone." She sighed. "My lack of family and connections has never helped with my appeal. Certainly, my parents' bookish tendencies do not. I cannot be choosy. Anyone at all would do for me at this point."

Aurora sighed. "Is it true that your parents once spent a night reading through the Duke of Exeter's library instead of attending the dinner they were the guests of honor for?"

"That is true. I was fourteen, excited to be home again, and they ruined it for me. His grace boasted that he had acquired a rare set of manuscripts before the first course was served," she confessed and put her hand over her face momentarily at the remembered embarrassment. "They fairly sprinted from the dining table, leaving me to make their apologies. That was not even the most embarrassing night out with them."

"I'm sure he won't make that mistake again," Eugenia promised. "He told me the tale with great amusement though so he wasn't offended."

"He might be the only one who isn't. Anyone who claims to know my parents should also know their attention span for people and conversation, especially upon first returning to England, is ridiculously short to the point of rudeness. I can hardly get them to notice *me*, and I'm always with them."

"Why didn't they leave you behind with family or put you in school since they seem rather disinterested in parenting you?"

She shrugged. "I asked them that once and do you know what happened? They told me to count to five, because I had raised my voice to catch their attention. When I repeated my question in a calmer voice, they claimed they had wanted to show me the world and then immediately went back to their work again."

"Worldly experience is something many would envy you for."

"But they didn't show me the world. They abandoned me to it, and to the care of indifferent servants. When I was older, I had to hire my own companions and they never cared to stay very long. I didn't bother replacing the last."

Charlotte really didn't know why her parents kept her around now she was older, other than the convenience of having someone to manage their household and see to it that their trunks were not lost on their journeys. Any paid servant could have done that for them. She was not special to them in any way, but familiar. Like a well-worn blanket or trusty parasol.

They started walking again. Aurora linked their arms and pulled Charlotte close to her side, likely in an attempt to cheer her up. Charlotte was usually better at hiding her resentment toward her parents, but every now and then it just came gushing out in a torrent. "I'm sorry. I shouldn't have said any of that to you."

"Nonsense. You can tell us anything and it's good to know how you really feel about things." Aurora suddenly laughed. "Our great adventure was the journey to London, and it must seem very minor compared to your wider travels. Our next adventure will be a visit to Lord Wharton's country estate."

"Yes, not long now," Eugenia murmured.

"I would gladly carry your luggage," Charlotte offered. "I so wanted to see Lord Wharton's estate. I've heard so much about it over the last months."

"I wish we could offer to go with you," Eugenia murmured. "It would break the duke's heart if Thaddeus left the country."

"I wouldn't offer to go with you," Aurora admitted, then

suddenly waved wildly to a horse and rider that thundered past. "There is just too much to my taste right here in London."

Even though the rider had been traveling at speed past them, Charlotte could easily tell the rider noticed Aurora's interest. That sort of masculine understanding had never happened for Charlotte and likely never would. She wasn't bitter about being overlooked by bachelors and scoundrels. Well, maybe just a little.

She wasn't hideous. Just shorter and rounder than most of her friends.

Charlotte turned to look around at Hyde Park's panorama and sighed heavily. "I will grieve for the loss of these views if I am forced to leave."

"Then we will do all in our power to help you stay in London with us, even if we have to take you in and hide you in the attics," Eugenia decided.

"No, I never want to be a burden to my friends." She lowered her gaze to the ground, cheeks burning with embarrassment at how tempting being hidden in an attic suddenly sounded. "But thank you from the bottom of my heart. It means a lot that you would offer."

Eugenia hugged her briefly. "I was afraid you'd say that. It will always be an option though. There's a ball to be held tonight. I'll speak to the Duchess of Exeter about adding you to our party. We'll pick you up after nine on the way there."

"I truly appreciate any help you can give. I can't expect any assistance from my parents."

Charlotte lifted her hand to brush the back of her neck and then swiftly looked around for a source of danger. The last time she'd felt such a sense of foreboding was in the presence of a hungry tiger.

She moved her gaze to the green lawns where others strolled, looking for any source of danger from that quarter. All she could see was a pair of horses being ridden across the green lawns at speed, weaving between couples and causing chaos and outcry from members of society.

Charlotte narrowed her eyes on them, attempting unsuccessfully to identify who they might be. "Aren't riders supposed to stick to the row and not the green lawns?" she asked her companions.

"They are."

She pointed the tip of her parasol toward the oncoming riders. "Those men are rather rude then. I do hope they stay away from us."

"I expect they'll be chased off before they injure someone," Aurora said, raising her hand to watch them a moment, too.

"Ho, wife of mine!"

They all spun about as Thaddeus Berringer swung down from his sweating horse and led it from the track in a rush to meet them. He didn't hesitate to kiss his wife passionately right then and there in front of everyone.

Aurora took the reins of his mount and fussed over the great beast.

Charlotte turned her back as well to keep track of those horsemen riding recklessly, giving the newly married couple privacy.

To her great surprise, the riders were much closer now. "What are they doing?"

Suddenly the horsemen stopped, seemed to consult each other, then pointed, it seemed, directly at Charlotte and her party. Her eyes widened as they took off directly toward their shaded spot.

Between Charlotte and the riders, however, a gentleman and an older lady strolled arm in arm.

And they were unaware of the danger headed toward their backs.

She gasped as she recognized Lord Hurlston, his aged

mother by his side. She cried out a warning to them, but Hurlston misunderstood and merely waved back at her.

"No!" she cried, as the horsemen bore down on the pair.

They were almost to them when Charlotte reacted with an instinct honed from her travels in dangerous places. She unfurled her parasol and thrust it ahead of her as she ran directly toward the earl and danger. Once past them, she twirled the parasol, hoping the swirling pattern might frighten off an easily startled animal like a horse.

Lord Hurlston and his mother cried out as the horsemen thundered past. So close, Charlotte could smell the sweat of the horses and feel the wind of their passage drag at her long skirts.

And then they were gone. Flying away across the green and out of Hyde Park entirely, without looking back even once or shouting an apology.

Charlotte snapped her parasol shut and worked to slow her breathing to normal, keeping close watch in case the horsemen returned. But the thrill of danger narrowly averted remained with her, and then worry soon settled in. She glanced behind her to make sure everyone was safe and that there were no other horses charging their way even now. "I think they are gone."

Suddenly, Charlotte was turned around by a pair of strong male hands on her shoulders. "What the hell were you thinking?"

She blinked up at Lord Hurlston, who seemed to be in a towering rage. "What was I thinking?"

His frown deepened, and he shook her once, gently. "Have you no sense? You could have been trampled!"

"At least it was only horses this time and not an unhappy elephant like the last time." She joked with a shrug and a nervous laugh.

No one laughed along with her, and she looked around.

Poor Lady Hurlston, though, held a gloved hand at her throat and her face was exceedingly pale. Fearing the woman was about to faint, Charlotte brushed off the earl's grip, and rushed to her side. "Are you all right, my lady?"

"I am not at all right!" Lady Hurlston cried, clutching Charlotte's hand tightly. "I would have been run down and killed but for you. Who were they?"

Charlotte felt the older woman trembling and looked about them for seating. But of course there was no place to sit a lady of her distinction anywhere close by in Hyde Park. She couldn't very well be asked to sit on the ground against a tree. Instead, Charlotte could only squeeze the lady's hands in hers. "I've no idea, but I am sure they have gone, my lady. You are quite safe now."

"My son might have been killed," Lady Hurlston nearly sobbed.

Afraid a complete collapse or faint was imminent, Charlotte risked putting an arm about the woman's back to support her. "He's as whole and as handsome as ever," she promised.

Charlotte urged the countess toward her son.

Mr. Berringer was standing beside Hurlston now and had his hands on his hips, staring off into the distance. "Bloody fools! The Park needs policing."

Lord Hurlston agreed and caught Charlotte's gaze. "I cannot believe a pair of riders almost ran us down in Hyde Park. They should have been on the row. Did anyone recognize them?"

Everyone demurred.

"I'm sorry. I never got a good enough look at their faces," Charlotte apologized. "They were moving too fast."

"Probably some ridiculous bet to be won," Berringer decided, shaking his fist at nothing.

"Yes, I suppose it could have been a wager of some sort," Charlotte agreed quickly. "They must have wanted to see how many people they could offend in under ten minutes."

"Ten?" Hurlston asked.

"I noticed them circling couples in the park not so long ago. Crisscrossing the lawn where anyone strolled," she told him. "Like most people, you didn't seem aware of them until they were almost upon you both."

That was probably the longest she'd ever spoken to Lord Hurlston about anything that hadn't involved mention of the weather. She glanced at his mother, who seemed much calmer now, and smiled.

Hurlston removed his hat and shuffled his feet. "I thought it was merely thunder."

Charlotte couldn't help but laugh, then quickly smothered it.

He frowned at her and put his hat back on. "What's funny in that?"

"Oh, nothing." She glanced up at the clear sky and then smiled at Lady Hurlston, who still seemed content with Charlotte's physical support. At least the lady was no longer trembling with fright. "I was just thinking of the weather at that moment. It's an otherwise lovely day for a stroll."

Hurlston looked up at the near cloudless sky above the park and grimaced. "It was a reasonable assumption on my part."

"Of course, my lord," she quickly assured him, though it was hard not to grin that an earl was defending himself to her. She was finally having a conversation with him. A pity it was too late to do her any good.

Hurlston reached for his mother's hand. "Mother?"

Charlotte let her arm fall away from the older woman's back.

"So much for the enjoyable stroll you promised we would have," Lady Hurlston said in a shaky voice. "I should have trusted my instincts and remained at home."

"This will never happen again," he promised, glancing Charlotte's way.

"Oh, I'm sure Lord Hurlston is correct," Charlotte added

with a reassuring smile. "Everyone is usually on their best behavior in Hyde Park at this time of day."

"Damn dangerous way to ride a horse," Berringer grumbled once more, before slapping Hurlston on the shoulder. "Well, they do look like they've gone, but we should keep an eye open in case the fools come back."

Charlotte agreed.

"I think we best return to our carriage and head home," Eugenia murmured, catching Charlotte's eye and nodding vigorously. Charlotte took that to mean they would continue their conversation later. "Would you care to walk with us, Lady Hurlston?"

The lady gestured to Charlotte. "I should be happy to, and I might never let this brave young lady out of my sight, so would someone please introduce us?"

Charlotte looked to Eugenia, but it was Lord Hurlston who performed the introductions, using her full name and mentioning her parents as well.

Charlotte quickly offered a curtsy.

"It is a pleasure to meet you," the lady said, but then her brow creased. "Your face seems familiar. Am I acquainted with your mother, perhaps?"

Charlotte nodded. Lady Hurlston and her mother were born in the same year. She knew that from studying the peerage during her first aborted season, when her interest in Lord Hurlston had been at its first peak. "Perhaps you came out together? Her name before marriage was Olivia Hemdale."

Her face brightened. "So we did, though I have not spoken to Olivia in many years now. I trust your mother is in good health. She always professed to have a robust constitution."

"Yes, indeed she is quite well," Charlotte promised. "My parents travel often, so it is not surprising you've not exchanged words in recent years."

"Miss Waters' parents are notoriously difficult to pin down

for conversation, Mama," Lord Hurlston murmured. "Don't ever mention additions to our library in their presence or they'll abandon you in an instant."

Charlotte winced.

But the lady nodded. "Is it because of their adventures that you encountered unhappy elephants?"

"Indeed, it is, unfortunately." She glanced at Lord Hurlston. His mother was quite upset. "Will you both walk with us, my lord? There can be safety in greater numbers."

"That seems a wise thing to do." Hurlston nodded. "Are you ready, Mama?"

"Indeed I am. I should never have let you persuade me to venture from the town house," she muttered softly to him.

Charlotte winced. She knew a fair bit about Lord Hurlston's mother, of course. Society loved to gossip about eccentrics like her parents, and recluses like his mother seemed to have become in recent years. Lady Hurlston was said to be deeply affected by the loss of her husband two years ago. She had mostly kept to herself this season, eschewing the usual London amusements for the quiet of home. But she always traveled where her eldest son went.

They fell into step, heading back the way they came, and surprisingly Charlotte ended up with Lord Hurlston on her other side.

"I am in your debt for the timely warning," he murmured quietly after a few steps. "Thank you."

"Think nothing of it, my lord."

"I could not do that. I wasn't paying attention, and I ought to have been."

"Hyde Park can be as dangerous a place as anywhere in the world," she promised him. "We must all do our best to look out for each other."

"Is that what you learned while traveling, frightening off elephants with just that flimsy parasol you hold?"

She looked up at him slowly. "It pays to never take your safety for granted anywhere, my lord. One must use whatever comes to hand, in Hyde Park, in a ballroom, and in the jungle. Parasols come in handy in many situations, not just for beasts."

"I'll keep that in mind."

"Good."

He frowned. "I trust you've never needed to try your hand at fighting back savages or scoundrels with that thing."

"Shallow-water fishing," she replied with a tight grin. Charlotte *had* fired pistol shots at the feet of a savage once. Not that anyone needed to know that part of her past. Was it any wonder she never wanted to go back to that life?

When they reached the carriage, Lord Hurlston's was signaled to draw up behind the Berringer carriage. Although Lord Hurlston urged his mother toward his, the old lady dug in her heels and turned toward Charlotte.

"You must come for tea, and bring your mother, too," she said. "As my son said, we are forever in your debt."

"That is very kind of you, but I assure you, you have no obligation toward me," she promised, blushing fiercely. Although the honor of the invitation was great, the chances of getting Mother to socialize with anyone on the cusp of leaving the country were slim.

"We do owe you a great debt," Lord Hurlston promised. "You must come for tea, even if you mother has other plans for the day."

Charlotte gave grudging agreement and murmured a goodbye to the older woman as she finally agreed to go.

Charlotte filed after the others toward the Berringer carriage, feeling unsettled still. Danger left her feeling out of sorts. Mr. Berringer swung up onto his horse, intending to follow them home. When it came time to enter the carriage, Lord Hurlston was suddenly by Charlotte's side again.

She nearly swooned as his fingers clasped tight on her elbow. "Anything," he whispered.

"Anything?" She looked at him in dazed confusion. Only inches away but oh so far out of her league. Her senses swam momentarily with the thrill of his presence.

His gaze softened as he squeezed her elbow a little tighter. "I'll grant any boon within my power to give."

She shook her head to break the spell he'd cast over her. What she wanted from him, she could never have. She must be content with the occasional smile in her direction in the years to come. "There's nothing you can give me," she insisted before entering the carriage.

Charlotte heaved a sigh as he disappeared from her sight as the door shut. It wasn't fair that he'd finally noticed her *after* he'd announced his intention to make a perfect match with someone else.

Chapter Four

Winston ushered his mother into his home and sighed in relief as the door shut behind them. "There you are, Mama. Home at last."

"And not a minute too soon," Mother murmured.

Winston was long over the fright of nearly being run down and moving toward feeling indignant about that. Never before had he been endangered by talking a stroll. Mother might have been hurt. His friends and Charlotte Waters, too.

"Have you time to amuse an old friend," a voice suggested out of nowhere.

Winston spun around in surprise to find Lucien Hunt, a country neighbor, standing just inside the open library doorway with a glass of wine in his hand.

Winston gaped. "Good Lord. What the devil are you doing in London, Hunt?"

Hunt grinned and rushed forward to shake his hand. "I've come to offer my congratulations to you and your beautiful future bride, of course. I understand a date has finally been set. I had to come and see myself that it was true, and it does seem the rumors are true."

"Indeed, they are. A date has been set but you didn't have to come all this way to congratulate us," Winston said. Lucien Hunt was exactly the last man he'd expect to travel all the way to the capital just to offer his best wishes on his marriage. "The wedding is not for weeks yet."

Hunt inclined his head. "I had other business to attend to in London as well."

"Oh, of course," Winston murmured.

"Lady Hurlston how wonderful to see you again," Hunt said, taking up mama's hand in his and kissing the air above it. "It's been too long, my lady."

"It has," she answered with a fond smile for their neighbor.

Hunt turned about before Winston could ask what business had brought him to London because Elizabeth was coming down the stairs.

"There's the blushing bride to be," Hunt exclaimed. "How do you do, Miss Elizabeth?"

"Very well, Mr. Hunt. I had no expectation of seeing you for weeks yet," she said, her cheeks turning pink as Hunt took up her gloved hand too and kissed the air above it.

"Why don't we all go into the drawing room," Winston suggested, moving to claim Elizabeth's hand. "Shall we?"

Lucien offered his arm to Mother. "Shall we join them, my dear lady? May I also say how well you look today. London clearly agrees with you and your future daughter-in-law. Why you've both never looked more radiant than you do today."

Winston caught his friend's eye. "I'm sure looking forward to your own marriage will put a glow on your own cheeks too, Hunt," he teased.

"Ah, I have my doubts I will marry at all now," Lucien warned, settling mother into a chair and claiming an armchair for himself. "Who would have me?"

Elizabeth winced. "Lady Hurlston, shall I call for tea?"

"Please do," mother agreed with a soft smile for Winston's future wife as she rang the bell. Mother turned her attention in their neighbor's direction. "Mr. Hunt, indeed it is a great surprise to have you join us in London at this time of year."

"Or any year, for that matter," Winston murmured. "I was starting to think you'd never come back."

"Well, Hurlston here has pestered me sufficiently and now here I am." He speared Winston with a smirk. "Come on. What exciting news do you have to share with a poor country bachelor? I suppose you've driven young Peter away with your lovey-dove ways."

Lucien Hunt had always teased them about their long-standing betrothal in terms that made Winston uncomfortable. And it seemed he would continue even now the marriage was announced. "Peter will put in an appearance sooner or later, I'm sure. Other than the banns being read, you missed nothing much else going on."

Mother clucked her tongue.

"No, nothing at all," Winston warned Mother. He had decided on the way home not to mention the eventful day he and Mother had endured to anyone. There was no point having Elizabeth worried about him, too.

Elizabeth cleared her throat. "When did you arrive in Town, Mr. Hunt?"

"Just this morning. I'm staying at Long's Hotel, on New Bond Street unless you've room for another guest."

"Of course, I do," Winston promised after a moment of consideration. But he was annoyed. Hunt had very neatly given him no choice but to agree to house him really or seem churlish. The London townhouse had room enough to play host to a dozen more country friends and Hunt had stayed with Winston before. Though entertaining his neighbor's was not how Winston had planned to spend the weeks leading up to his marriage.

"The more the merrier," Elizabeth agreed with a tight smile.

For a moment Winston wondered if he should have consulted her about the matter of housing Hunt. But Hunt and Elizabeth usually got along well enough when in the country. He could not imagine he'd be a bother to her now.

Elizabeth steered the conversation adroitly from one topic to another while they waited for tea to arrive. When a footman appeared bearing a heavy tea tray, Elizabeth was quick to catch the servant's eye. "Have a guest room prepared for Mr. Hunt."

The man looked confused for a moment and glanced at Winston's mother for instruction.

"Yes, please do arrange a room for Mr. Hunt," mother murmured, a little frown forming on her brow.

Elizabeth noticed the frown, too. "Forgive me, my lady. But Hurlston did say to make myself at home. I hope my occasional requests do not bother you overmuch before the wedding takes place."

"Of course not, my dear. I consider you my daughter already. You may do as you please here."

"Thank you," Elizabeth murmured before turning back to their guest. "What news do you have to share from home, Mr. Hunt?"

"You've only been gone a week," Lucien replied, laughing. "But I do know something that will amuse you."

Lucien began to whisper some tidbit of local gossip in her ear.

Winston didn't care much for gossip and turned to his mother to whisper, "There's no need to speak of this morning, Mama. It was only a little bit of excitement, soon forgotten."

"I hope so."

Winston smiled down at her worried face. "Do not fret about today. It could not have been intentional. As Miss Waters suggested, most likely some ridiculous wager played out in public. No doubt they realized the harm they'd almost caused and fled swiftly to avoid any unpleasantness over their actions."

Mother worried her lip still. "If not for that brave girl, I might have lost you."

Woman. Charlotte Waters was no child. She was a pretty *distraction,* too. "A bit of conversation now will do your nerves the world of good, I'm sure."

"You might be right," she conceded.

Winston sighed. If left alone, Mama would likely nurture her worry of further danger for the whole of the day.

Papa had been much better in drawing Mother out of her mopes than he was. But he was the head of the family now, and at least she would leave the country estate with him, even if she did not embrace her widowhood yet or a full return to society.

Hunt could be quite the flatterer, too, and Mother usually responded well to that. It was a pity Lucien had no luck with the ladies his own age though. He seemed destined to remain a bachelor forever at this rate. "How was your journey from home, Hunt?"

"Crowded," Lucien complained. "But that is the lot of those who must travel by public conveyances. A private carriage must be vastly more agreeable."

"We'll have to find you an heiress to marry while you're in London and then you can afford a fine carriage of your own to travel about in," Winston suggested with a wink for his friend.

"Do not tease him about marriage, Hurlston," Elizabeth snapped. "Not when Mr. Hunt has only just arrived in Town."

Winston wasn't unduly surprised by Elizabeth's sudden rebuke. She tended to overreact whenever the topic of match-making and marriages came up in conversation with anyone. "I was only teasing him, as he's always done to me over the years."

"Hurlston may tease me," Hunt promised, absently patting Elizabeth's hand where it rested on the arm of her chair. "What else could we expect but a matchmaking attempt from the man who will marry the most sought-after beauty in the district?"

Elizabeth blushed. "You're too kind," she murmured.

"It is a success I don't deserve but will cherish all the days of my life," Winston added with a gentle smile for his future wife.

"I desperately miss the serenity of the countryside," Elizabeth said suddenly.

"Everyone misses the countryside while in London, and London when in the countryside," Mama threw out.

"I know Hurlston prefers London over wherever else he might be," Lucien teased.

"Much like you are fond of the contents of other people's wine cellars," Winston noted.

"Speaking of wine cellars, when might you return to the country so I can visit yours again?" Hunt asked with an arched brow.

"I've no immediate plans to travel." He smiled at his neighbor. "As I was saying before, while you're here, I must introduce you around, help you make a good impression with a few notable families. You never know what might happen."

Mother cleared her throat. "If you will excuse me, I think I should retire to my rooms to attend to some long-overdue correspondence."

Lucien stood and escorted Mama to the door, whispering something that made her laugh before they disappeared from sight.

"Hurlston, when you go out this afternoon, do take Hunt with you," Elizabeth murmured.

Winston looked at her in surprise. "I never said I was going anywhere."

"Of course you were going out. No need to change your usual routine on my account. I have your mother for company and a townhouse to learn to run. My father will demand my company, too. You always go to your club on Wednesday and dine with your friends there later, don't you?"

"Normally, yes." Winston had not discussed his routine with Elizabeth yet. In fact, that was something he'd hoped to discuss with her that very day. He wanted to make sure their appointment books matched in the weeks leading up to the wedding. "Escorting you about Town is the privilege of a future husband. I was looking forward to showing you the sights."

"But now Hunt has come to Town, and is to stay, you cannot ignore him. As you said last night, nothing needs to change because I am to marry you," she murmured. "I have enough to keep busy with."

Did she not want to spend time with him before the wedding? But then he heard Hunt whistling as he returned. And with him around, Winston couldn't very well ask that question out loud. And it wouldn't do to quarrel in front of a witness. Winston had made a promise to be an easy husband. "Very well. Anything to make you happy, my dear."

She smiled quickly. "Good." She stood. "Now, I'm expected to accompany my father on an outing when he returns from his morning ride. Good day, my lord. Mr. Hunt, I will speak with you again later."

She whisked from the room before he could even say farewell.

"I can find my own way about London, you know," Lucien assured him. "If you've other plans for today, I can—"

"No. No. I'd made no great plans for the day," he promised. Not now, anyway. He'd have to make it clear to Elizabeth that he was at her service before and after the wedding. "So how long were you expecting to stay in Town?"

"As long as I'm not in the way until the wedding."

"You'd never be in the way," Winston promised, though he wasn't sure that was true. He would have to be added to every dinner, amusement or outing from now on. He might though be a good company for mother, too, on occasion. "Well, I suppose I'd best take you out."

"I do appreciate your sacrifice on my account." Lucien stood.

"It will be my wine cellar that's sacrificed the longer you stay in London," he teased. "We can go out now if you like. I'll just say a quick farewell."

Lucien laughed softly. "Oh, of course, do gain your mother's permission to leave the house without her."

Winston scowled and stalked from the room, annoyed by

Lucien's constant teasing. He was a good son by obliging his mother, so she knew where he would be.

He went up to Elizabeth's room first and knocked. At her call to enter, Winston slipped inside to find her alone. She stood in a sheer chemise, hair tumbled down around her face and shoulders as she rolled a stocking down her leg. Winston had never seen a woman, let alone Elizabeth, in such a state of undress before and froze, uncertain of what to do.

Elizabeth glanced up, saw it was him standing there, and then jerked the comforter from the bed to cover her near nakedness. "What are you doing in my chambers?"

He approached her slowly. They needed to progress past this initial awkwardness before they became man and wife, didn't they? He smiled gently at her. "I came to tell you Lucien and I have decided to go out."

"I knew that."

"Immediately." He narrowed his eyes on her and then looked behind him. "Who did you think was knocking at your door?"

"My maid, of course," she said as she flicked her hair back over her shoulder. "She is fetching an iron to curl my hair. I expect her back at any moment."

"Ah, well. I'm afraid you got me instead." He drew closer still, since she hadn't asked him to leave. He took in the creamy white shoulder peeking above the comforter she clutched to her breast. "Do you have any idea how beautiful you are?"

Elizabeth shook her head. "You must announce yourself before bursting into my chambers."

"I did not burst. You said to enter."

"That was meant for my maid."

"Ah, a pity," he said. "But I'm glad I have another moment to speak with you alone. You know, we should decide how we greet each other and say goodbye in front of others. It was a little strange to have my future wife walk away without ceremony just now. I felt I should have done something differently, even with Hunt there and watching us."

"Goodbye, my lord," Elizabeth said, dipping a curtsy as she used to do when they were younger. Of late though, she'd taken to merely nodding to him as his equal. He'd thought that was a sign of maturity in their relationship. Perhaps they had some way to go yet. "Can we not forgo the formalities when we are alone."

He reached for her face, lifting her chin so he could see her expression better. Her color was high, and her eyes were wide and bright. She wouldn't hold his gaze, unfortunately. Out of embarrassment? Unease? They were both feeling that…only she didn't understand his inexperience matched her own. "In private, I should like to kiss you goodbye the way my parents always did when they were married. And if there is company, I'd like to clasp your fingers at least and perhaps kiss the back of your hand."

He dipped his head slowly and let his lips sweep across hers. A tiny kiss. Their first since her arrival in Town and the banns being read.

He'd have liked to steal another, but Elizabeth stepped back swiftly at a loud knock at her door. "That will be the maid returned," she whispered. "I should not like the servants to see us together like this and gossip. Please retreat using the connecting door to the guest room next to mine."

"Yes, of course." Winston didn't like being dismissed but what choice did he have? "I'll see you for dinner later then."

She nodded. "Until tonight."

He used the connecting door to enter the empty, sheet-shrouded chamber next door. And after listening carefully for any noise from the hall, he slipped along to his own chambers to change.

But once alone in the privacy of his chambers, he glanced down. The fabric covering his groin had remained stubbornly unmoved when he had kissed Elizabeth. Admittedly, it hadn't been much of a kiss. Come to think of it, he had not even become even a little stiff at seeing her hardly dressed.

He raised his face to the ceiling, confused by that. He'd always expected that when the time came, he'd be eager for Elizabeth. Ready to make love at the drop of a hat, as so many other men claimed to be with their wives or lovers. But so far, his body was utterly unaffected.

Mind you, Elizabeth had been more startled than welcoming just now. Tonight, after dinner, he hoped things went better when they hopefully shared a longer good-night kiss.

Yet as he strode into his dressing closet, he wondered if there was something wrong with him. He had not the same urges other men seemed to have to slake their lust without any hesitation.

He was also still a virgin—and that was awkward at his age.

He changed and then went along to tap on his mother's closed door.

"Come in, Winston."

He poked his head through the door to find Mama not resting on her bed but seated by the window staring outside. "How did you know it was me?"

"A woman knows the steps of those she loves."

He crossed the room to kiss her cheek. "I came to tell you I'm going out."

"Where are you taking Elizabeth? Not to the park, I trust."

"I am not going out with her, but with Lucien instead."

"I'm surprised Elizabeth will let you go without her," Mother chided. "She wouldn't if you'd told her of our dreadful morning."

"There's no need to worry anyone, and it was her idea I take Hunt, since her father is due to return for her shortly. I'm sure to be home in time for dinner with you and the Mayflowers, and now Lucien, too, I suppose."

Mama nodded. "Be careful."

"Will you try to sleep, Mother?"

"How can I, when you will be away from home now?"

He wouldn't rise to the bait and change his plans to keep her happy. "Until later."

"I've just finished penning a letter, inviting Miss Waters to join me for luncheon. If you can spare the time, I should like you to join us to thank her personally again for saving your life."

"I've already thanked her." He nodded. "I should be happy to speak with her again, but I must consult Elizabeth, in case she has engaged us elsewhere."

Mother narrowed her eyes on him. "You're a good man to consider your future wife before making plans with me."

"I'll always do my best to accommodate both of your needs."

Mother nodded. "You know, I was quite taken with Miss Waters, even if she takes after her mother a great deal."

Winston couldn't see it himself. Mrs. Waters hadn't any of her daughter's warmth or pretty ways. "Mrs. Waters must have been very different as a younger woman then."

"In looks more than nature. Olivia was a very capable woman, and Charlotte much the same I suspect, though it seems she has tried to hide her resourcefulness behind a smiling disposition. I want to help her. She ought to be married."

Winston scrubbed a hand through his hair. "Yes, I suppose she is old enough."

"More than old enough." Mama frowned though. "Was there anything unsavory I ought to know about her reputation before I send this invitation?"

"No," Winston promised. "She's as kind and sweet as she appears. An excellent dancer. She has a laugh that…" He grimaced, remembering the musical, distracting sound from the sidelines at countless balls and dinners over the past season. "Well, she has a fine sense of humor."

"So, you like her?"

"I, um…yes, I suppose I do, not that I know her very well, of course."

Mama beamed. "Good. Because I think I shall make her my favorite until she is wed."

"Mother," he warned. "Charlotte Waters cannot be your pet."

"Why not? With a mother like hers, so wrapped up in her own interests, and who has dragged her heaven knows where, she must have been very neglected growing up. And I never kept a daughter to spoil."

Winston sighed. Mother's one regret was that she'd never borne a daughter who had lived beyond infancy. Winston did not remember what his sisters had looked like, but mother still spoke of them often. Their age, what they should have been doing at any given time in their lives. The experiences they'd never have. Mother spent a great deal of time in the past. "You'll have Elizabeth to spoil now."

"It's not the same." Mother nodded slowly. "I'm sure Miss Waters must have a dowry of a decent size. Why she remains unwed is a mystery. She's quite pretty."

Yes, she certainly was. Winston shook his head. Pretty and funny. That laugh of hers made him smile. "She's shy of men." Winston shook his head, trying to dispel thoughts of her. "You shouldn't concern yourself."

"I doubt she is shy of anyone or anything at all after what she did today. Why, Charlotte is so much like her mother used to be when we were girls. Independent and strong. A nurturing disposition that her mother utterly lacks, I'm sure. I would hate for her to marry poorly. Would you mind asking your brother to join us for luncheon when you see him?"

Alarm bells went off in Winston's head. "She's not for Peter."

"They will be chaperoned at all times."

All the anxiety Winston possessed came alert, sensing danger. Peter was a rake though mother would never believe that.

"Mother, I shouldn't think Peter and Miss Waters would suit at all."

Mother laughed softly. "Not as a wife for him. What an absurd suggestion. But he does know other bachelors' circumstances very well. If he paid her a little attention, it might lead to a budding romance for her with someone else."

"I know bachelors," he complained. "I can make all the introductions she might need."

Mother flicked her hand to wave away his suggestion. "All your friends are married or about to be married or scoundrels. What help could you possibly be to someone like Miss Waters? She gives with no thought to her own advancement or safety."

"Mother, you spent barely ten minutes in her company. How could you have concluded all that about her?"

"Sometimes it only takes a moment to know someone's heart, my son."

He thought about that statement. Winston couldn't dispute her belief that Charlotte might be an undiscovered rare gem. She was unusually easy company and that made her dangerous to him. But Miss Waters *had* been fearless today. A sign of her selfless and kind heart. And Mother was right to a degree. She was well placed to ensure Charlotte came to the notice of any bride-hunting bachelors they might know.

But the idea of Charlotte as Mama's project, married off to someone Peter recommended, sat ill with him. Charlotte needed a special man who appreciated her sunny personality… and her curves.

Winston winced, shoving that image out of his head fast.

No, he knew he should not notice that Miss Waters had enticing curves, or voluptuous full breasts that threatened to spill out of her evening gowns at balls lately.

No, he must not remember that her sunny laugh always brightened his mood…especially not when he was about to marry Elizabeth.

He pulled his thoughts back to Mother's plan to meddle in Charlotte's life. Perhaps thinking about someone else would be good for Mama. Surely the worst that could happen was a wedding day for Charlotte.

And if anything, or anyone, caught Mama's attention, that had to be all right with him. He was certain Charlotte wouldn't expect more attention from his mother than was proper.

Chapter Five

Charlotte had smiled and agreed all night until her face ached with the strain of pretending she was having a good time. And she'd have to smile a great deal more if she was to catch herself a husband in less than three weeks, too. "That is an interesting opinion, Mr. Lawrence."

"I tell you there is nothing more delicious than eating ice cream in the early afternoon." He glanced at the little dishes of food spread out before Charlotte in his aunt's supper room with an approving eye. It had become clear as supper progressed that Mr. Lawrence felt she should taste everything set down before her tonight.

Charlotte had eaten far too much already. She'd come to dance, talk, and tempt—not really to eat herself sick. Mr. Lawrence kept urging her to take just one more bite, unfortunately. It was time to put her foot down and move on to another gentleman. Perhaps someone less interested in her eating habits.

"I'm sorry, I couldn't possibly eat any more," she protested, glancing longingly toward Eugenia and Aurora, who were hovering not far away. Eugenia was acting as her chaperone, but Aurora was always at her side for moral support. "But please do convey my compliments to your aunt. Everything was so delicious tonight."

Mr. Lawrence's eyes fell from hers in reluctant acceptance. "I certainly shall tell her about you."

"Oh, I fear my dear friend wishes a word with me now." She started to rise from her chair. "Would you excuse me, sir?"

Mr. Lawrence lifted his girth from his chair too with a groan and bowed. "Of course. It has been a pleasure."

"For me too," she promised. Charlotte quickly retreated to the comfort of other women, hand on her belly.

Aurora captured her arm immediately. "Well?"

"I think he's looking for someone to feed more than a woman to marry. I fear I may cast up my accounts if I see one more slice of ham. Dear God, distract me from doing that."

Aurora pulled a face that made her laugh and, to her relief, she burped too, just enough to give her stomach some ease.

"It is to his credit that he is a man who doesn't care too much about the size of a woman's waistline," Aurora noted.

"Oh, he's interested. The larger, the better, I suspect." Charlotte looked into the ballroom with less eagerness than she ought to possess. She fought a desperate need to escape for somewhere quiet and to be alone. But she could not do that. Not if she wanted to catch herself a husband in the little time she'd been granted. She had a purpose in being here tonight. The Duchess of Exeter had graciously taken an interest in her and been so warm and excited about her joining them for a night out. "Who's next?"

Aurora rose up on her toes to look around. "Have you been introduced to Lord Somner?"

"Yes, in my first season, I think."

"He's over there with Mr. Berringer and company." Aurora beamed. "Let's go see if he remembers you."

Charlotte laughed as she was jerked into motion and towed into the ballroom.

They came to an abrupt halt and Aurora pouted. "Oh, drat, he has moved on and I cannot see him anymore. Never mind, we'll hunt him down eventually."

Charlotte giggled again. She'd never really hunted a husband like this before and it seemed easier to have a conspirator by her side for it. "I doubt that he'll remember me, but of course I hope he might."

Aurora winked. "We'll make sure he never forgets you after renewing your acquaintance with him tonight."

Aurora Hillcrest was a force to be reckoned with. At the rate they were going, Charlotte was sure to be reintroduced to almost everyone under forty years by dawn. A sudden thought occurred to her though, and she pulled Aurora aside. "I can't thank you enough for all you're doing to help me tonight, but I just want to be clear that I don't want to compromise myself into a hasty marriage."

Aurora beamed. "I agree. Everything will be done to maintain your sterling reputation and dignity."

Charlotte looked around quickly, noticing an absence. "Where did Eugenia go?"

"Do you see her husband standing anywhere about the ballroom now?"

She looked around. "No."

"Then that is likely where she's disappeared to. They're always doing that, now they are married, and also before I suspect. Not that I blame them. They're in love." Aurora laughed softly, her eyes lighting up with pleasure at the thought. "So, let's see who else was invited tonight that we can renew your acquaintance with. We must strike while your nerves last."

Charlotte was swept around the perimeter of the ballroom, and she smiled and greeted anyone she knew and everyone Aurora had a passing acquaintance with. "What our aim is tonight is to remind everyone that you're very pretty, intelligent, and still unwed. And you do have a good-sized dowry. Your parents are respected academics."

"Respected where?" Charlotte muttered. "They're hardly on anyone's guest list anymore."

"People who are not seen, or are not particularly talkative, are merely less desirable at a dinner party than others. I'm sure your parents would have a great deal to say to people who shared a common interest."

"No one ever seems to," Charlotte complained. "They are my parents and I must love them in some fashion, I suppose, but they're not an asset I can use to make a marriage to me more desirable."

Aurora patted her hand. "I understand. Ooh, look. Lord Sullivan is here. He's across the room talking with Lord Hurlston."

Charlotte had spotted Hurlston the moment she'd arrived but had resolutely turned her back on him. She could not admire him anymore, and she tried not to at every turn. Yet despite his upcoming marriage, she still foolishly dreamed of him. A man already betrothed would not want to kiss her.

"I said no to pursing Lord Sullivan, remember," Charlotte reminded Aurora again.

"Never hurts to be thorough," Aurora murmured. "Smile now; he's coming this way."

She looked around to see both Lord Sullivan and Lord Hurlston bearing down on them.

Although she smiled at Lord Sullivan, he seemed only to have eyes for Aurora. "How do you do this evening?"

"Very well, my lord," Aurora replied. "I'm sure you remember my dear friend, Miss Waters."

"Indeed, I do," Lord Sullivan bowed. "A pleasure to see you again."

But his attention immediately returned to the Aurora, the true beauty of the evening. And it wasn't the first time Charlotte had detected a partiality on his part for her dear friend, either. Charlotte had a suspicion, though she was sure Aurora would deny the idea, that Lord Sullivan's interest in Aurora was genuine.

Aurora, of course, kept offering him to other women.

Charlotte glanced up to find Lord Hurlston studying her

wearing a tiny smile. As usual, he looked very handsome in his black coat and breeches, with a simple gold pin holding his cravat in place. His attention flickered between Aurora and Lord Sullivan, and his expression registered a trace of anticipation, too.

"Good evening, my lord," she murmured, preferring that he not interrupt the other pair. If there was a chance of romance between Aurora and Lord Sullivan, Charlotte would not like to stand in the way of it.

His smile grew wider. "It *is* a good evening, Miss Waters."

Although brief, Lord Hurlston's greeting filled Charlotte with such hopeless pleasure that she shivered. He knew her name, and it really did feel like he was pleased to see her. Oh, how she hated that he was to marry someone else.

Tonight, the subtle hint of his cologne teased her nostrils as he drew subtly closer to whisper. "What do you think is going on there?"

"Where, my lord?"

His eyes flickered to where their friends stood deep in conversation and his eyes sparkled with good humor.

Charlotte hoped it was a romance in the making, but she wouldn't want to jinx it by speaking of it with anyone. "I have no idea what you're talking about."

"I'm sure that couldn't be true." His tone was teasing. "But by all means, keep your own counsel. Far be it for me to pry into a lady's opinion. I'm sure you have many."

Charlotte frowned, unsure if she was being accused of being a busybody or not.

"I only meant that you are more observant than most." He grinned and then asked, "Have you by chance spoken with my future wife tonight or know where she might be found?"

She shook her head, dismayed by the question. Of course, that is all he would really seek her out for. An observant wallflower saw much, sitting on the sidelines, ignored and bored. "I have not seen her or had the honor of an introduction, my lord."

He blinked slowly, as if he wasn't aware of that fact. "Well, then I will rectify that as soon as opportunity permits. Which sets are you engaged to dance?"

She looked away from him. She had met and talked with a great many guests here, but none of them had expressed an interest in taking the floor with her. Aurora, in comparison, had received plenty of offers to dance tonight.

So far, she'd had no nibbles, no suitors. No real interest from the opposite sex except for the occasional leer from libertines who could have no interest in matrimony. She had a decent dowry but when a woman was possessed of eccentric parents like hers, well…her chances of making a grand match had to be set aside.

Charlotte was short, rounded no matter how hard she tried not to be, and was already considered a wallflower at one and twenty. Hardly surprising she'd not found a husband with no help from her parents or their connections. She'd been late coming out at nineteen for her first season, and had only returned to London for her second season this year.

But if she was going to avoid traveling abroad again, she would have to push herself forward a little more. She was desperate to stay in England. This was where she belonged.

"I am not engaged to dance tonight." She peeked past the earl's wide shoulders, hoping to see an available man heading her way. Unfortunately, none were forthcoming, and a set was being called. She glanced at the earl, willing him away for the first time in her life.

"That is…" His gaze was sympathetic, though he seemed to take a long time to search for the right words to continue. Gentlemen did not line up to dance with her. They had to be persuaded to it by someone who liked her.

"It's perfectly fine," she assured him.

"I was going to say *disappointing* to hear."

"Think nothing of it, my lord. I've become an expert observer at *tonnish* amusements."

"That should never be the case for a lady as pretty as you." He gulped as soon as the words were out of his mouth and looked away.

She fought not to smile at the unexpected compliment. Lord Hurlston had just called her pretty, and that made her feel a little better. He hadn't meant to compliment her, she was sure, which accounted for the blush forming on his cheeks now.

Lord Sullivan convinced Aurora to dance with him, and she winced as her friend was led away. With Aurora gone, Charlotte would have to find Eugenia to play chaperone for as long as the dance lasted.

"Miss Waters," Hurlston said very quietly. "If you have no objection, I wonder if you would like to dance this set with me?"

She laughed softly, but she was blushing, too. "Did Mr. Berringer put you up to asking me to dance again?"

He laughed. "No, I am in the mood to dance, but Elizabeth is not to be found."

She grimaced at the news. Coming second to his future wife smarted. And if she danced with Lord Hurlston tonight, that was one less set she'd have available to dance with an available bachelor. But since no one had asked her yet, surely one lost set couldn't spoil her chances with someone else later. And besides, being on the dance floor meant others might notice she was quite a graceful partner. Being short had distinct disadvantages in a crowded ballroom. People tended to look over her head and not see her. On the dance floor she would be seen.

"Thank you, my lord. I would be honored to dance with you," Charlotte said quickly before she changed her mind. She held out her hand, fighting the thrill when Hurlston gripped her fingers tightly to lead her to the dance floor.

The strains of a waltz suddenly filled the chamber, and she smiled up at him in delight. Hurlston rarely danced, but he was clearly fond of it and danced well. It was a doubly special treat for her to be one of so few of his partners. She'd cherish the memory for the rest of her days, too, or at least until her heart was claimed by someone who might love her back.

They stepped toward each other, and she fit snuggly into his arms, heart racing. Her lips were level with his wide chest. Charlotte strove to calm her excitement with some difficulty. The cologne he wore was tremendously distracting, and the hand he placed high on her back seemed very warm.

They started to dance and, after a few turns in companionable silence, Hurlston cleared his throat. "Forgive my boldness, but I wanted to thank you for the comfort you gave my mother. She has not stopped singing your praises since we made it safely home. I'm very glad to hear you accepted her invitation to take luncheon with her."

Charlotte took a peek around his shoulder to see if anyone had noticed them dancing together. So far, society was more interested in everyone else. "Your mother was kind to invite me, and I was happy to offer whatever support she needed."

"Were you not frightened at all?"

"I was for you," she admitted softly.

"Thank you." Hurlston's fingers flexed upon her back, perhaps unconsciously urging her to draw closer.

Charlotte fought not to sink into his arms as the heat of his hand spread across her upper back. The blush warming her cheeks surged with a vengeance, which at least she could blame on the exertion of the dance. "You already thanked me enough."

"Your quick thinking saved our lives," he said, his grip tightening on her in a little more with every turn. "My mother's nerves have become delicate. She is more sensitive to shocks and unpleasantness than she used to be. Your reassurances and protectiveness went a long way to soothing her in ways I often struggle to meet. She's keen to know you better."

"My actions might have saved any one of our lives, my lord," she countered. "If I hadn't been already aware of the riders headed in our direction, I might have thought it thunder, too, and the situation may have become fatal for any of us."

"Still, I owe you a debt," he said in a whisper. "Tell me, is there really nothing you need?"

The smile on her face faded. Besides a kiss from him? A night in his arms? She'd once thought she could give up her virtue for one night with the unattainable earl. But...she had her pride. She stiffed her posture, remembering painfully that he was not for her to fantasize about anymore. "No."

"Well, if you change your mind, do speak up" he said, seeming to gulp. "You're an attractive young woman. Marriage must be on your mind. If I can ever introduce you to any eligible bachelors, find a way to let me know."

Charlotte closed her eyes, cut to the quick by his seemingly generous offer. It was kind of him, but she couldn't seriously let the man she still secretly loved help her find a husband she might never have feelings for.

With that realization firmly in mind, she decided then and there she probably ought to marry someone not acquainted with Lord Hurlston. "My lord, I must decline."

"Why?"

For a thousand reasons and all of them too embarrassing to share with him. Their dance came to an end, and she opened her eyes slowly to see a frown had formed on his face.

She curtsied to him. "Thank you for the dance, my lord. I hope you locate Miss Mayflower soon and enjoy a proper dance." She curtsied to him a second time, eager to escape him and return to her real friends to share the news of her change of heart. There had to be an adjustment made to her needs in a potential suitor. The man she married could not be titled, and therefore no close friends of Lord Hurlston's would do for her. It would be entirely too painful to be around him should their paths cross in society too often.

"The pleasure was entirely mine," Hurlston promised, bowing to her deeply.

They stood facing each other awkwardly afterward, and then she recalled herself and fled from him. She glanced over her shoulder, though, and saw that escape might not be hers immediately. Hurlston was following her, at a slower pace, toward their mutual circle of friends.

They parted, him angling toward Mr. Berringer and Lord Sullivan on one side of the chattering group. Charlotte headed for the comfort of Eugenia and Aurora on the other, aware he was watching her.

Aurora leaned close to whisper in her ear. "You looked lovely dancing with Lord Hurlston. Since he is known to be so particular, I'm sure everyone noticed the honor you received."

"Perhaps that will do me some good," she answered, though the thought brought no real joy. Her happiest moment had been diminished by Lord Hurlston's offer of aid to help her find a husband to replace him in her affections.

"I'm sure it will. I—" Aurora began but was interrupted when a gentleman came to take her away to join another set just forming. Others left, too, and after a few moments, she found herself standing beside Lord Hurlston again.

And she didn't know what to say to him. The man she loved. The man she'd adored from afar since first laying eyes on him in her first season would always belong to another woman.

Winston turned slightly, inching closer to her side. "Forgive me the blunt question, but are you one of those women who never intend to marry?"

Charlotte bristled. "I want to marry as much as any lady." Perhaps even more now. She was counting down the days until her parents' departure from England with dread growing in her heart that she'd have no choice but to go with them. "But I truly don't need *your* help."

He inhaled sharply, finally noticing her emphasis. "Everyone needs help to make the right match. My mother has expressed an interest in your future. I'm sure she will broach the subject of marriage with you tomorrow at luncheon."

She closed her eyes and clenched her jaw in frustration. Did everyone in London pity Charlotte's spinster state?

She opened her eyes slowly. Hurlston appeared to be waiting for a response, so she gave it to him—uncensored. "I never said I wouldn't seek the opinion of my closest friends and confidants," she stated, annoyed with his very being. The nobility had a much easier time forming alliances and making socially acceptable marriage. Love was not even involved half the time. Such was the case with Lord Hurlston and his future bride, too. "What would you know about making a good match? You were betrothed for years and only now are dragging yourself to the altar."

That seemed to give him pause because his cheeks drew dark, and his jaw clenched momentarily. The silence didn't last long. "I needed no help from anyone to do my duty."

Duty.

"A marriage should mean more to you than duty." Charlotte forced a smile. She'd heard the gossip, heard his friends joke about Hurlston's endless delays in setting a wedding date. But now he was weeks away from tying the knot, and he still believed it was a duty to be a husband.

And then she saw *his Elizabeth* gliding through the room on the arm of a man surely old enough to be her father. The woman was truly beautiful in a way Charlotte could never be. She moved through society with an obvious air of cold superiority, too. "Yes, you must be a dutiful fellow indeed to be forced to marry Elizabeth. By the way, your future wife is over there on her father's arm, I think, looking down her nose at everyone.

Excuse me, my lord. You have professed enough gratitude to an unworthy wallflower to appease your conscience. Please think no more of me ever again."

Charlotte turned to Eugenia and whispered that she was headed for the retiring room before she said anything else. She needed to cool her head before anyone noticed she was in a temper. Women with tempers were quite unattractive.

Chapter Six

Winston marveled that someone so tiny could have literally knocked him to his knees with so few words. Charlotte Waters fled from him in a temper, and he had deserved the set down, too. What did he know of courtship when he'd never had to bother with it himself?

He should have held his tongue and not tried to force his offer of help on a woman with so slight an acquaintance with his family. She wasn't flattered by his concern or that he wanted to help her make the right match. She'd been downright offended that he thought she needed any help at all.

Yes, it was in his power to introduce her to more bachelors than she could realize existed. But if she didn't want his assistance, so be it. He didn't need to be hit over the head to learn to hold his tongue around her.

He would forget the obligation he felt must be settled with her for the warning she'd shouted and the bravery of her actions in Hyde Park. It had been a selfless, instinctive reaction and nothing more. The concern she'd shown for his mother's fragile nerves after had seemed genuine, but what did he really know about Charlotte Waters? Very little really. And as she had said, it could have been any one of them trampled under the horses' hooves.

He made himself smile, trying to forget the lady he'd upset...with some difficulty, he found. "Warm night," he murmured to no one in particular, digging his finger under his collar to counter his unease.

Winston peered about the ballroom, discovering Elizabeth

and her father had disappeared again. They were not dancing. Perhaps they'd missed seeing him and gone to the card room together.

It was high time he joined them instead of seeking the company of a wallflower who didn't want to talk to him.

He sauntered from the ballroom, accepting congratulations for his upcoming marriage from those he met, hearing praise for Elizabeth too, as he had all night. His bride had impressed everyone he knew so far.

Except…Miss Waters did not seem to be impressed with Elizabeth. She'd complained that Elizabeth had looked down her nose at everyone. Yes, Elizabeth was reserved and unused to moving about in large crowds. Perhaps once the pair were introduced, Charlotte Waters might find they had much in common and like her.

He frowned. Not that Charlotte's good opinion of Elizabeth was vital. But they would move in the same crowds more often after they wed.

The card room was crowded. Some of his friends were already deep in a game at one table, and he moved past them, looking for Elizabeth. He found her and, surprisingly, Lucien Hunt standing behind her now, rather than her father.

Hunt and Elizabeth were so focused on her game that neither noticed him stop in full view of the table. Elizabeth eyes were heavy-lidded, signaling intense concentration, but Hunt's face revealed keen interest in the outcome, too. The game seemed to be going well, though. Expecting a good outcome, he started to circle the table, ready to congratulate Elizabeth when the time came.

But then he saw Charlotte again standing with her back to him. She was being introduced to an exceedingly tall gentleman across the way from him. She was smiling up at the fellow and nodding her head, clearly agreeing with everything he said.

Charlotte was so tiny she ought to have a sore neck.

Her hand rose then, and she rubbed her slender neck, disturbing a few strands of her glossy dark hair. He saw them settle upon her rounded shoulder and he let out a heavy sigh of envy. He ought to fix things with Charlotte and he would tonight if he could.

He started toward her, and she looked over her shoulder at him. A tiny smile appeared on her lips and Winston stumbled, tripping over his own feet. Unseen hands reached out to put him back to rights again and he thanked those around him.

But when he looked up and around for Charlotte, she was disappearing out the card door with the tall gentleman on her way to the ballroom.

He followed and was both pleased and disappointed to see her in another gentleman's arms. He would not have a chance to talk to her again for a while he supposed.

He turned to look for Elizabeth then, remembering why he'd come to the cardroom in the first place. Elizabeth was gone from the tables, and the room. So was Hunt.

Winston hurried to look for her again, berating himself for becoming distracted by a wallflower.

The pair were just joining Elizabeth's father at a supper table.

As Hunt helped her into a chair at a table set to the side of the room, he looked up and met Winston's stare with a bland expression.

Mayflower noticed him then and waved him over. "Hurlston," Elizabeth's father called out. "Do come and join us."

Hunt smiled. "There you are at last, Hurlston. I thought you'd abandoned us entirely for the company of your other friends."

"Not at all," he promised.

Elizabeth accepted tea from a servant. "Who was she?"

"Who?"

Elizabeth's spine stiffened and sipped her tea without looking at him.

Hunt tutted as he approached and drew him aside. "I've done my best, but I fear you offended your future wife tonight. She was expecting to dance with you, and you chose another lady. Bad form, old chap," Hunt chided.

Winston frowned. "I could not find Elizabeth for the first two sets."

"Well, she saw you whispering and then dancing with a stranger to her, and I told her it could mean nothing serious, of course."

"Of course it meant nothing."

"Oh, I believe you," Hunt agreed, looking over his shoulder to Elizabeth. "But I'll leave you to explain the facts of the affair to her."

Hunt patted Winston on the shoulder and then made himself scarce.

Winston tugged down his waistcoat and took the seat opposite Elizabeth, bristling with indignation over what he'd been unfairly accused of. There was no *affair* to explain. He'd done nothing wrong tonight in dancing with another woman. "Where have you been tonight?"

Elizabeth studied him rather coldly over a teacup. "With Father, of course, and entertaining your friend. Something you should have thought to do yourself."

He lifted a brow. "I would have been with you all—if you were able to be found," he countered.

Elizabeth stared at him. "At least *he* wants to keep me company. You charged off as soon as we arrived."

"Now, daughter," Mr. Mayflower chided. "It's not for you to question Hurlston over something so inconsequential. He's an important man. An earl."

Winston leaned forward, ignoring his future father-in-law. "Whatever you suspect me of is simply not true."

"Then why does the question I asked remain unanswered?"

He didn't like the tone of this conversation. He had been faithful to Elizabeth his whole life. "The lady I danced with is the friend of mutual friends. Miss Charlotte Waters is her name."

"Why have you not mentioned her before in your letters?"

He frowned. "There has never been anything particular to tell you about her."

That brought out a bitter laugh from her and a sigh from Mr. Mayflower. "Your letters are forever filled with countless recollections of balls and parties you attended, and always you taunt me with the names of my rivals for your affections."

He stared at Elizabeth, confused. He'd never knowingly done such a thing, but he did write to her whenever he was away in London. "I tell you about other women in anticipation of you coming to London to meet them. So you were prepared and knowledgeable of important people in society. Charlotte Waters is a wallflower."

Elizabeth's brows rose. "She's a guest of the Duke and Duchess of Exeter, and she even attended church the day the banns announcing our marriage were read out."

He blinked. "She did?"

"And cried about it, too."

Winston sat back, stunned by the accusation. "Surely not."

Elizabeth regarded him with something akin to pity. "I recognize misery only too well on a woman's face, even if *you* think nothing of a broken heart."

He leaned forward again. This was getting ridiculous. "Well, I did not see anything unusual in her behavior that day, or any other day, for the whole of our acquaintance."

"And how long has that been?" Elizabeth looked around the supper room at a sudden influx of guests with a sour expression. "It's easy to see you're a favorite among the women of society. Women watch you in the hope of catching your eye."

"Women look at me the way they always have. I've never pretended not to be betrothed to you," Winston argued.

"Forgive my daughter, Hurlston. The move to Town has unsettled her senses," Mayflower said, dismissing the matter. "She's imaging trouble where none exists just like her mother always did. What say we all forget tonight's misunderstanding and enjoy the party."

Winston wasn't about to let the matter drop. He would not allow such a ridiculous assumption to continue. "I met Miss Waters and her parents years ago, but I don't know the daughter at all well, which is why I have never mentioned her."

Elizabeth raised a brow. "She's to take luncheon with your mother, I understand."

"Mother arranged that, not I," he promised. "I'm sorry if Mother did not consult you about the luncheon. She will after we are married, I'm sure."

"Miss Waters and I are not acquainted," Elizabeth murmured, lifting her nose a little.

"Well, then I'd be more than happy to arrange an introduction tonight, and then you will see that your suspicions about her broken heart, as you call it, are entirely unfounded."

"That won't be necessary, Hurlston," she said, patting her lips with a napkin. "She's merely a wallflower, as you said, with a pitiful crush on someone far above her. She's no one worth knowing, as you say. I'm certain if you tell your mother to break the connection, she will."

He wasn't about to tell his mother anything of the sort, but perhaps it was best to keep that to himself. Elizabeth and Charlotte had no need to be introduced really. He didn't think it would be an acquaintance that would benefit a woman with a sweeter nature like Charlotte Waters had. Feeling a touch disloyal to Elizabeth, Winston stood and offered his arm. "Shall we dance now?"

After a moment, Elizabeth nodded and stood too. She

curled her arm around his, and it dawned on him that she might have been jealous that he'd paid so much attention to Charlotte Waters. He grimaced.

They left her father to amuse himself and returned to the ballroom.

Unfortunately, on his way to the ballroom floor, where a set was forming, he discovered he was looking for Charlotte everywhere in the crowd. She wasn't sitting among the wallflowers or standing about with mutual friends anymore.

And she wasn't dancing, either.

Where had she disappeared to now?

Winston danced with Elizabeth, trying to shake an odd feeling around his heart. Disappointment and confusion filled him when he thought of Charlotte's absence. But what should he care if she was making herself scarce on purpose?

She was just a friend of a friend.

No one important, as he'd led Elizabeth to believe.

And yet…he couldn't shake the feeling he ought to find her and make peace still.

When their dance ended, he escorted Elizabeth toward his friends. Charlotte was still absent, so he made sure Elizabeth was amply distracted before drawing Mrs. Berringer aside for a quiet word. "Your party seems to be one short. I hope nothing is amiss."

"An unfortunate circumstance. Miss Waters developed a headache and has gone home early."

"I'm sorry to hear that," he murmured.

He was both worried for Charlotte and exasperated by her, too. He suspected she'd not had a headache at all but sought to avoid further conversation with him that night by leaving early. Well, she would attend a luncheon with Mother soon. He planned to be there to clear the air between them once and for all, and also introduce Elizabeth to her as well. Damned if he would allow a wife to dictate who he could talk to at a ball.

If he wanted to be friends with a wallflower, he damn well would be. There was nothing wrong with Charlotte. She was sweet, lively and her laughter made him smile.

Elizabeth tugged on his sleeve suddenly. "I feel a megrim coming on. Would you mind if I left early? You don't have to come, of course."

"I shall be happy to call it a night, actually." He looked about his friends and bid them a good evening, offering his arm to Elizabeth.

Together they headed for the door, collecting her father along the way. Mayflower tried to get them to stay but Winston's mind was made up. If Charlotte had gone, he'd no reason to stay.

He shook his head, annoyed with himself for thinking of Charlotte still.

If *Elizabeth* wanted to go, he had no reason to stay and he was already wishing he'd never come out tonight. At this point in his life, so close to the wedding, he shouldn't be worried about other women. "I'll send a footman around to tell Hunt we're going."

"No need," Elizabeth murmured. "Hunt is behind us."

Winston turned to see it was true. Hunt was bringing up the rear, a smirk on his face and an empty glass in hand. He handed it off to a footman as they swept out the door.

Winston climbed into the carriage and Hunt followed, shutting the door. "Sorry your evening out has been cut short, Hunt."

"I am happy to go. I've seen all that interests me for one night."

Winston nodded. "Yes, indeed."

In the carriage, Elizabeth leaned her head back against the velvet squabs for the entire journey home. Once there, she bid Winston a swift good night and disappeared upstairs, as did her father a moment later.

"How about a nightcap?" Hunt asked immediately, once they were both alone.

"Yes, why not." But he might tap on Elizabeth's door later to make sure she was still in charity with him again and had whatever she required to ease her megrim.

He poured two whiskeys and sat down by the fire to study his old friend by firelight. "So, how did you enjoy the evening out?"

"Hmm, not really my idea of fun," Hunt murmured, swirling his whiskey around in his glass. "Bunch of pompous windbags, if you ask me."

"I think that exact same thing often." He laughed briefly. "You should hear the ruckus kicked up in parliament some days. Deafening and repetitive. There are many there who love nothing more than the sound of their own voices."

"Then why stay?"

"It is my duty to devote my life to the prosperity of my people and the country at large."

"Duty," Hunt drawled, much like Peter often did when they locked horns over his preoccupation with the business of being an earl. "Do not forget you'll have a wife soon, too. Nothing should mean more to you than her happiness."

He narrowed his eyes on Hunt. "The future Lady Hurlston's happiness is at the forefront of my mind at all times, I assure you."

"Is that right?"

Winston put his feet up on the low table between them, and let out a heavy sigh. Tonight had not gone as he'd planned at all. "Yes, indeed. She means the world to me."

"It hasn't always seemed that way to me," Hunt said slowly. "And even now it seems a pretty face and heaving bosom can still turn your head."

"My head pivots," he joked, "every which way I care to turn it."

Hunt pursed his lips though. "I hope so, for your sake. Elizabeth is not going to forgive indiscretions as easily as some women might."

"Ah, I heard you were back," Mama said as she entered the room. She looked about, and a flicker of disapproval crept into her gaze for Winston's feet on the table. "I did not anticipate you coming home so early and ate supper without you."

"That is quite all right, Mama." He smiled. "Elizabeth has suffered a megrim and has gone up to her chambers to bed. Hunt and I are just having a nightcap."

"I'm sorry to hear she's become afflicted. A megrim is never pleasant." Mother took a seat. "How was the evening out?"

"Thoroughly enjoyable," Winston promised.

"Yes indeed. Quite wonderful," Hunt agreed smoothly as he smiled. "And you're just in time to hear about the plans made for tomorrow," he said.

"What plans would those be?"

Hunt sat his glass aside. "Elizabeth has requested my company for an expedition with her father. Hope you don't mind my absence. It sounds like it will be a very long day away, in fact."

Winston had heard nothing of this from Mr. Mayflower or Elizabeth yet, but he was not surprised Elizabeth planned to shop. He had given her leave to send him the bills. Her taking Hunt along did not sit well with him, though. Why wasn't Mama going with them, too? Or had she been asked, and refused to go on account of Charlotte joining her for luncheon? "I can make myself available."

Hunt winced. "That will make it hard for Elizabeth to buy a surprise wedding present for the groom, though, won't it?"

"Ah, yes, I suppose it might," Winston agreed. He'd not expected a groom's present from anyone but he was touched. "I'll stay behind," he offered quickly.

"Excellent." Hunt downed the rest of his whiskey and bid them good night.

Mama frowned after Hunt left and then faced Winston with another disapproving glare. "You could still have spent a day with your betrothed."

"I couldn't spoil the surprise Elizabeth intends for me."

Mama looked down at her hands. "You're lucky she wants to give you anything at all. You avoided her for so long."

Winston groaned under his breath. He could have made it clear that *Elizabeth* was the reason their marriage had been delayed for so long, but what good would that do, other than cause friction between the pair? Instead, he gave a different response that she could accept. "Elizabeth has a streak of independence a mile wide. If she wants Hunt's advice about a present for me, that's her choice. He knows my tastes well."

Mama nodded. "I'm sure she'll want your company all the time when you are married. She'll want only her husband when she's carrying your child, too."

He shook his head. "I hope not. Our marriage is not meant to be a gilded cage for her. She has her own friends at home and has a fondness for Bath. She plans to visit there after we marry, by the way."

Mama frowned. "Bath is for the old and infirm."

"I would never have demanded you join her there," he teased.

"Good." Mama laughed softly. Her dislike of Bath was well known and of longstanding. Father had gone there to taste the waters as a remedy for gout, and Mother had only ever grudgingly accompanied him just to be certain he took proper care of himself.

She rubbed her hand on her knee. "Winston, I received a peculiar note from Miss Waters tonight and don't quite know what to think of it. As you know, she had accepted my invitation for luncheon, but tonight, just before you returned, I received a note saying she will not come after all."

"I was told she left tonight's ball with a megrim, too."

Mother seemed startled. "Her as well? I do hope there is not a sickness going round."

"I'm sure there isn't," he promised with a soft laugh. "Mother, you always worry too much about us all."

"Is that not a woman's duty? How do you feel?"

He laughed wholeheartedly then. "I'm in excellent health, Mama. As ever."

"What of Peter? I have not seen him in days."

"I've no idea, since I've not seen him either. Not since shortly after Elizabeth's arrival in fact."

Mother pursed her lips. "He's bound for trouble that boy, the way he carries on."

"Mother, he is a grown man now."

"With an expected inheritance that should have been delayed till he was thirty. At least."

"Thirty? Father would never have been so mean-spirited as to clip his wings for so long." When Mother puffed up, he spoke quickly. "I know you want to protect Peter with all your heart, but it's time to let go the leading strings. His birthday is coming up, and he'll receive the full sum Father bequeathed him then. We must have faith in his abilities to manage his own life."

Mama subsided. "You've always been a good brother to him."

"I still occasionally think about wringing his neck," he confessed with a grin he hoped Mother would laugh at. "Trust him."

"I suppose I've no choice now. He's grown so distant and secretive. Sneaking in and out of the house at all hours. At least I hope he still confides in you. I worry about the crowd he must be running with. Who are these friends of his? Why do they never join us for dinner?"

"Peter confides in me when he needs a second opinion," Winston promised. But that hadn't been often lately. Winston did not really know what his brother got up to anymore. It was something he wanted to talk to his brother about when the wedding was behind him. Peter might dislike Elizabeth, and be avoiding home to avoid her, but he still had family who loved him and wanted to see him.

Mama covered a yawn with her hand. "I think I shall sleep late tomorrow."

"I'll see you at luncheon," he told her. "Elizabeth is going out anyway, so I'll be in my study for the morning and join you later."

"Very well. I'll have cook prepare your favorite dishes," Mama promised, but then she sighed. "I was so looking forward to hearing of her travels."

Her being *Charlotte*.

Mama wandered from the room, appearing aimless and utterly disappointed in Charlotte's refusal to come. Now there was another person he'd like to strangle. Charlotte had no reason to snub Mama when her quarrel was with him.

Winston raked a hand through his hair. He really had put his foot in it with her tonight, if she thought she must avoid his mother over so slight a disagreement. But then again, he was used to quarreling with Elizabeth, who rarely held anything back when she had a chance to speak her mind.

He wasn't sure how he could fix things between Charlotte and Mother, or if he should make the attempt. Elizabeth had a ridiculous idea of Charlotte being heartbroken, which couldn't be further from the truth. He might be wise to let the matter rest, but it played on his mind as he sat alone sipping his whiskey.

Could it be true she admired him, as Elizabeth claimed? Cried over his betrothal announcement?

He'd never noticed anything untoward about her, except her occasional blushes and heaving bosom. But lots of young women, virgins, blushed around bachelors even if they wore gowns with bodices so low that gave any man an eyeful.

Charlotte had nice breasts. He'd like to…

"Has everyone gone to bed?"

Winston startled and opened his eyes as his brother slid into the room, quiet as a mouse. When had his brother learned to move so silently. He'd been for years telling him to cease stomping.

Peter looked a little worse for wear tonight and wild about the eyes. "Yes. Even Hunt has had his fill of my liquor and gone up to bed. What are you doing?"

"Getting a drink at last. Did Hunt leave any for me?" Peter rushed to the sideboard to the decanters and, finding them full, filled a glass of whiskey for himself. He gulped the first glass down and paused to refill it. "You need to have a strong word with your future wife, brother. You're not married to her yet, and I won't be ordered to bed by her, no matter what hour it is."

"What?"

Peter took another drink. "Just now, I was looking about for something to drink in your chambers and when I came out into the hall, I encountered Elizabeth. She blistered my ears for invading your rooms as if I have no right to roam the halls of my own home."

Winston shook his head. "They *are* my chambers, and it was my whiskey you were intending to drink, brother."

Peter set his hands on his hips. "Oh, so now sharing the occasional glass with me troubles you too?"

"No, it doesn't, but then I haven't before had a future wife under my roof before this week. You must have startled her out of her wits."

Peter downed the remains of his glass. "Well, she shouldn't be traipsing about the upper halls in her night gown in the dead of night. Seeing her like that frightened me out of ten years of my life!"

Winston scowled. "She has a megrim, and your rattling around must have disturbed her. I'd better go smooth things over."

"Yes, do run along." Peter said dropping untidily into a chair. Better you than—"

"For heaven's sake let it lie, Peter." He stood and glared at his brother. "There are plenty more spirits stashed about the house. Drink whatever you care for, but from now on, I suggest you keep out of my private chambers."

"Fine." Peter's jaw set in a mulish line. "How long is Hunt expected to stay?"

"I don't really know. A few weeks, I expect, at least. Is he teasing you about being the spare again? I told you just to ignore it."

Peter shrugged, and his eyes dropped. "Isn't it odd to you that he's come to Town now?"

"He said he had business in town. He's our guest because I asked him to stay, as well. But I doubt he'll manage to stay much beyond the wedding."

"Good. He's another I don't want to see traipsing the halls in his nightshirt again, either."

"When was that?"

"Just now. Came out of his room to stare and laugh while Elizabeth cut me to ribbons with that shrill tongue of hers. The pair of them always side with each other, no matter what I say to protest my innocence."

"Most often you're lying to a degree, brother. Everyone knows that—even Hunt."

Peter burst to his feet. "Well, I'll not stay to be slandered."

"Oh, don't be so damn touchy. I was only teasing you."

"Does seem that way to me." Peter shook his head and headed for the door. "I knew you wouldn't want me around anymore."

"That is not true. Come back."

Peter didn't.

Winston sank into a chair but refused to chase after his brother. It was an unhappy realization to discover that after two years of adjustment, Peter still resented him becoming the earl upon their father's death. Winston would have given anything in the world to have his father brought back to life. But that was not possible. All he could do was try to live up to his father's expectations for his life and hope that somehow Peter could forgive him for something utterly out of his control.

Chapter Seven

"Mr. McCarrick, you are too kind," Charlotte murmured, holding on to her favorite carriage hat as they rounded the corner into a stiff breeze.

"No. No. I am a man who says what is on my mind, and the way the sunlight catches the highlights of your hair is remarkable."

He was not saying Charlotte was remarkable. Just the color of her hair. So far, he had complimented her shoes, her modestly sized reticule, and the sturdiness of the parasol she carried with her for their outing to Hyde Park. She didn't exactly enjoy traveling in a high-perch phaeton but could hardly quibble. She finally had a nibble.

Mr. McCarrick was a business acquaintance of Mr. Berringer's, and he had only introduced them that very morning. It was a pity he'd not been invited to last night's ball, but Mr. McCarrick had immediately asked to take her driving that afternoon. She had been very flattered by his keen interest in seeing more of her.

But this was not quite the fashionable hour for a carriage ride. Indeed, they were likely an hour too early to join any of the *ton* for an afternoon of staring at each other's fine equipage and company and paying anyone a compliment.

She would have to explain a few things about the reason for the fashionable hour to the young man, should she manage to bring him up to scratch.

His first name was Taylor, she'd found out.

Taylor McCarrick was an amiable young man from a hard-working London family. He possessed neither grand fortune nor exceeding good looks. He worked in the city in a bank the Duke of Exeter had dealings with and dressed appropriately for his station in life. And he seemed genuinely interested in her so far.

When he passed the turn into Hyde Park, she stared over her shoulder in dismay. "I thought we were to drive into the park?"

"To the park and around it. Can't stand the way the aristocracy crowds in at the same hour every day to gawk at each other."

"That's why they call it the fashionable hour, but that is at five o'clock, not at four in the afternoon," she advised. "Which is the time now. The row should be almost deserted if we go back."

"Well, it's nobody's business if I have a lady in my carriage, or how long she's there, either," he muttered. "Cannot stand gossips. Don't know how Berringer stands it. We'll skirt the perimeter and miss the *ton's* ridiculous parade by a good mile."

"Oh." Charlotte felt deflated. It hadn't been every afternoon that she was invited to drive on a sunny day from the vantage point of a high-perch phaeton such as this. And since they were not actually entering the park at all, it was highly unlikely she'd be asked to take a stroll on his arm now, either. She patted the parasol by her side, disappointed no one would see the pretty new design of her latest purchase.

"You're disappointed," he observed after a moment.

"Yes, a little. But it is my fault I misunderstood your intentions for our outing today, I suppose," she admitted.

"It is better this way," he promised. "We'll have an easier time talking with no one eavesdropping on our conversation. We've much to talk about, and I understand you've not much time to spare."

"Oh?"

"Berringer warned me not to waste a moment, as you'd likely be leaving London soon."

Dismay filled her. She hadn't wanted to make a big deal of the urgency of her situation until it became necessary. "Oh, he told you I was leaving?"

"Yes, he thought it best to explain the situation before we went driving today. Before things went too far. I must admit, when we were introduced, I felt an urgency to learn more about you. I can hardly call upon you in Egypt, can I?"

"My parents are headed to Africa, actually."

"Even farther away still," he murmured, proving he'd no idea of geography or travel. "You have my sympathies. I can understand why you're so desperate to make a match."

Although he was correct about the urgency of her situation, Charlotte bristled a little at his comment about it. He was a blunt one. Blunt men tended to trample on other people's emotions and never noticed. "I have many friends in London, and I should like to remain behind to live my life here, too. Adventure is my parents' passion rather than mine. But they will not countenance parting with me unless I am wed. I'd like to be married, as well."

"You've always traveled with them?"

"Yes."

"They must love you very much, then." Mr. McCarrick nodded to a passing carriage. "Carting an infant about the world cannot have been an easy matter. I have six siblings, and you'll find out firsthand just how exhausting so many at a time can be when you meet them."

"Six?" She gulped. Had Mr. McCarrick decided to introduce her to his family already? "I'm fond of children." Charlotte wanted her own very much.

"Good. It's a tight fit at our present lodgings, but should I happen to marry a lady possessed of a dowry the size of yours, I'm sure we'd find somewhere larger to fit us all soon enough."

Charlotte swallowed a lump in her throat. He was already planning their future with a dowry like hers. He wasn't wasting time stating he had an interest. But she was not sure if it was her or her available dowry that suited him more. "May I be so bold as to ask where exactly you live, sir?"

"Home is near Lincoln Fields, above a milliner. It's a cozy place. Nothing at all what you must be used to in Mayfair, though. My old papa has the smaller room to himself overlooking the street, the children and I the larger at the rear. There's a kitchen of sorts, and a washroom off that in the middle, under the staircase."

Charlotte took in that description, quickly realizing Mr. McCarrick's accommodation was a good deal smaller than a single floor of her current home with her parents. "I see. Does Mr. Berringer know where you live?"

"Not certain it's ever come up in conversation," McCarrick said slowly. "The bank pays a decent wage for the work I do, though. I'm sure to advance up the ranks anytime now."

She gulped down her disappointment over his situation as best she could. Mr. McCarrick was not quite the suitor she'd hoped for. She wasn't even sure her father would accept a working-class gentleman into the family, either. But if she found she liked Mr. McCarrick enough to wish to consider marrying him, she would convince her parents that she would adapt to his present circumstances and persuade Mr. McCarrick to pursue advancement in his career as quickly as possible. Hopefully moving them to a home closer to Mayfair and her friends.

She looked up at his face, trying to decide if she felt anything for him yet. He was a plain, practical sort of man. He didn't make her heart skip a beat, though. She looked forward again. "I couldn't help but notice you did not mention your mother or older family members. Do you have many relatives?"

"Mama ran off after my last sibling was born. My cousins live below, behind the milliner shop they also run. We all help out with the shop. You'd be expected to as well from time to time."

Charlotte looked down at her hands. She had trimmed her own hats, but she'd never excelled at the art. Not enough to do the work for paying customers. "I don't come from a large family. There is only me and my parents. Do you attend the assembly rooms during the season?"

"Oh, yes. Every quarter, we all go. It's a jolly good night for all of us traveling together. The little ones especially enjoy it and invariably fall asleep wherever they can on the way home."

"You're fond of your family?"

"Isn't everyone?"

"Some do like their families more than others," she said carefully, not really believing that. "I come from a rather small family."

"Must be why you're so quiet and timid," he teased. "You've got to shout to be heard in a large family."

She shouted sometimes, but only to drag her parents' attention briefly from their dusty books and then she'd be reprimanded for it. Mr. McCarrick's life and family sounded so very different from hers. Would she enjoy it? Taking care of six of Mr. McCarrick's siblings and a father, too? Working in a milliner's shop from time to time? It certainly wasn't the life she'd expected for herself. A long step down in consequence for her, too. She hoped it wouldn't prove to be a step too far.

She appreciated Mr. McCarrick's candor, though. He was an honest man, it seemed.

"Berringer mentioned your father and mother were…"

Charlotte closed her eyes briefly and finished his sentence when words seemed to fail him. "Eccentric."

"Bookish," he suggested.

"Yes," she drawled. "They are that. Bookish and eccentric. There's no cure, I'm afraid."

Mr. McCarrick laughed. "I like to read. Frequent a lending

library when I have the funds to spare. I've spent many a night reading out loud to everyone before bedtime."

"My parents' choice of books certainly helped me fall asleep while I was growing up." She sighed. "Dull as paint drying. I must be equally honest with you, Mr. McCarrick. My parents are more than a little eccentric, I'm afraid," Charlotte admitted, wincing. "They are blinkered to all but their own interests. Always have been."

"Bookish men, historians, and explorers *are* blinkered. Every family has its oddities." He chuckled. "Take my own family. I have an uncle in the country who swears he could divine the location of fresh water using two chickens."

"That would have been useful on my third expedition to a desert. We had to line sandy hollows with canvas and by morning, there'd be just enough water to quench our thirst."

He laughed. "You really are a seasoned adventurer to know such a trick to gather water from only air."

"By necessity, not choice, I assure you. Adventure was forced upon me whether I liked it or not. I was never of an age where I could refuse to travel if my father orders it. I'm still not."

"So, you really would be happy to remain in England?" When Charlotte nodded, he continued. "I always hoped to travel to the seaside myself, but with the little ones to look after, it's a dream that will most likely never come true for me unless I marry well."

"I see," she murmured in as noncommittal way as possible. The sea contained ships that took one away from England. She had no interest in visiting any port ever again.

"You'll have to tell me your stories so I can share them with my family," he asked, looking at her with one arched brow.

She had years of experiences that were hard to put into words. But finally, she'd met a man keen to hear what she had to say. "I'll do my best to share only the most exciting ones."

Mr. McCarrick grinned, and he turned the carriage south toward Green Park. It was an area she'd rarely gone, and she looked about eagerly, drinking in the new views. "How similar it is here to Hyde Park."

"Not so similar." Mr. McCarrick flicked the reins suddenly to make the horse speed up. "A lower class of criminals obviously frequent it, though, so we'd best not linger."

She looked around. "How do you know there are criminals here?"

"Don't look."

"I—" And then Charlotte saw four men brawling on the edge of Green Park, while a fifth, his hat pulled low over his eyes, watched on from behind a distant tree.

One brawler stumbled and fell; his assailants were upon him immediately. Kicking at him with their rough boots. His hat went flying off his head as he tried to protect himself, and Charlotte recognized him instantly. "Stop the carriage!"

"I hardly think—"

"No, stop!" Charlotte rose despite the fact they were moving and it was dangerous. Her skirts might become caught in the wheels, but she was beyond caring. "Stop the carriage this instant! We have to help him."

"I don't want to put you in harm's way."

"I'll put *myself* in harm's way. That is Lord Hurlston on the ground!"

She snatched up her parasol and gathered up her skirts in preparation to fling herself out of the moving phaeton, if need be. Thankfully, Mr. McCarrick saw reason and brought the horses to a rough halt not far from where Lord Hurlston had fallen.

Charlotte wasted no time. She clambered over Mr. McCarrick's long legs and jumped down unaided to the roadway. She landed well and then darted into Green Park, little caring for the consequences of her mad dash.

Winston was being hurt.

She flew at his attackers, parasol swinging wildly, and struck the first fellow she came to a resounding blow about his head before moving on to the next man.

They roared in outrage, but her surprise attack gave Winston a chance to regain his feet. He seemed winded and in obvious pain. He clutched his ribs with one arm for a moment, then went on the attack, too. Striking out at two of his assailants.

Charlotte kept up her jabs and smacks to the third man until the moment he grabbed the end of her parasol by the tip.

"Unhand my parasol, you worthless cur!" Then she jabbed at him as hard as she could. The tip of her parasol was nicely pointed and apparently sharp enough to cause a break to the skin. A bright patch of red appeared on the man's shirt and he uttered a foul curse.

She stumbled back a few steps, assessing her situation as the man surveyed his injury. She was not winded, and her opponent was wounded and obviously angry. Uncertain what he might do next, Charlotte planted her feet. Her opponent glared threateningly at her.

Out of the corner of her eye, she saw Winston knock one assailant to his knees. He was doing better now that the odds were more in his favor.

Charlotte swirled her parasol about and smacked Winston's other attacker across the back of his head.

Her own wounded opponent quickly backed out of her range, dragging the second man with him. The third turned tail and fled without prompting.

Charlotte watched them hurry away, blood pumping wildly through her veins. "Cowards! That'll teach you for not having any gentlemanly manners and teaming up three against one," she complained.

Winston shook his fist in their direction, too. "Bad sportsmanship if ever I've seen it," he cried out. "Eh, Charlotte?"

"The worst," she replied, turning to grin at him. She scanned the park again, looking for the fifth man. But he'd vanished now, too. She turned back to the earl. "Are you all right, Winston?"

"Never better." But then Winston winced, his arms curling around his ribs.

Charlotte rushed to him. "You're hurt!"

"Bruised." He looked up at her from under his long fringe. "I'll forever consider myself lucky my assailant didn't carry an equally lethal parasol like yours. I wouldn't have stood a chance."

"*Miss Waters!*"

She turned to find Mr. McCarrick standing just beyond Winston and staring at her as if he'd never seen her before. She also got the sense that it wasn't the first time he'd called her name.

Mr. McCarrick strode over, grabbed her arm and tried to tug her away from the earl. "I must insist we leave this place now."

"Yes, of course. We must get Lord Hurlston on his way home immediately. We cannot wait for the authorities." She wriggled under Winston's arm to support his weight as he slowly straightened up. "Where is your carriage, my lord?"

"I walked here."

"Well, that wasn't sensible."

Winston made a half-laugh that turned into a full groan of pain. "I see the error of my ways now that you've pointed them out."

She smiled at him, but couldn't help noticing his handsome face was in utter ruin, and that tore at her heart. One of Winston's eyes was swelling shut, his nose was dripping blood onto a once pristine cravat, and he was listing to one side like a sailor under the influence of too much rum. "We'll take you straight home."

"Miss Waters, I must speak with you immediately," Mr. McCarrick announced.

She glanced up to see a look of severe disapproval on Mr. McCarrick's face. She took a moment to consider what she was doing. What she might have looked like to another person more concerned by appearances than she currently was.

She had fought beside Winston with a parasol, drawing blood on at least one of his attackers, and now she was draping herself around the earl's waist in case he was worse than he let on and happened to fall down. It was nothing she'd never done before on her adventures with her parents with an injured fellow traveler…but it was not something she ought to do in England, perhaps. "He is injured and needs our aid."

"This is distressing indeed, however, I think you'll agree with me that—"

She cut the young man off. "If you have difficulty with rendering assistance to a member of the aristocracy, then I am afraid we can have no more to say to each other after this."

"Charlotte," Winston warned.

"Hush. I won't abandon you." She looked up at her once potential suitor with resignation. McCarrick clearly disapproved of her behavior. But then he shrugged, at last coming to Winston's other side, and put an arm around the earl.

They shuffled to McCarrick's carriage which McCarrick had left tied to a tree, listened to Winston groan as he climbed up to the high-perch bench. "Oh, that stings."

Charlotte clambered up next and put her ear lightly on Winston's chest, listening to his labored breathing. It was impossible to tell if his ribs had punctured a lung through. He seemed to be breathing well enough for now. "You must see a doctor soon." She turned his abused face carefully toward hers. "Are you having great difficulty drawing in breath?"

Winston stared at her and then his fingers rose to touch her face as well. "That's not the difficulty I'm having."

Charlotte frowned. "What is the other difficulty? How can I help?"

He dropped his hand, and looked away. "Take me home," he whispered.

Charlotte looked down at McCarrick who had not yet taken a seat in the carriage. "We should go, sir, before they think to come back for him."

Mr. McCarrick clambered up to sit beside her. It was a tight fit to seat the three of them on the narrow bench, with her squeezed in the middle, almost on each man's thigh.

Hurlston tilted alarmingly away from her at the first corner, and Charlotte made a hurried grab for his leg to prevent him from tumbling out. "Hold on," she whispered to him.

McCarrick grunted again. "So just how well acquainted are you with this man, Miss Waters?"

"Oh, not very," she assured him, putting her hands back in her lap primly as soon as they were driving in a straight line again. "He is a friend of my friends. We've hardly ever spoken."

"It seemed just now as if you and he were more than that," he muttered, half under his breath.

"I'd render aid to anyone in the same situation," she assured him. But perhaps not as vigorously if it were anyone else. She hadn't given a thought to her own safety from the moment she'd seen Winston under attack. Those men could easily have pulled out a knife and slit his throat. She shuddered. She might have been wounded herself. Yet, she hadn't thought of anything besides saving Winston from harm.

Winston frequently groaned as they built up speed and the carriage began to lurch and bounce them with every change of direction.

"This will not do." She turned to Mr. McCarrick. "Could

you please take the next corners very slowly? I fear he might have broken ribs."

"What do you know about the care of broken bones?" McCarrick asked.

"I've treated my share of misadventures," she admitted.

"She's too modest. She's probably seen more misadventures than anyone in London, if half the stories I've heard about her travels with her parents are true," Winston added in a strained tone.

She looked at him in surprise for that statement. What had he heard about her? And was that the reason why men never sought her company?

But she pushed those questions aside as she noticed how pale Winston's face had become, and that it shone with perspiration now, too. She dug in his coat pocket, finding his handkerchief nestled directly over his heart. She held it out to him. "Bite down on this. It will help you bear the pain."

He met her gaze—what gaze he had left, because one of his eyes seemed to have swelled almost completely shut by then. He used the handkerchief to dry his brow instead. "You shouldn't have put yourself in harm's way on my account again," he complained.

"Would you rather they'd succeeded in stripping you of everything of value?" she asked, wringing her hands, unsure of what else she could do for him.

Winston shoved the handkerchief back in his coat pocket and showed her a bundle of notes from another pocket. "They took nothing from me. Too busy with their fists and feet. At least until you arrived. You were magnificent, by the way. A veritable tigress."

She ignored his praise, thinking hard on the fact that she had, twice in one week, managed to save Winston from danger. Of course, he was badly injured this time, but what were the odds of it happening at random twice?

Unheard of.

He groaned as they reached his square and suddenly clutched at her arm. "I need to get down from this carriage before I cast up my accounts."

"You'll not do that," she ordered of him. She grasped his hand tightly. His impressive London mansion loomed just ahead. "We're almost home, I promise."

McCarrick drew to a halt in front of Winston's grand house and jumped down. He helped Charlotte down to the pavement, and Winston nearly tumbled out, landing almost on top of her with his inelegant decent.

McCarrick, instead of Charlotte, hooked an arm round Winston's back and marched him up to his own front door and kicked instead of knocking.

Charlotte followed them inside as soon as the butler opened the door a crack. She had been inside Hurlston's home just once before. His study was to the right, his drawing room to the left. "To the right, Mr. McCarrick," Charlotte decided. He'd be more comfortable in his own private chamber. There was bound to be liquor there, too, to dull his pain.

A flustered butler followed them into Winston's study, spluttering out a demand to know who they were and what they'd done to Lord Hurlston.

"That is not our story to tell," she informed the distressed servant. "His lordship will explain what you need to know later." Charlotte stripped off her gloves. "For now, we'll need long bandages, warm water, and soft cloths. Quickly, man. Your master is in agony while you dither."

The butler scurried off as McCarrick eased Hurlston down onto a leather settee and stood back.

Charlotte leaned over Winston. "Let me see your face now," she murmured.

Winston looked up slowly as he slid back more comfortably into the seat with a groan. His right eye had swelled completely shut, and his nose was in danger of dripping blood onto his cravat still. She gently pressed her handkerchief to his nose, wincing as Winston hissed in pain from even that little pressure.

"Sorry," she whispered.

"Who are you people? What are you doing in my son's private chambers?"

Charlotte turned to meet the angry glare of Winston's esteemed mother. Realizing she was blocking the lady's view, Charlotte quickly stepped aside. "Your son has been hurt, my lady."

The woman rushed forward with a terrified wail. "Oh, my sweet boy! What's been done to you?"

"I'm all right, Mama." Hurlston promised, trying to avoid his mother's hands as they started to close about his abused face. "I'm all right. There's no need to fret."

"First those riders, and now this," she sobbed. "Who did this to you? Tell me."

"I don't know," he admitted, catching hold of his mama's hands and comforting her. "But they're far away now."

Charlotte backed toward the door where Mr. McCarrick waited, to give them privacy.

"Might I have that word with you now, Miss Waters?"

She nibbled her lower lip and nodded. "Yes, I'm at your disposal."

He stalked into the hall and Charlotte followed, assuming he was about to speak very bluntly indeed.

He spun about, his eyes blazing. "You know that man too well indeed. Don't lie to me."

She owed McCarrick nothing but thanks for his aid in bringing Winston to safety. "Of course, I know of him. He is the Earl of Hurlston, a popular figure in London society. Thank you for helping him."

"Is he so popular that everyone uses his given name rather than his title, or is that just you?"

"That was my presumption," she admitted. "I am fond of the name."

"And the man too, it seems."

She couldn't answer that honestly. "I did what I thought was right, even if you don't agree with me."

"Did you even bother to ask my opinion before you went charging in and endangering your own precious life?"

"That is not the way I was raised, sir. There was no time to waste. I have taken care of myself, made my own decisions, for as long as I can remember. I had to."

"Well, when you marry me, I'd advise you to start listening to your husband. It will be my responsibility to shield you from the unpleasantness of life."

She studied McCarrick. He was a good man, and he wanted to treat her in a way she'd always dreamed a man might. But she was ill-suited to doing nothing. Not when someone she cared about was in peril. "Thank you for an enjoyable drive today, Mr. McCarrick. I will be able to find my own way home from here."

"I am not leaving without you. Think of your reputation!"

"Lord Hurlston is engaged and no danger to me, and his mother is here now, so I am suitably chaperoned."

"The men who attacked him know your face," he warned. "I'll see you home and speak to your parents about the danger you foolishly put yourself in."

Charlotte sighed. She'd rather he didn't try to talk to her parents. When he did, he'd find out just how indifferent her parents were to her welfare. He would certainly turn tail and run then.

But as she considered his towering display of temper, she realized she wanted him to do exactly that. To be put off by her parents attitudes. She couldn't consider marrying McCarrick, after all. She wouldn't be happy with such a man.

Chapter Eight

Mama was beside herself despite Winston's reassurances, and she turned to Charlotte immediately when the young woman returned to stare down at him with such tender concern.

Charlotte, his unexpected savior.

Again.

"My lady, I suspect he's suffered no great harm," Charlotte soothed.

From what little he could see through his diminished vision, Mama was only somewhat relieved by Charlotte's words. "You were there."

"I only brought him home," she admitted, making light of her rescue. "Mr. McCarrick and I were luckily driving by and saw…"

"She saw that I had fallen down," Winston finished for her firmly. He could not allow Charlotte to embark on a long description of his altercation today. That would not do Mother's nerves any good. "So clumsy of me. It was just a bit of bad luck that I landed flat on my face."

Mama frowned, clearly suspicious of his explanation. But there was no way she'd bear the truth. A lie was a kindness for her nerves right now.

"Yes, he fell forward," Charlotte agreed in a rush. "Tripped and fell. Straight into a tree trunk," she confessed and then winced.

Dear God, Winston would have to live out that lie for the rest of his life. He could easily imagine the teasing he'd suffer for it, too.

"Mama, could you do me a favor," he asked quickly. "I was expecting to meet with my banker here later tonight. Given my accident, would you be so good as to send a servant to Jacobs and Sons and request a delay of a few days for our appointment? Please. I'd rather not be seen like this."

"Yes, of course," Mother agreed, nodding quickly, but she remained, wringing her hands. "Oh, I wish Elizabeth was not out still. She'd be such a comfort to you."

Charlotte's smile turned brittle and she drew Mama slightly away from him. "I'd be happy stay with your son until your return."

"We both will," said Charlotte's male acquaintance in a stern tone.

"Oh, thank you, both of you," Mama gushed. "Yes, I…I'll be right back."

When Mother went on her way again, Winston rushed to explain why he lied. "It will do her no good to hear what really happened to me." Winston glanced at the man standing just behind Charlotte. "I don't believe we've been introduced, sir."

"Mr. Taylor McCarrick. I'm an acquaintance of Miss Waters'," he said slowly. "And you are…"

"This is Winston Bell, the Earl of Hurlston," Charlotte said quickly, introducing them properly.

McCarrick's shake was too firm and made Winston wince in pain.

"Be careful with him," Charlotte cried out, rushing to take his abused hand out of McCarrick's grip. He still wore gloves, which she carefully removed for him. As she turned his hands over, Winston was relieved to see no blood or cuts upon his knuckles. They ached though.

Winston pulled his hands back to his lap and adjusted himself more comfortably on the chaise. But he regretted moving even that much. The carriage ride had been torturous. He felt much better on the soft chair close to the floor. Less distance to fall if he became nauseous and dizziness assailed him again. "I cannot thank you enough for your assistance, Mr. McCarrick. They almost had me."

"It was the right thing to do," Charlotte answered for McCarrick as the housekeeper and a pair of maids rushed in, their arms full.

Charlotte took charge of the servants and began giving quiet orders for what must be put where around Winston. Clearly, Charlotte had fooled him. She might act like a demure mouse when at society entertainments, but she seemed a take-charge kind of woman everywhere else. He was grateful for that today, yet he still couldn't believe how enthusiastically she'd rushed to his defense, beating off an assailant with just a parasol in hand.

He couldn't shake the feeling she'd done that before on her travels. She seemed completely at ease about her violent display, too. Something he could hardly fault her for when it had been to his advantage.

The housekeeper approached with a fistful of red-stained muslin cloth that carried the scent of blood upon it. "We'll need to apply steak to both your eyes, my lord."

"Yes, I thought you'd say that." He already couldn't see out of his right one, and what he could see from his left was becoming very narrow.

Behind the housekeeper, Charlotte and her male friend conducted another whispered discussion. He strained to hear their words over the next mutterings of his housekeeper, but then the fellow, McCarrick, stalked from the room, leaving Charlotte behind, hanging her head.

The housekeeper chose that moment to dump cool steak on Winston's upturned face. He let out an ugly curse for the shock and cold and fresh pain inflicted.

Charlotte, and he knew it was her by the light touch on his

shoulder, whispered from close by and the light scent of citrus she always wore. "Here, let me do that."

"You'll get blood on your hands," the housekeeper warned.

"Clearly you've never sat down to dinner with the Maasai of Africa," Charlotte mused. "Rare meat for every meal. Not a knife in sight or a fork. I'll do this while you fetch ointment for his cut lip."

Winston lifted his fingers to his face, noticing for the first time how his lip bulged and pained him when he touched it.

Charlotte gently moved his fingers away from the injury without a word.

"As you like," the housekeeper agreed. "I'll see what's keeping my lady."

"Thank you."

Winston tensed as the cold meat shifted on his skin. But now the pressure was lighter and more bearable. "Is that easier to bear, my lord?"

"The housekeeper could have done it," he complained.

"I know. But I wanted a moment to talk to you alone and thought this might be my only chance."

He felt her skirts brush against the inside of his thighs and tensed. "What more is there to discuss?"

"About my suspicion that someone is trying to do you in."

He pushed away her hand holding the meat to stare up at her in surprise. She was leaning right over him, frowning with a level of concern that only his mother could match. She was so close he could probably count every eyelash she had. He swallowed hard, overcome by unexpected desire thanks to her proximity and the innocent brush of her legs against his. "I'm just having a rotten run of luck."

Charlotte returned the meat to the right side of his face, leaving his left eye uncovered for now. "You could have died today."

"But I didn't." His pulse sped up as he lifted one hand to

brush against her thigh. For a moment, he imagined Charlotte poised naked over him, about to make love. He shook his head to dispel a tryst that could never be. He let his hand drop to his lap. "You saved me, remember?"

"Again. Winston, I cannot shake the feeling that someone seeks to do you harm."

He caught again the repeated use of his given name by her, but he would not chide her for the slip of decorum. He had been assaulted today, and Charlotte had been deeply involved. She might be unsettled enough to have forgotten propriety entirely. "They wanted my valuables."

"If they wanted your valuables, they would have held you down while the third man searched your pockets. Not kicked you over and over and over again."

He winced that she'd seen that. Charlotte may have a point about the viciousness of the attack being excessive for a robbery, but he could hardly agree that the assault was in any way planned. He'd been in the park alone on a whim. "It was a foiled robbery and the fellows like to rough up their victims first. Anyway, what experience do you have in understanding the mind of a criminal?"

"More than I care for," she warned, nibbling on her lip.

That did not sound pleasant. "What happened?"

"An unpleasantness. One of many." She shook her head as if to clear away the memory. "I am a seasoned traveler, my lord. I learned how to protect myself on my travels from a young age. Fight, if I have to. Surrender valuables if need be. Run if outnumbered by villains or thugs. You should have run at the first sign of trouble, and you really shouldn't wander alone anymore, my lord. It's not safe."

He drew in a deep breath, regretted it instantly as his ribs protested, and forced a smile to his face. She was kind to be so worried about him, but it was just bad luck that he'd been singled out today. He rarely went anywhere without a carriage and servants accompanying him. He'd only gone out today alone to prove his brother wrong about being entirely too predictable. "I appreciate your concern, but I'm sure you are mistaken about the nature of today's skirmish."

"Attack." She chewed on her lip again while she turned the raw meat, so the cooler side now chilled his skin. "What if I'm not wrong and someone really does want to hurt you?"

"Then you'll be proven right, I suppose."

She scowled at him. "I'd rather know you lived in perfect health. Promise me that you'll take the matter of your safety seriously."

"Miss Waters," he scolded. "I am grateful for your assistance today, but there is only so much fussing I can stand." He took the meat from her hand and stood, ignoring how different parts of his anatomy protested the stretch. It was time to end Miss Waters' speculation before Mother returned and took anything Charlotte might utter to heart. He looked down upon her upturned face and a pang of longing rushed through him. She had the kindest eyes and he lost track of time as he stared into them. He could drown in them, and her, if he were not careful. If it had been any other day, he might even have kissed her. But he could not. He was almost a married man. "Thank you for your aid and your concern, but I can look after myself now."

She stepped back—but then did something remarkable. Something no other lady of his acquaintance had ever dared. She wagged her finger at him. "You'd better be in perfect health when I see you again or else!"

She turned away to wash her hands and spoke quietly to the returning housekeeper. When she exited the chamber, parasol clutched tight in her tiny hand with her chin held high, he would have smiled except that would hurt too much.

He let out a frustrated breath. How could such an exceptionally complex woman have remained unnoticed among the wallflowers? Why hadn't he paid more attention to her either? He might have…

Winston groaned. *Women.* He'd never understand them as long as he lived.

He went to the window. Charlotte was being helped into Mr. McCarrick's phaeton outside, and he had to say, neither of them looked pleased to be together now.

It occurred to him only then that he'd probably interrupted their outing. And if McCarrick had actually been courting Charlotte, they'd exchanged harsh words about him. The fellow must have been shocked by the ferocity of Charlotte's actions today.

Winston winced. Clearly, Charlotte hadn't needed his help meeting bachelors. If he'd stayed out of her way, she might yet be in McCarrick's good graces. He feared that was not the case anymore and it was entirely his fault.

The housekeeper appeared at his side then and steered him back to a chair and forced him down in it. "Forgive me, my lord, but I must insist you rest." The housekeeper grabbed his hand and peered at his knuckles. "The young lady was right, wasn't she? You've taken a fair beating today, and you won't admit it to be in great pain. Shall I send for your physician."

"No. I only need to rest."

"The young woman feared you've damaged your ribs, my lord. Is it hard to breathe?"

"It was at first," he admitted sheepishly. "But it is getting easier now I'm sitting down again.

"She bid me watch over you closely for the next few days." The housekeeper smiled. "I expect you'll not care for it, but you must rest if you are to heal properly. I'll assign a footman to help your valet and to fetch anything you need, including as much drink as required to dull the pain."

The housekeeper was never usually so bossy. He nodded grudgingly because he *was* in a bit of a bad way. Charlotte had read the situation, and his feelings, very well indeed. "I promise to rest."

"Thank you, my lord." The housekeeper sighed. "Shall I have Miss Mayflower sent for?"

"No," he said quickly. He'd rather not have Elizabeth panic and rush home to wring her hands over his state.

A footman arrived carrying a tall glass and filled it with spirits, and Winston gulped down the offering, then sat back in a chair with the raw meat perched over both eyes while the alcohol worked to dull the pain.

"Forgive me if I'm out of line, my lord, but I thought you should know…your mother is in tears on the stairs just outside the room."

He feared someone might tell him that about her. He uncovered one eye and met the footman's concerned gaze. "Would you whisper to her that I've fallen asleep and suggest I shouldn't be disturbed for a few hours?"

The footman nodded quickly, kindly refilled his glass, left a decanter beside it, and quietly excused himself to deliver his message.

Mother sobbed loudly once and then it seemed that she was ushered away upstairs. She'd return when she'd composed herself. She had never been very good when he'd been injured in the past. Like the time he'd burned all the hair off one arm trying to recover a new hat that Peter had thrown into the flames. He'd suffered a month of coddling that time and Peter had been locked away in his room a whole month—even if Winston had promised it had been an accident.

Winston sat there alone for what must have been half an hour, undisturbed while he relived the assault at the park, rubbing his thumb over the heavy signet right on his left hand as he recalled every blow he'd delivered and received.

It *was* odd that none of his money or valuables had been taken by his attackers. He'd a decent number of notes upon him, and coin, too. He patted his chest where the thick wad rested and toyed with the heavy chain of his pocket watch. Why hadn't they stolen anything of value from him if they were vicious thieves?

To ask that question, he'd have to find those men again, and he was not keen to do that just yet.

Charlotte might be right about some being broken, after all.

Clever woman.

Fierce.

Stubborn…and awfully *attractive.*

He sighed in disgust with himself. Even beaten and bruised, he couldn't explain why only Charlotte Waters incited lust in him. And her hand on his thigh…dear God, that had felt so good and better not happen again.

"Isn't it a bit early to be sleeping off an excess of spirits, brother?" Peter yelled out loudly. "You really are becoming just like Father to need a nap so early in the evening."

Winston nearly jumped out of his seat, started by the interruption to his musings from so close by. He must have dozed off thinking of Charlotte's soft hand stroking across his thigh.

"Hush now, Lord Peter. Can't you see your brother deserves all the drink he can swallow today," the housekeeper hissed. "There's been such a to-do, you cannot imagine."

Winston pulled the meat from his face and turned to find his brother being blocked by the housekeeper at the doorway. "Let him pass," Winston requested as he met his brother's startled gaze. "No cause for alarm. I'll survive."

Peter rushed around the chair to peer at his face. "What the hell happened to you? Are you in pain?"

"It hurts a bit," he admitted, avoiding an answer about the source of his current injuries. He checked that Mother hadn't snuck into the room while he'd been sleeping, too. "As far as Mother should know, I fell down."

"How many times? Thirty?" Peter sat down opposite, peering at his face. "Tell me they were apprehended."

"No. They got away." Winston frowned. "Why do you think there was more than one?"

"Well, I can easily imagine you are more than a match for a single assailant, brother. All those hours at Gentleman Jackson's should have paid off against one."

He could hardly take credit for his defense today. He'd thought himself lost until Charlotte had recklessly thrown herself into the fray. Not even Mr. McCarrick had rolled up his sleeves in an attempt save him. The man had stood back holding his horse and carriage, as Charlotte should have done. "Yes, well. I managed," he muttered, deciding it best for Charlotte's reputation if he omitted her part in it all.

"Well, wherever they are, I hope they look as bad as you. That's not a pretty sight, your face."

Winston was not particularly vain about his looks, but if Peter described his face so poorly, he shuddered to think what Charlotte had thought of it when she'd leaned over him and tended to his injuries. So tenderly. As if she really had cared about him.

He owed Charlotte for saving his life a second time now. For putting her safety and reputation at risk for him yet again. That was becoming a habit of hers. How could he ever repay her this time? A few words of praise, when he was feeling better, hardly seemed sufficient after all she'd done for him today.

He'd try to think of something suitable while he rested. Perhaps he'd send her a present. Something not too expensive that it might draw unwanted attention. Something small and personal. Like the parasol she always carried. Yes, that is what he could do. Buy a replacement parasol in case hers had been damaged today during the fight. She had truly beaten those men well with her current one.

He'd been rather impressed by that, actually.

Heaven help the cur who tried to steal her virtue. He glanced at his brother. "What are you doing home at this hour?"

Peter's lips pressed together. "We were to have dinner."

"Ah, yes well. I did forget about that, and under the circumstances I'm not quite up to a proper dinner tonight."

"Then I'll leave then."

"You could stay."

Peter glanced toward the door, a sour expression on his face. "No, I'll only be in the way."

"I say, Hurlston, have you seen Mayflower about," Hunt asked, strolling into the room, looking down at the bottle of wine in his hands. "He'll appreciate trying this vintage, I'm sure."

"He's not returned yet," Winston told Hunt, wondering when the man would ever look up.

When he did, Hunt stopped dead in his tracks and stared at Winston's face. And then he came closer. "Devil take it."

"Indeed."

Hunt drew back. "Do I dare ask what happened?"

"He fell," Peter told Hunt in a flat deadly tone.

Hunt shook his head. "He always had two left feet as a boy. I thought he'd grown out of it. Do be more careful, old boy. You're the head of the family."

Peter scowled at that comment.

Winston winced and then squinted at Hunt through his one good eye. "I thought you were out with the Mayflowers?"

"I was for a while, but I saw something I wanted and left them to their own devices. Did you want some of this?"

"No."

"I'll have that," Peter demanded, taking the bottle from Hunt to inspect the label. "This is from Father's private collection."

A look of horror touched Hunt's face. "Was it? I had no

idea. I'm so sorry. I merely thought Mayflower would like to share a glass if he were returned."

Peter sniffed the open bottle carefully. "Seems fine to my nose but just to be sure, I'll take it to the butler. It is his duty to open all bottles from Father's collection to be sure they're safe to consume."

"Of course. Wouldn't want anyone to become ill from Hurlston's personal wine collection," Hunt murmured, filling a glass with spirits instead as Peter stalked from the room. "He's in a fine mood. What's wrong with him today?"

"I've no idea," Winston murmured.

"He's not still angry that you wouldn't buy him that phaeton, is he?" Hunt asked quietly. "Or is it the other thing? Your elevation to your father's title still getting under his skin. He's been sulking about that since your father died."

"He does not sulk," Winston assured his friend.

"He does, and you know it, too," Hunt warned. "He's grown so bitter in the last two years too that I hardly know what to think."

Winston sat up straighter. Was Peter bitter? He certainly wasn't the brother he'd once been. "I'm sure he'll come around soon."

He'd better.

Chapter Nine

"How did it go with Mr. McCarrick the other day?" Aurora asked. "You haven't said a word about him since we arrived."

Well, who could blame me?

Mr. McCarrick had given her a lecture on decorum yesterday on the drive home from Lord Hurlston's. He did not believe she ought to have involved herself in Winston's troubles, either vigorously defending him or worrying about his injuries later. His threat about talking to her parents had been an idle one. By the time they'd reached her home, he'd had enough of her and driven away without looking back.

Mr. McCarrick's lack of compassion for another human being was exactly why she hoped she never saw him again. She'd taken the precaution of telling the servants she'd not be-at home to him if he ever dared call again.

Compassion could not be taught. One felt it. Bone deep.

She glanced around Hyde Park now, surveying the familiar scene but sensing nothing to fear today. "Who is left to consider?"

Aurora moved in front of her. "McCarrick came highly recommended and had a good prospect in his profession for advancement. That was one of your requirements. Tell me what happened with him?"

Charlotte did not feel she could mention what had really happened that disastrous day. Especially not where it concerned Lord Hurlston's troubles. Not until she knew the earl was speaking of it first. She hadn't seen him in days. Her role in his rescue would be frowned upon by many, particularly potential suitors similar to Mr. McCarrick.

She thought back over her brief outing with McCarrick, trying to find a reasonable excuse to dismiss him that Aurora would accept without question. "McCarrick dislikes Hyde Park. He actually drove me around the permitter, with no intention of going in for the promenade, and he revealed a distain for higher society that was quite offensive to hear."

"The *ton* is an acquired taste," Aurora reminded her. "And it's not easy to feel at ease among the truly wealthy members of the aristocracy."

"I've never aspired to be the most popular woman in any room, but I have claimed my small corner and I'll not give it up easily."

"Then you might want to aim higher for a husband again," Aurora suggested. "I should like to see you made popular through a good match. Society women would be the better for following your kinder example of how to behave."

Not if they'd seen her defend Lord Hurlston in Green Park earlier in the week. Society women were taught not to exert themselves too vigorously. Perhaps she could be of use to society in changing expectations, though. She grinned at Aurora, imagining a roomful of women learning to defend themselves with their parasols. "Why not change the world? We could both strive to make a difference."

Aurora laughed heartily then. "Heavens, not by my example. I've no luck in love, and I wouldn't wish that poor prospect upon anyone—not even my worst enemies."

"I've no luck in love, either. And maybe you are right that I should raise my sights a little higher to be sure I'll never be deprived a chance to see my friends because of whom I marry."

A pair of horses thundered past along the row, and Charlotte envied the lady's ease on horseback at a canter. Charlotte was competent on a camel's back but not a horse, unfortunately. Horses felt insubstantial and dangerous by comparison.

"Ah, there is Miss Elizabeth Mayflower out early again."

Charlotte whipped around in the hope of seeing Lord Hurlston finally emerged from his home, where she assumed he'd been resting for the past few days. It seemed a little soon for him to be out and about, walking through Hyde Park again, and vastly unwise given her fears for his safety. What if he was attacked here again? "Where?"

"On horseback, dear," Aurora said, and turned her to view the pair of hard-ridden horses racing away on Rotten Row.

Charlotte shaded her eyes and squinted at a pair of retreating backs. A lady and a man, riding fast. She squinted at the man, particularly. "That's not Lord Hurlston with her, is it?"

"No, indeed it was not," Aurora murmured. "I get the sense that the lady prefers to go out without him most times."

"Why do you say that?"

"Personal observation. Lord Hurlston has declined to join his friends for several days in a row now, but his future bride is seen everywhere. I have hardly seen Hurlston and his bride out together since the wedding date was announced."

That was a relief to hear, given his injuries. She was glad he was being sensible keeping off horseback. But she desperately wanted to know how his recovery was progressing. She waited a moment to see if Aurora mentioned hearing of Hurlston being set upon by thugs and when she did not, curiosity got the better of her tongue. "Does that seem odd to you? Hurlston not being seen about Town, I mean."

Aurora shrugged. "Hurlston about to be married seems odd to me. I kept hoping to hear the betrothal was called off until the banns were read."

Charlotte nodded. She had hoped for that, too, but there was no gossip she'd heard of Winston harboring any doubts about his impending marriage. And since there was no gossip about him being attacked in Green Park, she had to assume his injuries had been less serious than they'd first appeared to her. But why was Elizabeth not with him? "I always thought Hurlston would make a good husband."

"Yes, but in an arranged marriage? Such a draconian state of affairs, and it's obvious it's going to be no loving marriage already."

"Why do you say that?"

"This is the third morning in as many days that I've seen Miss Mayflower out with that particular gentleman."

Charlotte hadn't gotten a good look at the man, just his back as he'd rode away. "Perhaps it's a groom riding with her."

"On such a fine horse? I think not. He's a gentleman born to the saddle," Aurora warned. "Perhaps he's her lover."

Charlotte gasped in shock. "Don't say that."

"Why not? Half the *ton* marriages go that way eventually anyway. A love affair here, a secret family there. If there's no love in the marriage to begin with, husband and wife inevitably live separate lives very soon after tying the knot. It's a forgiven thing among the aristocracy for a husband to keep a beloved mistress, too."

Charlotte blinked. "I cannot imagine him doing that to his wife."

"You always think so well of everyone, but no doubt Hurlston is just like every other man. A rogue deep down. If he were to fall desperately in love with a lady not his wife, I think he would move Heaven and Earth to keep her as a mistress."

Charlotte's stomach knotted. She'd accepted losing Winston to a wife long ago, but the idea that he might take a mistress soon after marriage, and love that woman instead, would break her heart. "I hope he can love his wife, if not now then later. I would pity the mistress, kept aside like a dirty little secret."

"Most wives seem not to care one whit about their

husbands' scandalous liaisons I've found. Openly flaunting them at amusements."

"Yes," Charlotte acknowledged. "I have noticed that the few times I've attended the opera."

Charlotte heaved a sigh. *Love.* An elusive ideal. But she squared her shoulders. She had more pressing concerns than a lack of affection in her own life. "Now, back to the business of ensuring I stay in England. Tell me everything you know about Lord Sullivan."

"Lord Sullivan?" Aurora appeared startled. "But I thought you were not keen on him?"

"Well, if I want to marry a man with funds to spare and an appreciation of higher society, he'd be a good choice for a husband. As you've said before, he loves his late wife still, and although he might never love me, I imagine he'd be a considerate husband and not embarrass me by taking a mistress, too. He's quite handsome to look at."

"Dull as paint," Aurora warned.

"He smells nice."

Aurora's breath caught. "Do you often go around sniffing gentlemen?"

"Of course, and you do it, too," she teased. "I've seen how you inhale deeply whenever he comes near you."

Aurora gaped. "I do not."

Charlotte curled her arm through Aurora's. "I think you like him more than you want to let on."

"I definitely do not like him in that fashion," Aurora protested. "I inhale because I'm planning my escape from his tedious conversation."

"And yet he still seeks you out at every ball for a dance, and you do dance with him." Charlotte laughed softly. "It's all right. I'd never tell anyone if you fancied him. There are worse men to admire." She nodded to a married couple passing them by. "Lord Loftus?"

"Too old for you." Aurora leaned close. "I'll not permit you to lose your innocence to a wrinkled old man who stinks of gin."

"Lord Holloway, then?"

"Is expected to announce his engagement to an heiress any day," Aurora reminded her. "You knew that."

"I can't compete with an heiress of her great fortune," Charlotte conceded.

"You shouldn't have to."

She inhaled and turned around, looking down the length of the park. In the distance, she could just see the first of the finest aristocratic homes. Some of the oldest families in England lived close to the park, and that thought gave her a new bachelor to consider. "Lord Preston Bain."

"No," Aurora said in a decidedly firm voice.

"He's invited everywhere. He owns a town house overlooking the park not far away. Why had I never thought of him before?"

"Because he's an utter drunkard?"

Charlotte shrugged. "A little rough around the edges perhaps."

"He drinks until he's unconscious at almost every ball."

"Yes, he was sipping from a flask the last time I saw him, too, I admit," she said slowly. "But drunkenness is his only vice as far as I've heard. No long-term mistress," she added. "And no engagement, either."

"He's no use to you. When a man drinks that much, it's likely he'd be unable to rise to the occasion to be a dutiful husband in bed."

Charlotte sighed. The pleasures of the night in her marriage bed might have to be given up in that case, but she hoped not. How else might she have a real family of her own if she did not have intercourse? However, challenges aside, she was undeterred from considering Lord Preston Bain.

A husband with an unfortunate drinking habit was not utterly repellant. She'd never heard of any violence in him, but he *was* most often at the end of evenings seen being carried out to his carriage by a pair of servants while he slept on, oblivious to his relocation. "A lack of interest in women and lovers is actually a point in his favor. I would have less competition for catching his eye. He couldn't be more perfect for my needs right now. He tends to stay in London year round, too."

"He is said to be exceedingly wealthy," Aurora conceded. "Not that an excess of funds is required for your needs."

Charlotte chewed her lip a moment, but had already made up her mind to embark on a renewal of their acquaintance. "He might abstain from spirits long enough for the getting of an heir."

Aurora gaped. "You cannot be serious."

Charlotte shrugged, fighting a blush. "What other choices do I have?"

Aurora sighed. "None."

"At least if I left him to his own indulgences, he'll likely leave me to mine."

Aurora looked at her with something like shock written all over her face. "Are you planning to take a lover upon marriage, Charlotte?"

She laughed at the very idea. Men did not consider her in that light. "Gracious no. I just meant I could keep his house the way I liked, expect to raise our children with little interference from him, and see my friends as often as I wished to."

"You really *are* serious."

"I am. I'll never marry for love, so I may as well get what I want out of the match. He'll just be like a great shaggy dog is after a good meal."

"As long as you're not the meal," Aurora warned. "Will you tell him what you're about? Why you want to marry him?"

"Yes, I intend to be completely honest about my situation

and hope he likes what he hears. Let's go. I want to see him today."

She turned about, heading toward the park entrance, nearly dragging Aurora off her feet in her haste. They'd come far on foot today, leaving the carriage and servants behind at the southern entrance to the park. It could be a simple matter of crossing the road and walking up the man's front steps and knocking on his door.

They paused just outside the park, and Charlotte looked up. She'd always admired his town house's location so that was another advantage of marrying him. But did she dare cross the road to put her foot in his front door to meet him?

Just then a large carriage turned away from Hyde Park.

"There he is." Charlotte rushed to follow the carriage; eyes fixed upon the darkened windows in the hope of catching Lord Bain's eyes should he look out. The carriage rolled slowly down the street, expelling gentlemen as it went on its way.

"I'd say Bain has had a long night of drinking with his friends. Come, Charlotte," Aurora urged, tugging on her arm to draw her back to Hyde Park. "It might be better to approach him when he has a clearer head. The start of a ball should be early enough for him not to be pickled when you speak."

Charlotte was not to be deterred. "I've never actually seen him during the day. Maybe he's sober now?"

"Unlikely."

When the carriage came to a complete stop before a grand looking home, the grooms dropped to the street and walked forward to tend the horses.

The rear of the carriage was unattended. This was her chance to learn more about him without him knowing. She took a deep breath. "It's now or never."

Charlotte rushed to the rear of the carriage and hid there, listening to whoever was talking inside.

"I'll get you the blunt," Winston said suddenly.

Charlotte blinked in utter shock to hear Winston's voice coming from within. She'd never known the pair to consort.

"All of it, and no running to your brother to pay your debt."

Brother?

Charlotte breathed an immediate sigh of relief. It wasn't Winston talking in the carriage, but likely his younger brother, Lord Peter Bell. She had no idea they sounded so similar, but then she'd not been near Lord Peter in a good long while. He usually avoided the *tonnish* events his brother attended. She wondered if they were very much alike in other ways, too.

"I can pay my own way," Peter claimed.

Charlotte risked a peek around the carriage and then looked back at Aurora. Her friend had paused a short distance away, pretending to remove a stone from her shoe.

As Charlotte listened to the conversation going on inside the carriage, she discovered Lord Peter owed Lord Bain money, and Charlotte soon found that the longer she listened, the more she didn't believe Lord Peter capable of making a full repayment on time, either.

"Unless you want our business known, you'll be back here in three days with my money," Lord Bain demanded. No trace of a drunken slur in his voice, she noted. "All of it. Now get out. I've seen too much of you with no satisfaction to be had."

"I'll get you the money," Peter promised again and then burst out of the carriage, rushing down the street, past Aurora as if the devil was on his heels.

Lord Peter's departure was followed by a roar of masculine laughter from the carriage. "Did you see his face?" Bain chortled again. "Sniveling pup. If he thinks his brother's title will protect him, there's no greater fool in London."

"Yes, my lord. I'm sure he's terrified of displeasing you again."

"God, I love how gullible young men and women can be," Lord Bain continued.

"It *is* the game you play with society, my lord."

"I find my amusements wherever I can. Now hurry up and find me a filly to warm my lap. Perhaps a brunette, or three. I have the most tedious ball to attend tonight, and I'll need to prepare for that, too."

Charlotte rushed away from the carriage without looking back. She grasped Aurora's arm and drew her away from Lord Bain.

Aurora did not complain. "What did you hear that's turned you so pale?"

"He is no mere drunk," she warned. "He is another devil, like all the other scoundrels."

Charlotte would spread the word to her friends among the wallflowers to ensure they knew never to think Lord Bain a mere drunkard ever again.

Chapter Ten

Winston hugged his ribs as he straightened up to put away his quill. He'd had his first half day at his desk after three days of lounging around, which was all he'd felt capable of when he'd stumbled down the stairs in search of breakfast that morning.

The swelling to his eyes had faded almost completely but the odd pain he felt in his body endured. His ribs were not broken, but they had been strapped firmly that first night, and every day since. He was hesitant to face his horse or any serious exertion yet.

Thankfully, Elizabeth hadn't asked too many questions about his injuries. She had been well occupied learning about the running of the London townhouse and keeping her father and Winston's mother company while he recovered.

"Ah, there you are," Lucien Hunt said as he strode into Winston's study without knocking. "I've been looking all over for you."

"Well, here I am." Winston sat back. "How can I help you?"

"By saying goodbye," he asked.

Winston climbed to his feet and moved around the desk. "You're leaving?"

Hunt smiled. "I've other matters to attend to than watching your face return to normal."

Self-conscious, Winston raised his hand to his cheek where the last of the bruising lingered. "I'm almost healed."

"Excellent. No doubt you'll be out and about soon too and enjoying yourself thoroughly again."

"I expect so."

"Good. Now I really must be going. I've a long journey ahead of me and the mail coach waits for no man."

"That is true. But…what if you took my traveling chaise? It will be a faster return trip and a damn sight less crowded in my carriage."

"You'd do that for me. Loan me your own carriage."

"Of course. I'm always more than happy to help out a friend in need."

Hunt inclined his head. "That's very gracious of you. I believe I'll accept."

"Good." Winston headed out the door to find his butler and make the arrangements. He returned back to Hunt in the study almost ten minutes later and found Hunt had taken a seat before his desk. "Sorry to keep you waiting. The carriage should be ready in no time. I trust you've said your farewells to mother and the Mayflower's already."

"Naturally."

Winston gestured to the sideboard. "Care for a drink while we wait?"

"Better not. It's a long journey I must make." Hunt held out his hand. "If you don't mind, I'll take my leave of you now and leave via the stables. But I'll see you again soon."

"Take care, Hunt. I'll see you out."

"No need. I know where to go," Hunt suggested but Winston would not have it. He walked his friend as far as the rear door.

Hunt strode across the paved courtyard to the stables, his hat under one arm and a small satchel tucked under the other. It was odd to see Hunt go and not hear the man tease him one last time. Hunt had been a bit subdued the past few days they'd spent together. Winston could only hope that seriousness continued upon his return to Town for the wedding.

Winston retraced his steps and returned to his study but

found his brother pawing through the papers he'd left spread across his desk. "What are you doing, Peter?"

His brother jumped around, startled by Winston's question. He put his hand to his chest and scowled. "What are you doing down here, startling me half to death?" Peter complained. "I thought you'd be in bed still."

"No. I have had enough coddling," he promised. "I've been in here for hours."

Peter looked toward the door. "Is Mama about? Elizabeth?"

"Is that why you're skulking into my private chambers? Avoiding them? Elizabeth is out with her father and Mama is somewhere about the house."

"Don't tell me Elizabeth is shopping on your account again? She'll bankrupt you if you're not careful," Peter complained. "That's every day since the day after the banns were called. She's not even your wife yet."

Winston shrugged. "I can well afford the additional expense, and happy to pay, too. High expenditure is quite common in the first years of marriage, I'm told."

"You're not married to her yet." Peter tapped the papers on the desktop. "Looks like you're plump in the pocket. Buying another property, I see? That's not far from here. What's it for?"

"None of your business," he replied, pretending the purchase was an inconsequential matter.

Peter laughed. "Planning to set up your mistress within easy walking distance from home, are you?"

"I don't have a mistress, nor do I plan to get one," he told Peter briskly. "A wife will be enough."

His brother made a choking sound. Winston resumed sorting the long and complicated legal documents back into order, ignoring the urge to defend his intention to honor his upcoming marriage vows for the rest of his life.

He stacked the papers in a neat pile and sat back with a sigh.

Peter Bell, at one and twenty just today, would never understand sacrifice and duty or Winston's deep-seated need to take care of his family. There was nothing he would not sacrifice for them. He looked up at his brother and smiled. "By the way, happy birthday."

Peter shuffled his feet. "Thank you."

"I do have a present for you but it's not quite ready to pass over."

"I didn't expect anything."

"Nonsense. Everyone likes to receive a gift on their birthday. You'll like what I found for you," Winston promised. He'd bought his brother a townhouse. The property would be a perfect place for a young bachelor with few responsibilities. On the small side, perhaps, but manageable for a young man with a modest inheritance if he didn't waste all his money gambling. "You used to love having the family gathered around for a party."

"That was a long time ago." Peter looked at him. "I'm older and I don't want a fuss made of my birthday anymore."

Winston sighed. "Speaking of older." He glanced at the mantle clock. "Don't you have a meeting with our solicitor today at his offices?"

"Oh, Woolsey won't mind if I'm late. He'll earn his pay either way."

"It is an important meeting, Peter."

"I don't see why it couldn't be held here."

Because here, Peter would forever feel like a second son. His inheritance was surely less than Winston's had been. He might feel embarrassed or slighted by the lesser amount he was to receive. He needed to do this on his own.

Winston rang the bell perched on the corner of his mahogany desk. When a footman appeared, he said, "Have my brother's carriage brought round."

"Make it the phaeton," Peter requested instead with a smirk.

"Bring out the town carriage and be quick about it," Winston repeated, standing firm against his brother's contradiction. He walked to the door and shut them in before facing his brother. "I would appreciate you not attempting to change my orders in front of the servants anymore."

"A phaeton is a young man's carriage," he complained.

"The phaeton was not purchased for your use, but for Elizabeth and me. You are not to ever take it out, is that understood?"

Peter scowled. "I wouldn't have to beg to borrow yours if I had one of my own?"

"What you purchase after you meet with the solicitor today will be for you alone to decide," Winston reminded him. Father had described only in the broadest of terms the provisions made for Peter's future. Unfortunately, he had left his youngest son no property of significant value. That was why Winston had bought another London town house he did not really need to give away to Peter. Winston planned to surprise his brother with the gift of living there indefinitely, free and clear. "I look forward to hearing how your meeting goes tonight."

"I'll be out tonight," Peter told him. "My friends have something special planned for me."

Winston was disappointed to hear they wouldn't dine together for yet another night. He'd hoped for a few more family dinners before Peter went his own way entirely. "Don't stagger back here singing at dawn. You'll wake Mother," he warned.

"Yes, wouldn't want to ruffle the old bird's feathers."

Winston clipped his brother across the back of his head. "I have told you before not to speak of our mother in those terms."

"You're just like her. No sense of humor anymore."

"Ridiculing the woman who gave us life is no laughing

matter," he warned. Winston despaired for his brother some-times. "Your carriage should be ready. Off you go."

Peter stood, smoothing back his hair as if he were nervous. "What can I expect?"

Winston shook his head. "I was not privy to the details. It will all be very standard I'm sure. Read everything carefully and make sure you understand what Father has offered you before you accept a single penny. There may be strings attached."

There had been for Winston. Not attempting to break free of his betrothal would earn him an additional two thousand pounds in the year he married. Money that he'd decided to pass along to his wife in the near future.

Peter scowled. "You always understand this sort of thing better than I do."

"If it concerns the Hurlston estates, yes. But your business today has nothing to do with the title or the estate."

"Of course," Peter muttered. "Why would anything that affects me interest you anymore?"

"I am interested but you're a smarter young man than you give yourself credit for. You'll figure it out."

With a subtle push, Winston propelled Peter on his way. An hour with the family legal firm, sorting through his inheritance, would hopefully give him a glimpse of his future and his options. Peter would likely need a career if he was to make something great of himself, something beyond a spare's inheritance. He couldn't very well lounge about Hurlston House or at the country estate all the days of his life. Soak up gin and dally with women aimlessly forever. The sooner his brother was settled in his own life, the better.

"Do you think he'll be all right?" Mama asked, coming up behind him.

Winston turned with a smile. "Of course. Peter is a Bell, after all. We're all born into a great family, and not one of us has ever failed to exceed all expectations set," he said, quoting an off-used phrase in his family. There were uncles, younger sons, and cousins who had become men of distinction through the ages.

"Yes, but…he's such an innocent lad."

Winston just barely held back from rolling his eyes. Mother was blind to her youngest son's true nature. Lord Peter Bell was no innocent young man. He had taken his first lover at fourteen. Their father had arranged a visit to a brothel for him and encouraged other reckless indulgences, teaching him to gamble, until the day he'd suddenly died of a heart seizure. "Was there something you wanted?"

"I…" She shrugged. "I suppose not. Should you be out of bed?"

He walked toward her and smiled. "I am quite recovered from my fall, Mother."

"I'm glad to hear it. I've been so worried."

He kissed her brow. "Hale and healthy again," he promised.

It might have been a slight exaggeration. He was not keen to ride his horses yet or do much of a strenuous nature. He would not attend Gentleman Jackson's for a good long while or dance if he could avoid the activity. He'd planned a great deal of staying in, working at his desk, and reading in Elizabeth's company. "How about a cup of tea?"

Mother brightened and rushed to pull a bell for a servant. "We can discuss tonight's dinner for your brother's birthday."

Winston drew her into the drawing room, asking a servant to fetch tea as soon as they appeared. "We're going to put off the dinner for a few days. Peter has no idea when he will return and is going out with friends."

Her face fell.

"He's grown up now, Mama. Dinners with the family no longer appeal to him."

"He could have waited one more year for that," she

complained. "Or until I had grandchildren to bounce on my knee to replace him."

"It's best we do not stand in his way now," Winston suggested. "Let's talk about something else."

"We could talk about your wedding day," she said.

Winston groaned. "Mother, really. You go from one extreme to the other. Shouldn't you be having this conversation with Elizabeth."

"She's never around of late," she murmured. "It should not be unexpected that I want to know you'll be happy together. Your father and I were married by your age. You were born in the first year of marriage."

Winston leveled his gaze on his mother's smiling face. "Not to be indelicate, Mother, but it was because he got you pregnant with me that you wed so young," he murmured. "Your father planned to shoot Papa for the insult to your honor. It was only luck that he had become an earl shortly after when his brother passed unexpectedly. Your quick marriage into a titled family allowed the family rift to heal."

Mother waved the old scandal away with a flick of her hand as if it didn't matter. "He always loved me."

Mother liked to rewrite her own history on occasion. "Eventually, but he was none too happy to be wed at first."

She smiled a trifle smugly. "He came around in the end and that is all that matters."

Winston laughed. Mother had been an insufferably happy person until Father had been taken from them. He still saw glimpses of that woman from time to time. But not often. He was pleased to see her talk of the past so easily today. "He never stood a chance resisting someone as lovely as you."

Mother blushed. "You'll feel the same one day about Elizabeth. She really is perfect for you."

Perfect, yes perhaps she was. But for him? Winston squirmed, fighting down a niggling doubt. He and Elizabeth did not have a close relationship yet. They knew each other well from years of meetings and conversations, but he couldn't say he felt very much for her still. He supposed eventually they'd become closer. But that would be after he made love to her, most likely. After they were wed.

Unfortunately their wedding date was still some time away.

Mother turned to him. "I had a note from Lady Cartwright this morning. She said she heard Elizabeth expects to only be in London a few days after you wed. Why didn't you warn me you were leaving Town almost immediately?"

He blinked in surprise. "I wasn't informed of any travel plans, Mama."

Her face fell. "Oh dear. Have I gone and spoiled Elizabeth's surprise of a wedding trip?"

They'd talked about the need to remain together, but a discussion of where they'd spend the first weeks of married life had not come up yet. Perhaps a trip to Bath wasn't a bad idea. It would mean they'd have a great deal more privacy than they had here with their family about.

Winston captured his mother's hand and squeezed it tightly. Mother so loved surprises and would hate that she'd ruined one meant for him. "I can pretend I don't know for Elizabeth's sake."

"Would you? You know how she can be. Always a bit prickly about me telling you what she does with her time."

He gaped. "Was there something I should know."

"No, of course not. I'm sure she's already told you everything you need to know, and if she hasn't yet, she will. Who else should a woman confide in if not the man who will be her husband?"

Elizabeth *was* a private person, she kept a lot to herself. Clearly, she was that way with Mother, too.

Mother sighed. "You'll go out after our tea, I suppose? Now that you're feeling better."

"I hadn't planned to go anywhere today." He studied his mother. Mama ought to be getting out more herself. "What were you going to do today?"

"Oh, I don't know. Embroider, perhaps."

He winced. That sounded like what she had done yesterday. "What if we went out together instead of staying in?"

She smiled in obvious delight at the invitation. "Where can we go?"

"Let us forget the tea and go for ices instead at Gunter's." He spun Mama about, grinning. "After that… Anywhere. Everywhere. Why don't you go change into a pretty gown, gather up a cloak in case it becomes cold, and let me surprise you with an impromptu adventure?"

He'd surprise himself, too, if he could come up with something amusing at short notice.

"All right. I'll be right back."

Mama hurried off, clearly eager for the distraction of an outing. Now, all Winston had to think of a good excursion in the time it would take her to return. Nothing that would be too strenuous, of course, on account of his ribs. If Mother saw that he suffered, she'd make him take her straight home again.

So, it had to be something safe and private.

Indoors.

Charlotte would want him to be cautious.

He frowned.

Charlotte.

The little woman trickled back into his immediate thoughts again, and he conceded that she'd hardly ever left. Was he really in danger or was her warning the product of a wallflower's too-active imagination? There'd been no further danger he'd stumbled into since. Not that he'd gone out anyway in the last few days. He couldn't very well spend his whole life hiding in his town house, though, just in case she was right. It was time to venture out again.

But he would be cautious, ensure he was always on his guard for danger. And when he saw Charlotte again, he'd inform her that the only danger to his health was her sweet smile and soft caress.

He set his head back and groaned at the ceiling. He truly *had* to stop thinking of her. He was almost a married man.

Chapter Eleven

Charlotte offered a friendly smile to the large, muscled man blocking her way into the Royal Grand National Menagerie. "How much to view the beasts today, sir?"

Beside her, Aurora twirled a lock of hair around her finger and smiled flirtatiously at the man in the hope of getting in free of charge. It was a trick Aurora often deployed to great success, but not today.

The fellow held out a hand. "Two shillings for pretty ladies like yourselves."

Charlotte promptly handed over the few coins, impressed that they were paying less than the usual full entry fee charged to visitors. "Thank you very much, sir."

"Can I interest you in a tour of this fine establishment for another shilling?" he asked after tucking the coin away. His gaze slid to Aurora. "You'll have an adventure you've never had before with me as your guide."

Charlotte narrowed her eyes on the fellow. He had an engaging smile and might have been interesting to talk to about the animals, but he was paying too much attention to Aurora, and she did not care for his presumption.

"That won't be necessary," Charlotte replied primly, grasping Aurora's arm firmly. "I know my way around animals."

Aurora allowed herself to be led away from temptation, but she looked back over her shoulder at the fellow as they left him. "Speak for yourself," Aurora complained. "Why did you rush away? He was interesting, in a brutish sort of way."

"He's not the right man for you, my dear," she reminded

her friend. "The only thing on that man's mind would end in your ruin."

Her friend turned resolutely toward the menagerie room. "Yes, I suppose you are right. A man like that wouldn't have been keen to wed a lady he met here. And he must meet a great many more gullible women than us to be so bold."

"Exactly!"

Charlotte knew her way about the place from previous trips and showed Aurora, a first-time visitor, the way round. The menagerie housed beasts from foreign lands in cages and fed them each night. At this time of day, most should be sleeping peacefully with full stomachs. That was the only reason Charlotte had agreed to bring her friend here today. She did not want to watch the lion devour anything that had once lived and breathed.

"Charlotte, it smells," Aurora complained before they'd even sighted one single animal, lifting a scented handkerchief to her nose.

"That is the way of caged beasts," she warned. "It will be worse deeper inside." Charlotte squared her shoulders. "The lions come first; the screeching monkeys are housed above."

She led Aurora to the lions to get the viewing over and done with first. Charlotte did not like lions. One lioness opened a sleepy eye, studying them. She yawned, showing extremely sharp teeth. Charlotte shuddered.

Aurora stared at them. "Oh," she said eventually.

"Now you see why I care not to find one running wild through my canvas tent again."

"Yes, I do see your point." Aurora grasped her arm tightly. "You're staying in England even if I have to hide you under my bed to keep you safe from such a creature." Aurora glanced farther down the wall and pointed. "What is that?"

"Leopard. A skilled hunter in the wild and very hard to see

at night, of course, because of its color and stalking habits. You'll never hear or see them coming."

Aurora turned away quickly. "There are birds!"

And a sad and sorry lot they were, trapped in their small cages. They'd no room to soar as they could in the wild. "They are prettier in their natural surroundings," Charlotte admitted, holding a frond of seed grass out to a parrot to see if it would nibble. Her offering was ignored. The poor thing had probably been overfed all day.

Aurora craned her neck and looked around. "Where's the elephant?"

Charlotte had been hoping Aurora would not want to see that particular animal straight away. But that was why they were really here. "They call him Chunee, and he is housed in another chamber."

"Can we go see him?"

"Of course, we can." They headed out of the first chamber. One of the lions rumbled as they passed, and Charlotte shivered.

Chunee was a great beast trapped behind heavy iron bars, a thick chain bolted round his ankle. His gray skin seemed dull to her eye, and of course he stank of musk. He was also rocking back and forth in his cage. Restless, impatient, longing to be free, most likely. "We ought not to get too close."

"I wasn't going to suggest it."

"See his trunk? It is strong enough to carry fallen trees, you know. But they are very dangerous animals. He could catch you with his trunk, lift you up, and you'd not stand a chance of escaping if he threw you aside."

"But if you had a parasol handy to scare him off with, that might help, yes?" a lady asked from behind them.

Charlotte turned slowly and discovered Lord Hurlston and his mother were poised to view the elephant, too. She curtsied quickly, and Aurora did the same. "My lord. My lady. What a delightful surprise to find you both out and about."

The lady gestured to her son. "Hurlston convinced me to come out for a day of sightseeing and here we are."

Charlotte nodded. "That is very good of him. Have you been here long?"

"We've only just arrived," Hurlston drawled, looking past her to the elephant without meeting her eye.

Charlotte shivered at his tone. His mother drew close, though. "I take it you were not exaggerating about facing unhappy elephants, my dear," the lady asked. "You look decidedly uncomfortable standing here today."

"Yes. I suppose I am," she agreed, but her gaze flickered to where Lord Hurlston stood. He seemed uncomfortable as well. "Chunee here—that's his name, if you did not know it—is a great strong beast and is ill-suited to idleness. Spending his time indoors, caged in so small an area like this, cannot be good for his temper. He needs an occupation and more room to move."

"My brother and Chunee have much in common then," Hurlston remarked dryly. He stepped around Charlotte and drew closer to the bars. Closer than Charlotte was comfortable with. She kept her eye on Chunee.

"What do they feed him?" Hurlston asked.

"Incautious earls," Charlotte warned.

Hurlston turned to look at her then and one brow lifted. "Really?" he drawled.

She gulped. Something was off about the earl today. The friendly man she'd grown accustomed to running into about Town was gone, and in his place was...well...just another top-lofty member of the *ton* with no patience for exchanging pleasantries with someone beneath him.

She wet her lips and turned to the older lady, who was asking Aurora about the welfare of mutual friends.

While the pair talked, she risked a peek at Hurlston, only to find him staring back at her now. His gaze slipped away slowly, and he turned on his heel to stroll to the other end of the chamber, far from them. Far from *her*.

But Charlotte sighed in relief to see him moving about so easily. He looked much better than the last time she'd seen him, when he'd been clutching his ribs. As he returned, Charlotte moved to intercept him. "How are you feeling today, my lord?"

"Recovered," he said curtly.

"I am glad to hear it. I have been very worried about you."

"You shouldn't have troubled yourself," he chided.

"It was no trouble. None at all."

She glanced at Lady Hurlston and Aurora to check that they were still occupied and not paying her any attention. "Have they found the men who attacked you?"

"No," Hurlston said

She shook her head. "I had hoped the Runners would have found one of them by now."

Hurlston flicked a speck of dust from his sleeve. "They have not found them because I did not trouble them with the trifling incident."

Charlotte gaped at him. "Trifling?"

"I suffered no lasting harm save the embarrassment of being upstaged by a young woman who should have known better," he drawled again. "And no one in society had better hear about that incident."

"Not from my lips," Charlotte promised, but then she realized there had been a harsh rebuke in his little speech. "Upstaged?"

"You ought not to involve yourself in matters best left to men."

She gaped at him, outraged by his attitude. "If I had not intervened, your body would have been found on that grassy lawn not ten minutes after we passed that spot. I was under the impression you were grateful for my help."

"You misunderstood the depths of my gratitude," he said.

Charlotte blinked, her temper rising to boiling point. "To think I wasted my time worrying about you," she hissed. "I should have left you there, as Mr. McCarrick wanted to do from the very start. I shouldn't have bothered with either of you actually."

"Well, don't blame me if you've frightened off your suitor."

Charlotte clenched her jaw together and by sheer will, avoided stomping her foot—on his, most likely—by a narrow margin. "I see we've nothing left to say about the matter."

"None at all."

She nodded, sucked in a sharp breath, and smiled. But it was merely a baring of her teeth, just as monkeys sometimes did when threatened. It didn't mean she accepted his remarks as fact. She was sure pleasure wasn't reflected in her eyes, either, because he suddenly took a pace back from her.

The earl was an ungrateful, idiotic, horrible, awful, ungrateful… She stopped as she realized she was repeating herself to herself, and remembered she must not care about him anyway.

He was an engaged man.

What did the sudden loss of his gratitude matter? What reason did she have to continue to care about him?

There was none now, and if he wanted to put her in her place, well, he'd been successful today. She'd started to think they might have become friends. *Foolish, foolish, Charlotte.*

If this was how he treated a lady who only wanted to help him, then she hoped they'd return to being strangers to each other forthwith.

Charlotte returned to Aurora and put her friend between them. To Lady Hurlston, she said, "Do excuse us, my lady. We've much yet to see."

"I know. Your dear friend has just been telling me of your plans and has invited me to join you both for the tour, and then to take tea. I hope you don't mind that I accepted."

"Mother," Hurlston said in a harsh tone. "I thought we were spending the day together?"

"Oh, don't pretend you'd rather not be elsewhere. Today is your night for visiting your club with friends. I heard you grumble as we came in, too. Miss Hillcrest has offered to share their little adventure, and I should like to join them. You're always trying to get me out and about and now you complain?"

Hurlston looked only at Aurora when he spoke. "If you don't mind her company."

"I wouldn't have made the suggestion if it was an imposition, my lord. We're going to call on Lady Wharton after this for tea. She'll enjoy seeing another friendly face."

"We have a great deal to talk about, too," Mother promised. "I haven't had a chance to tell her our plans for your upcoming wedding yet."

"Yes. That is true," he conceded. His gaze darted to Charlotte and away again. "I'll see you at home then, Mama?"

"I expect it will be late. Enjoy the rest of the day without me, my son."

"I'll do my best," Hurlston said slowly. He nodded to his mother, then his gaze lifted to Charlotte. "Take good care of her."

Charlotte nodded, and otherwise ignored his departure.

Lady Hurlston let out a sigh. "I don't know what's come over him today. One minute he's laughing and the next so sour. He's not usually so moody. I don't think he liked the stench of the place. He almost turned about when we first saw the elephant."

"He does have a strong odor," Aurora agreed. "But then, all men do."

Lady Hurlston laughed at that. "That has been my experience, as well. Getting them to bathe regularly is a full-time occupation when they're members of your own family. Is that not right, Miss Waters?"

"I wouldn't know. Mama manages my father's bathing habits, not I." Charlotte shook her head, her mind stuck in the immediate past.

Lady Hurlston had said her son's mood had taken a turn for the worst when he'd come into this part of the menagerie. She doubted it was the stench of the animals in their cages that caused that, given how he'd spoken to her. He should be used to the smells of livestock. He attended parliament.

No, he was most likely offended by finding Charlotte here. Something about her presence had set him off today, and he'd made sure she'd known all about it, too.

She shook her head again. He wasn't the kind man she assumed him to be. He was moody, changeable, and aggravating—just like all the rest. She was glad to finally have her eyes opened to his true nature.

But toward his mother, the earl seemed inordinately protective and gentle.

For the next hour, Charlotte answered Lady Hurlston's every question as best she could. Aurora, too, had the lady laughing often, as she regaled her with tales of society amusements the older woman had missed by staying in more often than going out.

"Charlotte, of course, loves the balls best of all," Aurora teased. "And to dance with handsome bachelors like your son."

"As do you, my dear friend," Charlotte reminded her.

The older woman smiled. "You sound like firm friends. How long have you known each other?"

"Only this season."

"I was away last year when the Hillcrests first came to London," Charlotte rushed to explain. "I should have been very honored to have known them longer than I have."

"Ah, yes. The elder two have landed on their feet very well indeed. One engaged to a marquess and the other married now to a future duke. Your family has taken the *ton* by surprise, snapping up the most eligible bachelors to be found."

"My cousins found love where they least expected it," Aurora promised. "We hope for the same for our dear friend Charlotte," Aurora said, casting Charlotte a determined smile. "There has to be a man worthy of her somewhere in society."

Charlotte blushed. "You like to think there's someone for everyone but yourself."

Aurora nodded. "I do believe there's someone for everyone. But expectations and available choices are not so easily matched."

Charlotte nodded. "Indeed not."

Lady Hurlston looked between them with a shrewd smile. "The marriage mart is a difficult place to be. Are you acquainted with my other son, by chance?"

"I've seen very little of him," Charlotte murmured. And she didn't want to see him, either, if he was anything like his brother.

Aurora denied meeting him as well.

"That is his loss, I see. But I imagine neither of you lack for attention from the opposite sex. You're both besieged by suitors, I'm sure?"

Charlotte couldn't help but laugh at that. "I would gladly suffer an overflowing drawing room."

"Not I. All I require is a single suitor with a marriage to me on his mind," Aurora confided, surprising Charlotte completely with her confession.

Most of the time, Aurora acted as if suitors were utterly unwanted in her life.

Lady Hurlston moved a few steps ahead of them, and Aurora winked and drew closer. "It's what older women expect to hear from us," she whispered. Aurora grasped her arm. "Shall we carry on to Wharton House and see what excursion about the town house Lady Wharton has been scolded for embarking on today by my cousin?"

"Yes, of course," Charlotte said. Lady Wharton was not supposed to exert herself still after her surgery. "Lady Hurlston, have you seen all that interests you here?"

"Yes, it's all so fascinating. Particularly the stories you tell so well of your travels. I should dearly love to hear more one day. Perhaps over luncheon tomorrow?"

Charlotte's first instinct was to agree, but then she remembered Hurlston's behavior toward her today, and thought better of agreeing to anything that involved a member of his family. "The next adventure awaits."

Lady Hurlston linked her arm through Charlotte's and the three of them swept from the menagerie and out to the street, where it was the work of a moment to call up their carriage.

Charlotte studied her hands once they were underway, more than a little downcast. Lord Hurlston's words had upset her more than she cared to admit. She couldn't forget the way he'd studied her. Like a creature that had fallen far short of his expectations. His behavior today, after last week and Mr. McCarrick's criticisms, had just about convinced her to wash her hands of all men.

There seemed something wrong about every man she met, even now Hurlston. What was the point of trying to impress anyone by acting as if she was always proper and good? Shouldn't she be good enough as she was right now?

Hurlston was blinkered, imagining he could do no wrong in taking care of himself. Well, she'd let him fight his own battles now. No matter what happened, when another attack came, he was on his own.

She looked across at Lady Hurlston. There was no way to avoid the afternoon with his mother, so she'd make the best use of the time. She would smile, listen politely if she sung her eldest son's praises, and hope to hear of another man who was in want of a wife. But she would do her best to avoid the woman forever after that afternoon.

Aurora caught her eye. "Is something wrong, dear?"

"No," she answered, seeing that Lady Hurlston was watching her in concern. "Merely thinking about the future."

"Looking back is a more comforting pastime," Lady Hurlston told them. "But young women must think of the future more, I suppose. You'll want a husband and children to comfort you in your old age."

"Love," Charlotte whispered. "I want to be loved."

The old lady patted her hand. "I wanted that, too."

"Were you loved by your husband, my lady?" Aurora asked.

"Eventually, yes. But I knew I loved him on first sight of him strutting about society. He hardly knew I existed."

Charlotte looked at the older woman in surprise. "How did you come to marry him then?"

"Well, the usual way, I suppose. One thing led to another, and we were wed."

"It wasn't an arranged match?"

"Gracious no."

Aurora sat forward. "And yet Lord Hurlston's marriage was arranged. From infancy, I hear. May I ask why?"

The countess' smile faded a little. "My husband wanted an alliance with a neighboring family, and my son wants that, too, now he's old enough to understand what is at stake. The additional land he will inherit upon his father-in-law's death, since he has no heir, will increase the family holdings considerably."

"So the alliance is an investment in the future then," Aurora murmured, sitting back again.

"I suppose it is in a way. But they've known each other so long I cannot imagine they shouldn't be happy with each other."

Charlotte offered a smile to the countess that strained her

abilities to mimic happiness. "Then it will all work out for the best, I gather."

Lady Hurlston smiled quickly, "I'm sure it will."

The last remnant of hope within Charlotte's heart withered and died there and then. Today, Winston had been warning her not to expect even friendship from him. She'd do well to remember that not all dreams were meant to come true.

Chapter Twelve

"Well, that's me done for the night," Lord Scarsdale murmured to Winston, giving the young woman sitting on his lap a shove up so he could rise from his chair. "I'll see you all in a week perhaps, unless you change your mind and join me in the countryside for shooting," he said more loudly to the men seated farther away.

There was a murmur of discussion, but no one changed their mind about going shooting. Winston hadn't.

Scarsdale caught the young woman's hand and drew her close to whisper in her ear. Whatever he'd said must have been agreeable because he was successful in luring her toward the brothel's staircase. The bedchambers where a man and his lover might while away the hours were directly above them.

Winston lowered his attention to his nearly empty glass. Scarsdale obviously planned to spend the night here, as many of Winston's friends had announced in the past few hours.

He shifted in his chair, feeling out of place. His friend's casual attitude toward intimacy was completely opposed to his own. He waved a bottle of French brandy at Berringer. "Another round?"

Berringer shook his head. "Not for me, I'm afraid. His grace wants to go riding at first light."

Winston was disappointed but understood. "Ah well, better to go home with a clear head than risk falling off tomorrow on horseback."

Berringer agreed and stood. "I'll see you tomorrow perhaps."

Winston nodded and glanced at his remaining companions. Both had women perched on their knees. Pinner and Brandestock were quite accustomed to that sort of company. But Winston was not, and being the third wheel held no appeal for him at all. His friends would probably make use of one of the brothel bedchambers above later, too, and he'd be left alone sitting here drowning his sorrows.

But no matter how much he consumed, food and spirits, Winston was still left to wrestle with his guilty conscience.

He'd been curt with Charlotte, rude, and she had no idea why.

He hardly knew what he'd been about until he'd had time to reflect. The harsh, dismissive lies he'd let tumble from his lips in her presence were not even remotely true.

But the last woman he'd wanted to see today was the woman he couldn't seem to forget. And the fact that Charlotte's face had lit up upon seeing him, too, hadn't helped improve his mood. Because he'd known being around her would be wholly unwise for a man about to marry another. Charlotte had no idea the confusion she caused in him.

And the lust. Damned if he didn't wonder if giving up his celibacy for one night with her might not ruin him for his long-expected marriage.

But he couldn't do that. Ruin Charlotte. Pursue Charlotte. Betray Elizabeth.

He could never *not* marry Elizabeth. The price would be too high if what he felt for Charlotte was merely an aberration of feeling. And he utterly hated that he was doubting himself on the cusp of the most important change in his life.

"Gentlemen. I'm heading off home," he announced. He'd find no answers here or in an empty glass tonight.

"Oh, no," Brandestock cried. "You should stay. Find yourself a woman and end the night with a bang or two."

He fought to keep his face from coloring. "I came only for the beef and brandy."

"Both were excellent," Pinner agreed. "But the beauties are worth staying for, too. Don't you think?"

"Another time," Winston answered with a forced laugh and a wave as he strode out of the brothel, shoulders back, stride committed to leaving.

The fact that he'd never once lain with a woman had escaped his friends' notice, something for which he was forever grateful. He expected them to tease him mercilessly, which would be utterly humiliating. He'd prefer his friends believed him more experienced like them.

He collected his coat and hat from the doorman and asked for his carriage to be brought up promptly. While he was waiting, Pinner and Brandestock ushered their lady friends up the nearby set of stairs.

Winston envied them their ease with seducing women. It was a skill he feared he might never learn.

A footman returned, appearing apologetic even before he spoke. "I'm sorry, my lord. There's no carriage of yours waiting out there."

He tugged on his gloves. "Damn it all. I specifically asked them to remain until midnight."

"I looked in all the usual places but there are actually few carriages waiting in the road outside." The fellow scratched his head. "Shall I flag down a hack for you, my lord, or would you prefer to wait in the salon until yours returns?"

He glanced behind him, seeing if anyone he had an acquaintance with might be leaving at that moment. He should have left with Berringer when he had a chance, but he'd expected his carriage to be out there still. "No, I won't stay. Please do see what you can find for me."

The footman scurried back outside, and Winston did consider returning to the salon and having another drink while he waited, but there was no one left he wanted to talk to.

And if he sat alone drinking, he would only return to remonstrating with himself for thinking about Charlotte Waters again.

And the worst thing was…he liked thinking about her.

Her life and adventures abroad fascinated him. Not out of any longing to travel himself, he'd taken a grand tour as a younger man, but to know how she felt about the sights that she'd seen.

He took a deep breath and let it out slowly.

He had Elizabeth to go home to. He ought to want that more than to have Charlotte in charity with him again. But he'd whipped her with the lash of his bad mood at the menagerie that very afternoon. He was certain he was the last man she'd want to talk to again.

A burst of raucous masculine laughter reached him from beyond the velvet curtains dividing the club. A woman squealed with delight in response. Things were becoming rowdy in the salon already. They usually did at this hour. Definitely time he headed for home and his bachelor's bed.

Since the footman seemed to be taking too long, and there was no other servant to complain to about it, Winston let himself out of the club and stopped on the quiet street out front to look for the fellow.

Glancing left and right along the shadowed road, he saw no carriages, and no servants belonging to Madam Bradshaw's either. Odd for this time of night…and where the devil had the footman disappeared to? Was he even trying to find him a carriage?

Winston took a few steps into the dark street and instantly became aware of a sound nearby.

A gasp.

A groan.

He rolled his eyes. Having had enough of the amorous antics inside Madam Bradshaw's, he had no wish to be subjected to the sound of them out here. It was probably the footman from Bradshaw's with a lady of the night.

And yet there *was* a subtle difference… He peered into the dark where the grunts and groans seemed to originate. The gasps had become more of a gag now. He took a few more steps in that direction, and then more again.

The sound came from an alleyway that ran along the side of Bradshaw's. Halfway down the establishment's side wall, a couple wrestled in the grip of rough lust.

But then a chill of unease swept over him.

Something wasn't quite right about the pair and what they were doing. He may not have taken a woman to bed, or up against a wall, either, but he understood enough of intimacy to know that the pair were not having sex after all.

Both of them were male, too.

One of them fell to the ground untidily. Spent?

No.

He was injured…or mayhap dead.

"The watch is on the way," Winston called out, lying in the hope of scaring off the one who remained on his feet.

The fellow turned slowly to look at him—and Winston's blood ran cold. He sensed he was a threat even without seeing the man's face clearly.

Winston took a step back and turned, intending to return to the brothel and raise the alarm. He was only one man facing an unknown assailant without a weapon upon him to defend himself.

Not even a parasol.

Charlotte would not be happy when she learned he hadn't carried anything he could use as a weapon out with him tonight.

He'd gone a handful of steps before another shadowy figure

appeared directly before him. Blocking his way back to Madam Bradshaw's doorway.

Someone chuckled.

"We've been waiting for you, Lord Hurlston," the man said. "We'll be quicker this time. No chance of escape tonight."

A chill went through him because, in the moonlight, Winston could just make out that the fellow was holding a long, tapered knife. He turned suddenly, remembering there was a man in the alley behind his back, too.

The pair were here to kill him. Charlotte had warned him he was in danger, and he *really* should have believed her.

Winston darted sideways, putting himself in the middle of the street, but unfortunately it placed him farther from Bradshaw's front door. He frequented none of the other businesses on this street, and all others were shut up tight for the night.

When the pair followed, stalking him, Winston gulped in the grip of panic. These men seemed about the same size and shape as the ones who'd attacked him without provocation in Green Park. Then, their attack had been sudden and unexpected, and he'd barely survived. His fists had been no match for this pair last time, and he'd had Charlotte, too. They had the element of surprise yet again, but tonight they seemed to want to torment him first with the threat of what was to come.

When he saw two other men emerging from the shadows and join the slow stalking of him, Winston figured they were not here to help him do anything but to die faster. There would be no reasoning with them for mercy. No bargain to be made. No Charlotte brandishing her parasol at the last moment to beat them into submission and force them to flee instead.

There's no shame in running if you're badly outnumbered.

Winston swallowed, remembering Charlotte's words after the last attack. When she'd uttered them that first time, he'd felt it cowardly to run away from any fight. But now, alone in the dark—with the odds stacked even further against him—he wasn't sure he hadn't been stupid to stand his ground and take a beating he'd not deserved the first time.

He was the bloody earl of Hurlston. A man with responsibilities to his family, his tenants. A future as a husband. He couldn't die in the gutter. Too many depended on him to make their lives better.

If Charlotte thought he should have run when he'd been attacked in Green Park by three, what would she think he should do now that he was so surrounded by four and without a weapon still?

He glanced at the fellows drawing closer, intending to surround him and prevent his escape.

Run now and don't look back!

"Good advice," he said out loud.

Winston shot off into the dark, leaving behind a startled burst of shouts from his would-be attackers. A shot rang out, and he stumbled, but his legs propelled him to greater speed. In school, he'd been one of the fastest sprinters whenever there had been footraces against his classmates. As an adult, he'd kept reasonably fit, but he'd not run anywhere in years. He'd not had reason to.

He ran hard, veered to the left and then right, and then tacked down a shortcut he knew well. St. James' Square was a blur as he raced through it, taking the most direct path home. He couldn't hear any sign of pursuit yet, but that didn't mean they were not following.

They'd followed him to Bradshaw's.

They'd been waiting for him to come out so they could end him, they'd said.

They knew who he was—and likely where he was heading, too.

Winston saw a carriage coming toward him just then. A great lumbering barouche headed God knew where at this time of night. He quickly darted behind it, hoping its bulk would hide his change of direction, and once past, darted down a servants' staircase tucked beneath a pair of badly painted front doors, panting hard.

He needed a moment to think.

He wiped his sweaty face, desperately afraid that his luck had finally run out, and sucked in a deep breath.

He nearly groaned out loud because he'd forgotten all about his tender ribs in his mad dash. He hugged his chest and made himself breath shallow so they hurt less.

He glanced around, trying to orientate himself. He'd run a good way home. He had a battalion of servants in his town house, and weapons, too. All he had to do was keep going.

If he could.

He carefully peeked out to look at the street again. The lumbering carriage had stopped a short distance away, and the coachman was leaning down from his perch. Winston realized the fellow was talking to someone standing beside the carriage.

One of Winston's pursuers?

No, more than one. There were half a dozen men surrounding that carriage now.

The coachman pointed down a road Winston had not taken. The men conferred and then rushed off in that direction.

Winston sagged in relief at his brief reprieve, sent out a silent thanks as he watched the coach resume its journey down the dark street.

But his safety was surely only temporary. Those men might get smart and turn around when they failed to find any sign of him ahead of them.

If they found him, they would catch and kill him. The ribs that had been bruised were now complaining and it was becoming harder to breathe again.

Those men knew where he lived and might be waiting for him. He couldn't go home, or anywhere else he frequented often. If they'd waited for him at Bradshaw's tonight, a last-minute decision on his part to attend, it was possible they might follow him to other places he went to as well.

Yet he couldn't hide here in the dark all night. The arrival of dawn would reveal him, a lord in fine clothing, as a man out of place in this part of Town.

But where should he go if going home was just as dangerous a road to travel?

He wiped the sweat from his brow again and absently dried his hand on his breeches. He needed to go somewhere he'd never been before. Somewhere he'd be safe until help could be summoned. But where was that?

Where in London would the Earl of Hurlston never be expected to go? Certainly, he couldn't go to any of his friends' homes. He'd risk putting their lives in danger, too.

No, he needed a place to lie low and take stock of this situation. There was only one place that sprang to mind—and he was absolutely sure no one would imagine he'd seek help there.

He checked the street and slipped out of his hiding place and hurried in the opposite direction of home as fast as he could manage.

Chapter Thirteen

Charlotte was almost asleep when a scratch at her door woke her. "What is it," she grumbled, rubbing sleep from her eyes.

"Miss, there is a situation downstairs," their butler, Davis, whispered through the door. "You must hurry!"

Charlotte flew out of bed and threw a wrapper over her nightgown and shoved her feet into her slippers. "Is it Mama? Did she take another fall?"

"Your mother is sound asleep still. I thought it best not to rouse her," the butler confided.

Charlotte hurried into the hall and shut the door behind her quietly. "Did Father cut himself with his penknife again and drip blood on her notes? The last time he was beside himself for ruining those precious words."

"No, miss, this does not concern your father, but there is blood. A stranger is at the door and is demanding to see only you," Davis warned. "He would only say he's Winston."

"Winston? Here?" Charlotte flew ahead of the butler and peered down the dark staircase at the entrance hall below. Yes, there was Lord Hurlston, standing in a pool of candlelight, leaning against a wall in her home. She nearly fainted to see him at this time of night but rushed downstairs to meet him, wondering why on earth he would call.

When she got closer, she saw the blood the butler had mentioned splatted all over his clothes; his hands and face were smeared with it, too. She approached him slowly.

He lifted his head and met her gaze with a deep sigh. "At last."

She drew closer, reaching out, but was terrified to touch him. "What happened?"

"You were right," he said, setting his head back against the wall. "Someone shot at me. I ran."

She gulped and put her fingertips lightly on his chest. "You ran? From where?"

"Perhaps we had best get the gentleman into a chair first, miss, before you question him?"

"I feel fine," Winston promised. A ridiculous statement, given the way he looked. "Didn't try to fight them this time as you warned me not to do. I heard you in my head, and I ran here to tell you—you were right. I think someone wants me dead now, too."

With the butler's help, she guided Winston to a chaise near a smoldering fire and urged him to sit down. She could not see a wound in the firelight but there was so much blood every-where, there was no doubt he was wounded. He seemed dazed, too, and as the butler lit candles about the room, she saw the pupils of his eyes were huge. "I'd say they almost succeeded."

"No. No. I ran away, so they couldn't get me," he promised, raking a hand through his hair. It came away bloodier than it had been, which had been bad to start with.

Charlotte caught the earl's wrist and held his hand up before his face. "Winston, there's blood and it's all over you."

He blinked several time. "How did that get there?"

"I'd say from the wound on your head," the butler murmured. "If I may take a look?" he asked quietly.

Charlotte grasped Winston's bloody hand in both of hers to keep him still. "See if you can find where the blood is coming from and how serious the wound might be. He might need a surgeon if the pistol shot penetrated his skull."

Winston jerked in her grip. Charlotte squeezed his hand, hoping it wasn't the case at all.

But when Davis tried to look though Winston's hair, the

earl shied away from the butler's touch and his grip on Charlotte tightened. She gently eased to her feet and slipped around the earl and the chaise. "Perhaps you would permit me to inspect your head? I promise to be very gentle."

"You're always gentle with me," Winston murmured, but Charlotte heard his words slur. "More than I deserve."

Charlotte slowly lifted her hand toward Winston's hair, discovering the dark strands coated in sticky redness. She worked her way slowly from front to back and discovered a long, tapered wound running across the surface of his skull on the right side, from front to back. "Here," she said to the butler, pointing out the injury.

"He has bled a lot, but it seems to me that the wound appears not very deep," he murmured.

Charlotte exhaled a pent-up breath. A flesh wound wouldn't kill Winston if it didn't fester. He would not need a surgeon for this, but it would need to be cleaned and the blood flow stopped. She met Winston's gaze over his shoulder. "Do you have any other wounds besides this one? Do you have pain lower down your legs?"

He reached up and winced as he touched his head. "I didn't know I had *this* one. There was no pain from it until you mentioned it just now."

"Perhaps the fright of the danger distracted you from it," she murmured. "Could you stand up for me?"

"Why?"

She hurried around the chaise to face him. "I want to check you for any other wounds."

He put a hand on her shoulder, and on Davis' too. "All right. Don't want to expire from sheer bloody ignorance."

"No. I wouldn't like that very much, either," she promised him.

He seemed to take being shot in his stride.

She helped Winston stand because he was now trembling a

bit. With the butler's help, they removed Winston's coat and waistcoat, making a proper inspection of each garment—looking for holes. Finding none, she checked the shirt he was still wearing for any large blood spots on the fine linen. "There's a bit here at the collar and down his shirt front, likely dripped from the head wound."

"What about the rest of me?"

His trousers were dark, and she had to rub her hands up and down each of his legs and, of course, across his rear to find out if he were shot anywhere lower down. There were dark spots on his usually pristine stocking hose. More drips.

Her fingers came away smudged with blood from his thighs, where she quickly concluded he'd only wiped his bloody hands.

The rest of him appeared completely unharmed.

She stood back, relieved, and wiped her fingers on a cloth the butler handed to her. "You'll live."

Winston collapsed into the chaise behind him. "Guess I still possess a bit of luck."

"You do seem blessed with an abundance of it lately. Except for your poor head," she murmured. "Davis, would you fetch water and clean clothes? He'll need to wash and change. Perhaps something from one of the taller footmen would fit him. My father's clothes would never do, and I cannot allow him to arrive home in blood-soaked garments. His poor mother would faint clean away."

"Yes, miss." Davis paused a moment. "Should I wake the housekeeper or a maid to chaperone you?"

That would be the proper thing to do, but…given her last conversation with the earl… She shook her head. "I think the fewer people aware of his presence, the better for all concerned. Best not to mention this to my parents."

The butler nodded quickly, and rushed off, leaving them alone.

She turned her attention back to Winston, puzzled. Why

had he come to her tonight? And injured? He should have gone straight home and called the magistrate to start an investigation.

Charlotte pulled a footstool close to Winston and sat upon it. She stared at him and forced a smile to her face. She hated seeing him this way, but she was also mindful of their last conversation. He'd told her not to worry about him.

She wet her lips. "Why have you come to see me?"

His eyes grew sad. "I know after what I said to you earlier today that—"

"Think nothing of it," she snapped, cutting him off. "Why are you bleeding? You said someone shot at you?"

"I was at Bradshaw's, leaving, and my carriage was nowhere to be found."

She knew what Bradshaw's was. A house of ill repute. Wine, gambling and fallen women to be had for a handful of coin. She'd thought a betrothed man would have given up debauchery, especially since his future bride was staying under his roof until the wedding day. "So, you found a hired hack to take you home?"

"Yes. No. I was going to. But..." His eyes grew serious, and he stared at her. "Bradshaw's footman was dead in the alley beside the building. They were waiting for me out there in the dark."

She gaped. "Waiting specifically for you? Are you sure?"

"Yes. I recognized them. They called me by name and taunted me that they'd make it quick this time. They were led by the same men who set upon me in Green Park."

She took hold of his hand, concerned by that development. She'd really hoped she was wrong about the threat against his life. "How did you escape?"

"They had learned their lesson after last time. They brought more men tonight."

"And yet here you are with me," she reminded him.

He gazed into her eyes, fingers lacing through hers tightly. "I would have died but for you."

She pressed her hand to his brow, worried for his state of mind, but felt no fever burning on his skin. "Winston, I wasn't there with you."

He leaned into her touch and then the fingers of his other hand rose to tap against his temple. "You were in my head. Telling me there was no shame in running away. I was outnumbered. I had no weapon."

She smiled. "Winston, that wasn't me. That was simply common sense. Anyone should have run away in your situation."

He shook his head, face set into stubborn lines. "It was you. You saved me. Again."

She laughed at his delusion, even while noting the stickiness of his brow. His skin was becoming cold and clammy. She'd known a man to go into shock after a fright and fall into a stupor for days on end. She reached for a blanket and placed it over Winston's knees, determined to keep him talking until the butler returned. His wounds must be attended to before she sent him home in their carriage. "Tell me about Bradshaw's?"

"It's a club."

Charlotte tucked the blanket tighter about him. "So, you were with a woman at a brothel and then decided to come here."

"No. I…" He frowned. "I was drinking with friends there. Berringer had left to go home to his wife, and the others each had women. I had no reason to stay."

"I'm sure you didn't," she said dryly. Men were all the same. Foolish and stupidly brave and full of lust.

"I don't…do *that* with the women there."

But everywhere else was likely fine? She stood and went to where her father kept a bottle of whiskey hidden in a desk drawer. She poured the earl a generous helping and carried it to him.

He was watching her, and then he smiled. "I know what you're thinking—and I don't do that with *any* women, anywhere else, either."

She shrugged. So, he wanted her to believe he was chaste. *Wonderful.* Just the thing she wanted to hear in the middle of the night. "Drink," she urged, nudging his hand upward. Winston didn't need much prompting. One sip led to another until the glass was almost depleted.

She watched his face carefully, pleased to see that soon after his color improved thanks to the effects of the spirits.

He looked up at her suddenly, jaw set. "Someone is trying to kill me."

"Who?"

"I don't know. Not yet."

"I can send a servant out for the watch and the magistrate to escort you home. They'll find out soon enough and you'll be safe."

"No," he said quickly.

She frowned. "What do you mean, no?"

"There's no reason to kill me."

"Surely there is." She held up her hand and counted off a few. "Did an angry lord lose money to you at cards? Did you unfairly dismiss a servant who seeks his revenge? Have you a jealous lover, angry at the thought of being set aside upon your marriage?"

He met her gaze. "No. No. And definitely no."

"Then there is only one other reason I can think of. You are a titled lord and in possession of a great fortune in funds and property. Only one person truly stands to gain from your demise."

"You mean my younger brother?"

"And you and your brother haven't been getting along so well of late," she noted.

He frowned at her. "Why would you think that?"

"I, um…it's fairly common knowledge."

"No. It's not as bad as that. He wants to gamble and chase skirts. Waste good money on sin and vice. I refused to increase his allowance when he asked me to last, and we've quarreled about that on and off for the last year."

"He should be made to live within his means."

Winston nodded. "On that we agree. I have a town house to offer him the use of now as his principal place of residence."

"So, you are kicking him out?"

He scowled. "I'm giving him a chance to be truly independent."

"Does he know?"

"Not yet. I wanted to surprise him with the news on his birthday, but he's made himself scarce."

She sighed. "Well, we'd best clean you up and send you on your way so you can make sure it's not him."

She stood, intending to find out what was keeping her butler from returning, but Winston grabbed her hand again. He pulled her down, almost onto his lap. "Don't go."

"My lord, your family is better suited to comforting you than I am," she chided, inching away from him so they didn't touch anymore.

"You might think so, but you would be very wrong." Winston had kept hold of her hand and now caressed her fingers with his own, comparing their difference in size.

He brought her hand to his face and pressed his cheek against her palm again. "You're so different from anyone I've ever known." He drew in a deep breath and then his eyes fixed on Charlotte's. "I desperately want to know everything about you."

She shivered at the expression in his eyes. The longing she

saw there affected her, too. Even angry with him today, she'd still loved him. "But you're to be married."

A regretful expression appeared on his face. "That's the worst part of being already pledged to another. I cannot have everything I want."

She stared at him while her heart almost burst from her chest. Did he have *doubts*…and was that feeling she got when they were together not just her problem alone?

"I want to know you better, too." She grinned at the prospect of a future where Winston cared about her.

But he shook his head. "*Hell.* My brother couldn't want to kill me, Charlotte."

Charlotte pulled her hand back to her lap, clenching her fingers tightly together as she considered Winston, and the reason he'd come to her. "If it's not Peter, then think—did the property you purchased nearly go to someone else? Have you voted against a lord in the House who holds a grudge?"

"It's possible. But the town house I purchased, well, I had no competition on the sale. Mine was the only interest."

Davis finally appeared, bowl and washcloth in hand, and clothes tossed over one shoulder. "I had to take the footman I borrowed the clothes from into my confidence and Cook as well. She was still in the kitchens, despite the late hour, and caught me rummaging through her cupboards," he admitted with a wince. "She swears to keep the secret, given the danger to your friend." Davis wet a cloth. "If you could hold still, I'll wash the blood off your hands and face."

Charlotte scrambled out of the way and left the butler to act as valet. She could, of course, tend Lord Hurlston herself. She was not squeamish about blood, and she had an interest in his recovery. But she needed a moment to settle herself. She couldn't forget that Winston's moods changed like the weather.

Tomorrow, when he'd had a chance to think again, he might regret everything he'd said to her tonight.

She moved to the window and carefully peeked out to study the darkness beyond. No shapes moved in the quiet street before her house, and she prayed Lord Hurlston had not been followed all the way here.

She turned and let the drape fall. What was she to do with the earl? How could she possibly help him? She obviously had to send him away with as many servants as she could muster at this hour, for his protection.

But she would worry the moment he walked out her door. She had vowed not to care about him anymore just that afternoon, but it seemed she could not escape him yet.

It took a while but eventually Davis managed to wash enough blood from Winston's face and hair that he looked completely normal from the chin up. The wound on his head wept lightly now and was cleaned with only the odd curse being uttered by the earl.

Davis eased Hurlston out of his shirt in preparation for donning a clean one. Charlotte drank in every moment of his undressing. Admired the play of muscles across Winston's sleek back as he lifted his arms high. There were bruises, almost faded completely now after his assault in Green Park. Although she supposed she should have averted her eyes, Charlotte felt no shame, only the continuation of her fascination with the man.

Finally, any trace of blood was gone, and he stood in her home freshly dressed but obviously weary.

The butler excused himself to remove the soiled clothing, leaving them alone again.

Winston met her gaze, and his expression was grim. Charlotte returned to sit by the fire near him. "What will you do now?"

He drew in a deep breath, rubbing at his fingers, which had so recently worn the stain of his blood. "I don't know. That's why I came to you, I think."

Charlotte folded her hands in her lap. "What more do you imagine I can do to help you this time, my lord?"

"You're the most rational person I know in the midst of a crisis."

"I'll take that as a compliment."

He nodded. "It was meant as such. You *are* the only person I know who I feel I can completely trust right now, too."

She frowned. "I'm surprised to hear you say that."

"I feel safe here with you." He shifted suddenly in his seat and put his hands in his lap. "I'm afraid to go outside again."

"There's no need for haste. You can stay as long as you like."

His smile returned. "You never returned for your second season. Where were you?"

She blinked in surprise at the change of subject, and that he'd noticed her absence at all. "Places I wish never to see again."

He cleared his throat. "So, I hear your parents are planning another voyage? When will that be?"

"In about two weeks, they'll depart." She nodded. "There is a slim chance I won't leave with them this time, though."

"How slim?"

She shrugged. "If I marry, I'll remain in England."

Winston's expression grew tight. "Is there someone else? I mean…are you being courted?"

"No. But it's always been a dream of mine to be wed. A hope to have a home I never need leave and a family to care for." She lowered her face, hiding her embarrassment that she'd always wanted that with him. "But I have no one particular courting me."

He exhaled slowly and slumped back. "I need time. If I go home, and my mother sees me like this…"

"She will become very upset."

"Worse than last time," he agreed. "And that has been very bad."

She noticed he had failed to mention Elizabeth's reaction to his last injury. "Once your hair dries and you change back into your own clothes, your mother and Elizabeth might never notice the injury. Unless…well, if Elizabeth runs her fingers through your hair, she might notice a wince of pain from you for a few days."

Winston stared at her. "That won't happen."

Charlotte nodded. "All right. You may stay as long as you need to then."

He looked about suddenly. "What about your parents?"

"They're already abed." She shrugged. "If you're gone before dawn, they'll probably never realize you were even here."

He glanced around, eyes narrowing. He stared at the front door a long time "This room feels too exposed. Where else might I stay in the house?"

"Do you want to sleep?"

"No, I think it unlikely I could close my eyes after the events of tonight, but I am not going back outside while it is dark."

"Oh!" She gaped at him. "You want to spend the night here?"

He swallowed and then nodded. "Very much."

"We do have a guest room," she admitted. "No one has stayed in that room for a long time, but I can have a maid make up the bed for you."

"I need *you* to hide me, Charlotte."

She blinked. He was quite welcome to spend the night in a guest room, but was he really suggesting he stay with *her*? In her room, too?

"Yes, with you, if you will have me. There are some things I need to explain to you. In private."

All the air left her lungs. She was shocked but also intrigued. What was there left for him to say? He'd made his disapproval of her behavior quite clear already.

But she stood, wiping her damp palms on her robe and quickly glanced down.

Dear God, I am in my nightclothes.

Sitting in front of the earl I love in night attire!

She closed her eyes briefly, shocked at herself. Now she really *was* ruined, and he hadn't even touched her.

But Winston hadn't seemed at all concerned by her lack of attire. And it was possible she *could* sneak the earl up to her chambers, and hide him in her dressing room for the night, and no one might ever find out. Her parents rarely checked on her.

Davis returned then, and his gaze fell on the earl immediately. "Shall I call a carriage now?"

Thinking quickly, she replied, "Could you ask cook if there was anything left from dinner for him to eat? I fear my friend may go into shock from his misadventures tonight. Some food in his stomach might make him feel so much better before he leaves us," she murmured.

"I'd be glad to fetch him something," Davis replied with a nod before leaving to complete the errand.

As soon as he was gone, Charlotte grabbed the earl's arm and tugged him up to his feet. "Quietly now."

They tiptoed to the stairs, and Charlotte drew him upstairs and along to her bedchamber. She pushed him inside, promising to return as soon as she could, then hurried back downstairs. Once in the front hall, she opened and shut the front door and then stood about, waiting for the butler's return.

Davis seemed surprised to see her in the hall, but he carried the promised plate of food. "It is the best I could do at this hour."

"I do appreciate your efforts, but unfortunately the gentleman suddenly decided he had to leave." She glanced at the door and chewed on her lower lip. "I do hope he'll be all right."

"I hope so, too," Davis agreed, as he made sure the house was securely locked up for the night.

Charlotte caught a whiff of the food on the tray and her stomach rumbled in response. She put her hand out. "Waste not, want not," she said. "I think I'll take that plate up to my room and eat it before I go back to sleep. I'll leave the plate outside my door when I'm done to be collected in the morning," she promised.

The butler, used to her occasional requests for midnight morsels, gladly gave over the plate. A slice of cold pie from dinner, a little ham and cheese. Food perfect to be eaten with only her fingers.

She climbed the stairs calmly enough, but her senses were on fire. She had an earl in her chambers. Not even in her wildest dreams had she ever imagined that happening.

She let herself into her chambers and turned the lock on the door. Winston was seated close by the fire, staring into the flames. "Any problems," he whispered.

"None," she answered, also in a whisper, before depositing the plate on his lap. Then she took a seat beside him and waited for whatever came next.

He put the plate aside and turned to her. "I didn't mean a single thing I said to you at the menagerie. None of it."

She stiffened as she remembered the pain his words had inflicted but did not dare look at him. "Then why say it?"

He sighed. "I cannot explain why, only that I thought it was important at the time."

"And you've changed your mind now? Will you change it again tomorrow?"

"I've come to my senses."

She glanced at him now and raised one brow, as he'd done with her earlier that day, waiting on an explanation or an apology.

He inclined his head. "I am more sorry than you can imagine, Charlotte, for the hurtful things I said. I was unforgivably rude, ungrateful and foolish today."

She lifted her chin. "Yes, you were. I thought the very same thing of you at the time, and a dozen other unkind descriptions, too."

"I saw that. You've every right to be angry with me and knock me on the head with your parasol, too, if you wish."

She glanced at his head. "I think your poor head has taken all the beatings it can stand for this month."

"Charlotte, there's no easy way to explain but…" He sagged slightly. "I want to show you what I *really* felt today when I saw you standing before the elephant."

"All right."

"Hold very still," he whispered, as his hand came up beneath her chin and he turned her face toward his.

The next moment, his lips descended upon hers.

She froze under the gentle assault of her lips.

The earl was kissing her, and she wanted to kiss him back as the brush of his lips continued. Charlotte was only human, and very weak where Winston was concerned.

She parted her lips—and suddenly found herself wrapped in the earl's strong arms, pulled onto his lap. She clung to him, breathless, her senses overwhelmed by a passion that seemed to have come out of nowhere.

Winston suddenly drew back with a sigh. "*That's* why I was cross today. I don't want to have the thoughts I have when I see you…but I do."

"I did nothing different today," she promised, gazing at him in utter shock.

Winston desired her.

"It's me. I can't stop thinking about you," he admitted. A slow smile turned up his lips before he removed her from his lap. "You didn't stop me."

"No. I wanted that kiss." She'd always wanted to know how he tasted.

He nodded slowly. "Leave me to figure this out, sweet Charlotte, and go to bed. I need to think about what I've just done, and what happened to me earlier tonight. Pretend I'm not here, so no one suspects you're not alone anymore."

Charlotte didn't want to leave him but perhaps a little distance might prevent her from making a fatal mistake. She had dreamed of having Winston all to herself. Now that she had him, she wasn't sure she was ready.

She got to her feet and climbed into her bed full of conflicted hope, but more excited than she'd ever been in her life. Winston had kissed her with such sweet passion that she was nearly trembling with hope that she might yet have her dream come true.

A happy ever after…with him as her husband, perhaps. But only if he wasn't killed first.

Chapter Fourteen

Winston crossed off another name from his list and cursed under his breath at the futility of his solitary morning. He still could not fathom why anyone would want to shoot him, run him down with their horse or beat him to a bloody pulp.

He'd been at it all night and all morning. Writing down the names of acquaintances, and good friends, too, at Charlotte's urging, had been a futile endeavor.

In retrospect, he'd been under threat for some time and not realized it.

He could no longer pretend he was lucky to have escaped his near misses. There was a persistent danger circling him, and the methods had become more extreme over the last weeks.

The only thing he was sure of was that Charlotte was willing to do anything to help keep him alive. Even ruin her reputation and perhaps her chances of making a match.

He glanced around her cozy chambers, wishing and worrying about her safety now, too. She had gone out, determined to learn if any word of his recent misfortunes was being gossiped about by anyone in society. She'd assured him that no one paid any attention to inquisitive wallflowers.

But he had.

His attackers might have, too.

Winston had noticed Charlotte in her first season, but she hadn't come back for a second. And now this year, he'd been in her company due to their mutual friends—and he couldn't overlook the reason for his interest in her anymore.

He liked her too well to forget her. He'd kissed her last night, and wanted to do so again today when she returned.

He was meant to marry Elizabeth, had been betrothed even when he'd first noticed Charlotte. But then she'd gone away, missed a whole second season, and he'd thought his interest an aberration.

When she'd come back, he'd convinced himself the excitement of seeing her again was only anticipation for the stories she'd share of her travels.

Last night, she'd let him kiss her, and she did not seem all that worried about it this morning. She had slept not six feet away from where he'd sat all night, pondering his future—if he had one to live at all.

He peeked out the window of her room to the street below, observing passing carriages through the filter of lace curtains. Charlotte had been gone a long time now, and he was truly starting to worry about what was keeping her away from him.

He made himself sit back down at her writing desk for the umpteenth time to study the lists he'd made. Too many names on them had been scratched out and he was still no closer to finding an answer or reason for last night's attack.

His current servants had been with him a long time. His closest friends were above reproach. He could not surely be under threat from his own mother, or even his brother, as Charlotte had first suggested he might be. It could not be Elizabeth. She was to be his wife.

Yet, out in London somewhere was an extremely angry person with a motive he couldn't fathom.

The front door slammed shut one floor down.

Winston was on his feet in an instant. He scooped up his notes, made sure there was no sign of his presence left behind in Charlotte's bedchamber, and rushed back into her dressing closet—his hiding place for the day. Although he'd intended to leave before dawn, he'd not gone. Yet he couldn't be discovered here. Not if he wanted to protect Charlotte's reputation.

It wasn't long before the bedchamber door opened, and he heard Charlotte's voice—loud and clear and sounding aggrieved over something. "Just give them to me and I'll put them away myself," she ordered.

"It's no bother, Miss Waters," replied a maid, he assumed. "At least let me lay them out on the bed so they don't become wrinkled. They're fresh from the ironing table."

"Oh, very well. And then I really want to be alone," Charlotte grudgingly agreed. "My head…"

Footsteps rushed across the room. "Shall I fetch you a powder, miss?"

"No. No. I just need a bit of peace and quiet. Just ask everyone to stay away from my room."

Clever Charlotte.

He heard the rustle of fabric just beyond the dressing room door and shrank himself a little smaller behind the traveling trunks. "Did you see any handsome men while you were out today?"

"No," Charlotte replied shortly.

"You deserve a beau of your own."

Winston hung his head in embarrassment. Charlotte deserved better than a betrothed man lusting after her.

"That will be all," Charlotte snapped at the maid with a firmness to her tone Winston had never heard from her before. Not for the first time, he wondered what sort of life Charlotte wanted for herself. She'd mentioned marriage to avoid leaving with her parents, but was that all she wanted a man for?

Soon he heard a set of footsteps leave the room, then there was silence in the bedchamber for several long moments. So long, he feared Charlotte had gone out again, too.

But eventually, Charlotte's steps could be heard slowly moving about in the chamber before she stopped close to where he hid. She tapped on the dressing room door before flinging it open. She carried a yellow gown and slowly met his gaze. "Well?"

Winston studied her face, relieved beyond measure to see her, while also noticing her cheeks were quite red. "Well?" he replied.

"I half expected to return and find you'd slipped away." She bustled into the small space and hung a gown on a peg beside his head.

"I would not leave without saying goodbye."

Charlotte smiled softly. "I visited Aurora Hillcrest, Mrs. Berringer, Sylvia Hillcrest at Lord Wharton's, and several Bond Street shops. Anywhere I might bump into mutual acquaintances. No one is talking about you in particular today, and not a word was in any of today's newssheets about a murder near Bradshaw's, either."

Maybe the Bradshaw's footman had survived. He hoped so. "Did you see anyone from my home on your travels?"

"No, unfortunately not. I passed your town house on foot, too. I had hoped to see your brother or mother entering or leaving. But all seems quiet there."

"Mother hardly ventures out alone anymore." He slumped against the doorway, watching a blush climb Charlotte's cheeks. "She will have realized by now that I've not come home and will be worried, though."

"I might have a solution for that." She stopped in front of him and gestured him to move aside. She dug into a drawer behind his back and removed a neatly folded pelisse. "I have received another invitation from your mother—to join her for tea this very afternoon."

Winston followed Charlotte into her bedchamber so he could continue to speak to her in soft tones. "I had wondered if she might ask again. She was quite cast down that you sent your apologies for the luncheon, and I'm sure she enjoyed the tour of the menagerie better than if I had stayed."

"I wasn't feeling well the first time," she said, trying to hide that her cheeks were turning a fiery shade of pink.

If he had to guess, Charlotte was lying about the reason she'd declined to come. He moved to stand close behind her and put his hands lightly on her shoulder. "Whatever disagreements we have, I trust you will not snub my mother for them ever again."

She shrugged, dislodging his hands. "If I go to her today, I could tell her you are safe. Set her mind at ease." She turned around and looked at him. "I would not, of course, tell her that you were fired upon. That might be too much for any mother to hear about their firstborn."

He thought about it a moment. "She would be relieved to know I was safe and well, but I think it best you do not reveal you know my location. She'd ask too many awkward questions and assume the worst of us."

"I understand the risks to my reputation depend on keeping your presence here a secret. Do you have any objection to me accepting her invitation?"

"No." He frowned at her. "Would you normally have hesitated?"

"No. I am honored to be invited. Your mother is very sweet. But your future bride is there, and…"

"And I kissed you last night," he finished for her.

"Exactly." Charlotte winced and turned away from him. He watched her rifling through her wardrobe choices before lifting out two very different gowns. It appeared as if she couldn't decide between the yellow gown she'd first carried in, or the virginal white already hanging in wait to be worn.

He leaned against the doorframe and his gaze swept her from top to toe. Charlotte was…nicely rounded, in his opinion. In the past, she had not always seemed as confident as she was now. Especially not at balls. She'd usually kept company with the wallflowers, but of late, thanks to her expanding circle of friends, he'd seen another side of her, a bolder, more confident woman, and that only added to her appeal. "If you're open to suggestions, I vote for the yellow. The color always becomes you."

Her lips pursed as she looked over the yellow gown again. Winston had the sudden urge to dash across the room and steal a kiss from those rosy buds.

He turned away as his cock stirred to life. Only Charlotte did that to him it seemed. To his chagrin, he'd never been moved in that fashion by Elizabeth. Not even once that he could ever remember. He shook his head at his ill-timed discovery of lust. When he found out who was behind the attacks on him, he'd have to do something about his attraction to Charlotte. "What time did Mama invite you for?"

"Five o'clock. Quite late for taking tea, isn't it?"

It *was* late. Most of society would be headed to Hyde Park for the promenade at that hour. What was Mama doing? Was she trying to make Charlotte's visit a secret? But from whom? From him or Elizabeth? "Mama has become a bit of a recluse in her old age."

Charlotte nodded. "It must be hard for her, knowing she'll soon be replaced as the lady of the house."

"I hadn't noticed any sadness about that. Quite the opposite, in fact."

"Women don't always reveal their every thought the moment they have them," Charlotte confessed with a wry smile. "We might be boiling mad or sad, yet say nothing outwardly to give away our inner turmoil."

Winston's heart hurt for the misery in her voice. "I'm sorry to hear your parents are going."

She nodded quickly and moved to the desk, glancing over

his lists briefly and then putting them down again. "I'm doing everything I can to stay."

"I'm sure you'll succeed," Winston agreed, but he worried about her marriage plans now. She shouldn't marry because she was desperate.

Charlotte returned the yellow gown to the peg in the dressing closet and returned to lay the delicate white muslin gown upon her bed. He watched her again from the doorway, choosing ribbons and shawl and any number of things women needed to go out into the world.

He wanted to go with her. To protect her, and to walk about with her on his arm…but how could he ever do that? He was engaged to marry another. Had been all his life. A love match it wasn't, and he wondered if it could ever be more.

It couldn't if he was drawn to Charlotte this way.

He cursed under his breath, uncertain of what he was supposed to do about his unexpected cold feet.

Wanting someone you couldn't have seemed to be painful.

Charlotte turned to him suddenly, but without a smile. "I need to send for my maid if I am to be ready to meet with your mother this afternoon," she informed him briskly. "Could you please hide in the dressing room behind my trunks again, and be very still? My maid might need to venture into the dressing room, though I'll try to stop her or warn you somehow."

He nodded and withdrew from the room, pulling the door almost completely closed and again taking his papers with him. He slipped behind the tall stack of traveling cases. It was scant protection, but enough that he was hidden from a fleeting glance if he crouched down.

When the maid came into the bedchamber, he shrank himself as small as he could and decided he couldn't possibly stay another night here in Charlotte's home. He was putting Charlotte's reputation at too great a risk. She shouldn't suffer, too, because someone wanted to murder him.

But he was uncertain of where to go. Home was out of the question if his brother wanted him dead. But he couldn't imagine why Peter might feel that way. He should have all the facts of his inheritance by now and be satisfied he'd blunt of his own. Aside from disagreeing about gambling, whoring, and not buying him the phaeton he'd wanted, Peter and he had once been close.

Though now he had to wonder if that were really true anymore. People changed, revealing facets of their personality that were sometimes unpleasant or uncomfortable. Peter had become secretive.

He could go to a friend for protection. Berringer and Wharton would gladly take him in. They'd surely lend their assistance and protection until the culprit was found and apprehended.

But Winston would prefer to manage the situation himself. Would it make him seem weak to admit he couldn't always protect himself? It would be bad enough if anyone learned about Charlotte's small but heroic parts in his troubles.

"Winston?"

He poked his head around the trunks to see Charlotte redressed and appearing ready to go meet with his mother. She appeared…breathtakingly innocent when she wore white. He gulped, deeply affected. He wanted to go to her and wrap her tight in his arms. To hold her and never let her go. He pushed that selfish thought aside. "I was wrong about the color of your dress. You look lovely in everything you wear."

Her smile was instant. "I've thought of a way to deliver a message to your mother without revealing I have any knowledge of where you are."

"How?"

"Write a note to her, as if it were written yesterday. I'll drop it in your front hall on my way inside to meet your mother. Or I could discover it somewhere in the drawing room perhaps, and pass it to her then and there. Tell her in your letter that you'll return to London in a few days, most likely."

"She'll want to know what I'm doing. What do I say? I'm always honest with her. I cannot very well tell her I'm hiding in your dressing room."

She beamed. "Tell your mother that you decided to join Lord Scarsdale for a week at his hunting box. You were invited, were you not?"

"I was, but Scarsdale knew I wouldn't go because of Elizabeth being in London for the wedding. They would have all left this morning at first light."

"Indeed, they did," Charlotte promised him. "But not as early as first light. Scarsdale looked a little seedy as he stumbled out of his town house when I was passing by."

But Charlotte's idea was a good story to tell Mama. He could claim he'd followed them but missed the turn or gotten completely lost. He only had the vaguest idea of where Scarsdale and company were heading, after all. He nodded. "A message of that nature would be enough to relieve her mind for a few more days. Well done."

Charlotte nodded. "What should I do if I see Miss Mayflower? She must be worried, too."

Winston thought about that long and hard before he answered. "Elizabeth will be content with whatever Mama shares with her from my letter."

He ducked around Charlotte and went immediately to her writing table, aware that Charlotte was giving a look that screamed of curiosity. He didn't go around kissing other women or worrying about what they thought of him for it. She'd no idea he'd hardly ever kissed Elizabeth.

He scratched out a note, as if he were hurried when he wrote it, explaining he'd return to Town in a few days, and begged her forgiveness for not speaking to her about it in person. He signed the letter "her loving son" and folded it imperfectly.

Charlotte appeared at his elbow and whipped the note from his hand. "I'll make sure she's seen it before I leave your town house. I won't let her worry longer than she needs to about you. I will also try to find out where your brother might be, so you know that he's safe as well."

"I thought you were keen to accuse him of trying to kill me?"

She bit her lip. "I did, but I have been thinking about why you are being targeted. Is it all about you or your family as well?"

"It had not occurred to me that Peter could be in danger, too. Mother and Elizabeth, as well."

"Better to discuss an uncomfortable suspicion than leave it unsaid and miss a vital clue." She winced. "Until we discern a motive, and where the threat originates, there's nothing I can do except worry about you."

He stood, grateful for her concern and equally eager for word from home. "Thank you for doing this."

"It's the right thing to do." She shrugged. "Well...until tonight, my lord."

"Not Winston anymore?"

"No. That was a slip I must never make again," she whispered. "You are to marry Elizabeth still."

"If I tell you that Elizabeth only calls me Hurlston, will you call me Winston again?" He leaned down and pressed a kiss to Charlotte's cheek. He leaned his head against hers for a moment. "Be very careful out there."

Her head turned, and their lips connected. Winston didn't hesitate. He stole one kiss, then another, and more besides. When he finally stopped, he somehow had Charlotte perched on his knees, having once more sat at her writing desk. His hand cupping her cheek and her fingers in his hair. She'd managed to miss the tender wound on his head and seemed to be completely out of breath.

"That was…the best kiss of my life," he told her.

"Mine too." She slowly wriggled off his lap and went to the mirror.

"Did I muss you?"

"No." Her smile grew. "Try harder next time, will you?" And then she covered her lips to giggle. "I have always wanted to say that to a man."

"I'm glad it was me and not someone else."

"There's *never* been anyone else." Her eyes misted momentarily, and a strange smile appeared on her face, but then she shook her head before picking up her reticule. "I will be back with news as soon as I can."

"I'll be waiting right here," he promised.

A soft smile lifted her lips and then she was gone out the door.

Winston rushed to the window and carefully peeked outside. When her carriage drew away, he let out a frustrated sigh. What was he to do about his need for Charlotte's kisses when he couldn't possibly offer her a respectable future?

Chapter Fifteen

Lady Hurlston was so welcoming when Charlotte saw her that she felt bad about her deception in being there. Charlotte hated being here on false pretenses, but keeping Winston safe was vital to her own happiness too. "Please, I only did what any decent person would have done in that situation."

The older lady nodded as she refilled her cup. "If my son were with us today, I'm sure he would dispute your claim. You were very brave indeed. I would have said so yesterday again, but I did not want to embarrass you in front of Miss Hillcrest."

"Thank you." The endless praise from the lady was making her blush, and she looked about the elegantly appointed chamber. Hurlston had excellent taste, or perhaps it was his mother's taste she was seeing around her.

The old lady frowned and glanced toward the door with a look of longing on her face. "My son might consent to join us later."

Winston had better not show his face today, or their plan to avoid his attackers would utterly fall apart.

Charlotte glanced at the door to the front hall herself, though for reasons of her own. The reason she'd come at all was to reassure this woman her son was all right. She had dropped the note on the hall table immediately after she'd arrived. Was the Hurlston butler blind?

Charlotte sipped her tea, resisting the urge to tap her foot and reveal any impatience. Her time here would soon be over, no matter how slowly she sipped tea and chatted about her travels. She'd promised Winston she'd ensure that his mother had read the note by the time she left today. "I was very sorry to hear of the loss of your husband two years back. I had the pleasure of an introduction in my first season."

Lady Hurlston nodded. "I keep expecting him to walk through that door still to tell me of his day."

"I'm sure this must be a difficult time for you."

Lady Hurlston smiled sadly. "It is, but I have my sons to comfort me. At least one of them."

"Is one of them proving difficult?" she asked carefully, not willing to reveal her keen interest in the younger one. She did not know him well, but she'd learned he was well on his way to ruin if he were running up debts he couldn't repay. She ought to tell Winston about that. She would, if he kept his promise and waited for her at her home.

"My youngest," she murmured. "Winston says he's become too old to care about spending time with family."

"I'm sure that's not true. But doesn't every young man stage a rebellion against his duty at a certain age?"

"Winston did not. Now Peter's reached his majority I've barely seen him to wish him well."

Charlotte winced. She hoped Peter's rebellion never amounted to more than being too busy to spend time with his mother. Everyone outgrew their parents at a certain point. Some earlier than others. "But you have important guests staying with you. That must be a wonderful diversion."

"Yes, we do have guests." But Lady Hurlston's smile slipped away, and curiosity ate at Charlotte. She glanced around. The house had seemed eerily quiet when she'd arrived. It still was. Was Winston's bride-to-be even at home or flittering about London with her mystery man? Lady Hurlston had barely mentioned the woman. She wet her lips and decided to be more direct. "Will Miss Mayflower join us today, do you think?"

Charlotte didn't miss the disappointment in Lady Hurlston's

tone when she answered. "No. She gone out with her father again, I believe."

Charlotte glanced at the clock on the table, just beside Lady Hurlston's elbow. Ten minutes to six o'clock. It was almost time to make her way home. She delayed a little longer and asked the countess about her plans for the next day, and when the hall clock chimed the hour, a magical sound echoed through the entire house. When it ended, the silence left made her shiver deliciously.

"My husband gave me many clocks for our wedding anniversaries. That particular one on the day we married. It makes me remember of the life we shared."

"I love the sound." Charlotte put her cup down. "Well, I hate to say it, but I must be on my way. I do thank you for the tea and the conversation, my lady. I mustn't intrude any longer."

"I enjoyed your company immensely, and the stories you tell." The old lady nodded. "Thank you for humoring an old woman today by joining me. Do give my best to your mother and father. Perhaps next time, your mother might be persuaded to leave aside her books and join us."

Next time? She doubted she'd have reason or time to call again. "I'll try my best to persuade her to come."

The old woman seemed delighted by her promise. Charlotte stood, curtsied, and walked slowly toward the drawing room doors. They had remained open a crack while she'd taken tea, and when she stepped out, there on the floor was still the note she'd dropped on her arrival.

The butler hadn't even seen it!

She scooped it up and returned to Lady Hurlston. "Forgive me, my lady. But I found a note on the floor out there in the hall. I thought you should see it. It might be important."

Lady Hurlston frowned at the paper but accepted it from her hand and unfolded it slowly to read.

The happiest smile appeared on her face, and Lady Hurlston's posture changed to one of relief. "Well now. That explains everything. Thank you, Miss Waters. This is just what I needed to see."

"I'm glad I could be of assistance." Charlotte curtsied again and then sailed out the front door. Her mission successful, she hastened her steps toward home and Winston.

At home, it was clear her parents had no idea she'd left the house because they asked where she was going to as if they actually cared. Charlotte didn't bother to correct their mistake today. What was the point? She'd prefer it if they didn't take any interest in her right now. But she asked them if they'd eaten yet, and when they promised they were not hungry at all, she wished them a good evening and left them to their study of matters more boring than words could describe.

She climbed the stairs to her room, fighting the same sadness and anger that she'd felt all her life about their preoccupation. Her parents would never pay enough attention to her. Even as a child, she'd been forgotten and handed off to servants.

Charlotte let herself in her room and closed and locked the door behind her, leaning against it while she collected her thoughts. She could not bear another year of living with her parents this way. And with Winston here, she could not concentrate on seeking out a marriage to another man.

When she lifted her eyes, Winston was emerging from the dressing room, wearing a huge smile of welcome on his face. "You're finally back."

"Yes." She hurried to him so she could whisper. "Your mother appears well, but sad also. Is she always prone to prolonged low moods?"

"Yes." Winston took her reticule from her hands and her shawl from her shoulders. "Ever since my father died, she's been hard to cheer up."

"You were right that she'd noticed your absence. She read

your note and it was easy to see her relief." She grinned. "Are you her favorite, by chance?"

"Yes, but she shouldn't have favorites," Winston said as he caught her fingertips.

"At least you have a parent who cares about you," she noted, feeling a little touch of bitterness creep into her soul again, even with Winston's hand sliding up her arm.

His hand stopped at her shoulder and squeezed. "What's happened?"

"Nothing that hasn't happened a thousand times before." She moved away from his touch, unwilling to speak of her parents. "I saw no sign of your brother. Your mother hasn't seen him at all."

Charlotte retrieved her reticule from him and kicked her slippers under her bed as she always did upon returning home.

She scrunched up her toes on the rug, then stretched up on her toes. Homecoming ritual over, she wandered over to her writing table and set her reticule down upon it.

Hurlston had taken over her writing table in her absence again and seemed to have used up all her blank pages, too. She'd have to fetch more from her parents' study later if she was to write any letters of her own. "Any new discoveries made while I was gone?"

"I've a lot of acquaintances, and I cannot recall every conversation I've ever had with them all."

She sat down at her window seat, studying the names he'd scrawled down. "Are these all potential enemies?"

"No. It's a list of everyone I've spoken with in recent weeks."

"The cream of society indeed. Not so surprising since you're everyone's favorite."

"You sound like my brother though I've no idea why he thinks such a thing."

"Because you're easy to talk to and your mother tells everyone you are."

"You've heard gossip about me?"

She shrugged. "Wallflower's gossip all the time."

"Bachelors do, too."

She looked up at him. "Oh, I'm well aware of the devastation a rogue's tongue can do."

He grinned and leaned down to kiss her. "No one gossips about you. I never would," he promised when he pulled away.

"Even after this?" She gestured between them with a smile. She was not sorry she let him kiss her. It was nice. He was delicious.

"No one will ever know about this," he promised, and she believed he meant that.

Besides, no one would ever believe Charlotte Waters had kissed so distinguished a rogue. "I can't promise you the same, I'm afraid. I sometimes speak without considering my audience first."

He grinned. "Like the night you announced you were desperate to be ruined at a ball?"

Charlotte put her hand over her face. "I was hoping you hadn't heard me say that."

He reached up and tucked a strand of her hair back from her face. "It's been on my mind ever since."

"Has it?"

He nodded, and slid his fingers down to caress her throat, then slid across to her shoulder, before he clutched her tightly with both hands. "Promise me you won't give yourself to someone unworthy of you."

"Who should I give myself to, then? You?"

His gaze lowered from hers immediately.

"That's what I thought." Charlotte turned away. "No one wants me."

"That's not true."

"I'm too short and round to even be seen, most nights."

"I see you. And what I could say about your delightful curves might even warrant a slap," he warned her.

She laughed. "Oh, that was cleverly said. Now I'm both dying to know what you might have said, and prevented from slapping you should I find it offensive."

He grinned. "I would never say anything about a lady that wasn't entirely complimentary."

"Perhaps that's our problem. You're too nice and I'm too bold." She shook her head. He was here for one thing only. To save his life. She picked up his list again. "Tell me about Lord Montrose. You circled and then crossed out his name."

"I was at a dinner with him once and he was the target of a jest made in bad taste." He drew closer, his thigh pressed against hers on the window seat. "Do you really think I'm nice?"

Charlotte ignored his question. "You've another name circled and crossed out. Lord Belmont. Tell me about that."

"His current wife flirted with me before they married." He shrugged. "I thought at the time she was trying to make her late husband jealous. But Belmont was there that night too. Now she's married to Belmont I wondered…"

"Married women are often neglected," Charlotte noted. "The late Lord Barnes kept a string of lovers all over town. But Belmont is rumored to have consoled Lady Barnes during the unhappy years of their marriage."

"Surly that incident is not enough to kill me over. It was nothing more than an awkward kiss I never sought out."

"Well, a kiss means nothing to many, but to a lover easily made jealous it means something far worse. Belmont seems a possessive type of man."

"I had no idea they were lovers."

"Its only suspicion and rumor. Most likely unfounded." She found a clear corner on a sheet of paper and wrote out Lord and Lady Belmont's names on the top of a new list. "Lady Belmont is hosting a masquerade tonight, too, though I wasn't invited to that one."

"I was."

"Good. I hope that means both have forgotten about that kiss. Who else did you write down and have doubts about?"

"You're going to question me about all of them, aren't you?"

"Was there some other woman's bedchamber you planned to hide in tonight?"

He bit his lip and then laughed. "Maybe."

"You're going home to Elizabeth." She faced him, heart sinking. It was past time to go their separate ways. "I understand."

"No," he promised, catching hold of her again. He toyed with her fingers a little before he sighed. "But I wonder if it wise for me to remain here. There is something I'd like to do again. And again. With *you*...so perhaps I should take my leave instead."

She regarded him through narrowed eyes, wondering why Winston was so hesitant with her. When they had kissed, it seemed certain that he'd enjoyed it. But then he stopped and seemed to be conflicted. Was he plagued by guilt and felt he betrayed Elizabeth? "What did you want from me?"

"What I want," he started, but then he turned away. "It's a bad idea for you."

Charlotte reached for his arm and turned him back to face her. "Winston?"

He reached for her face. His hand was warm and gentle as it cupped her cheek. "I want to kiss you."

Charlotte's face burned hot. She stretched up to touch his face, too, ran her fingertips over the stubble of his cheek lightly. "There is nothing I want more than that, too."

He leaned down, bridging the gap between them. His kiss was hesitant at first, but soon she found herself wrapped tight in his arms. Charlotte curled both her arms about his head, loving the press of his larger body against hers. The heat of him and excitement. This was where she always wanted to be.

He picked her up suddenly and carried her away to the chaise by the fire, where he settled her on his lap. "I won't ruin you."

She was almost disappointed by that statement. "Then you'd better start kissing me and make it a good one."

He laughed. "I'll do my best, my dear."

His hands clamped gently around her skull as he drew her down for another taste of his lips. Charlotte kissed him, and then darted her tongue between his lips. Winston groaned and Charlotte took advantage of his reaction to launch a passionate assault of her own. While she rained kisses over his willing lips, she teased her fingers into his hair, avoiding his injury, but holding him to her so he would not stop. Loving him the only way she could. Completely and without reservation.

Winston pushed her back suddenly, his breath loud and rough. He stared at her, and Charlotte shrugged. Then rose, hitched up her gown, and straddled his lap.

Winston leaned back in the chair and smiled up at her. "Brave Charlotte," he murmured.

"Only for you," she promised as she leaned down to kiss him again.

Winston's hands wandered, captured her gown, and tugged her closer, then moved to caress her thighs. He watched what he did, where he touched and, when he reached her bare knee, he looked up with a question in his eyes.

"Yes," she gasped, hoping she understood his intent.

His fingers slid under her gown, teasing, exploring the sensitive skin of her thighs. Charlotte looked up at the ceiling of her room as the caress of his fingers neared her sex, and made craving more of his touch. So much more. She was more aroused than she'd ever been by her own hand at night when thinking of him. With Winston touching her, she feared she would not last long before she cried out in pleasure.

His fingers brushed her curls and her sex twitched in anticipation. She sank down toward his hand, seeking more of his touch.

"Charlotte," he whispered.

"Winston," she answered, shifting restlessly toward his fingers, "I wouldn't mind if you ruined me."

"You cannot mean that." He cupped her face suddenly. "I can't. The engagement…"

Charlotte froze, stung by the reminder now of all times. For a moment she had forgotten that in a short while, another lady would have the pleasure of his kisses and caresses. Elizabeth probably had been blessed with his attentions in bed already. The woman was currently his guest.

She climbed off his lap immediately, and although Winston tried to catch her hand, Charlotte evaded his grip to put a distance between them as she struggled to control her desires. She'd been so close to what she'd always dreamed of that was hard to set those feelings aside.

"I do want you, Charlotte," he promised, stealing up behind her. "You know that. But not like this. Not now."

"I understand." She walked to her writing desk and picked up his list. It could have been now but most likely never. They were destined for other people. "You came to me for help."

"I came to you because I needed you," he whispered, leaning down to nuzzle her cheek. He slowly wound his arms around her and despite her knowing it wouldn't do any good she allowed him to embrace her one more time. "My life is a little complicated right now," he whispered.

She stiffened. So was hers just by having him here and still loving only him.

"You should never have been a complication in my life, Charlotte. I'll find a way to make that up to you soon…"

There was no way to do that. She pushed out of his arms. "Your lists. We should go over them again."

She sat down without looking at him and picked up his pages, pretending to find his handwriting fascinating. She did. He had excellent penmanship.

Winston finally sat down beside her to look over his lists again with her, but the passion they'd just shared simmered just under her skin and made being with him now so much harder.

Chapter Sixteen

Winston leaned close to whisper, "Are you sure this is necessary?"

"Absolutely," she whispered back.

Winston glanced about as they moved toward the crowded ballroom. "I admit Lord Belmont is not a man to cross, but I still dispute anyone I know would be willing to kill me over some imagined slight that happened years ago."

"People will do anything for love. Gossip says Whittle is in dire straits. *Financially.* If the lure was great enough, they might certainly consider murdering someone to solve their own problems. Someone could have put them up to it. And Lord Bain is not as he seems. That's why we're here tonight. To discover if attempting to shoot you has changed their behavior at all."

He looked at Charlotte in shock. "I had no idea you were so cynical."

"You hardly know me," she reminded him.

But he was learning more about Charlotte every day, thanks to her agreement to keep him safely ensconced in her private chambers. He'd been with her for two days now, completely undiscovered.

It was a bit odd, he found, deferring to the wisdom of a wallflower. To rely on someone so unconnected to his home or family. But he was coming to appreciate Charlotte in dozens of new ways. She was the most resourceful woman he'd ever met, and he trusted her completely. How she'd managed to feed and clothe him and house him undiscovered was a spectacular accomplishment. She had put herself and her reputation at risk to keep him safe. She had urged him to be cautious at every turn, and he intended to do just that.

His scalp itched under his turban, and he started to raise his right hand.

"Don't even think about trying to scratch your head," she warned. "Keep to your disguise.

Not even his own mother would recognize him tonight. Winston's right arm was hidden beneath his long swirling robes, near a weapon Charlotte insisted he carry strapped to his thigh. To others, it might seem he was left-handed and perhaps lacked a right arm. He wore a long, tapered blade from his left hip, too, also within easy reach. She'd insisted he wear real weapons as part of his costume, just in case they were set upon.

The most awkward moment of his life had been when she'd knelt at his feet to help strap them on. He'd gotten a clear view at the bounty of her full breasts, and his erection had been swift and long lasting.

He wished that he could have continued to make love to Charlotte last night, in her chambers. But his conscience wouldn't allow him to ruin her completely.

He was betrothed. Had given his word to marry another a long time ago. It was a situation and a promise he couldn't avoid.

He caught sight of himself in a mirror and marveled at the outward change. It was his face that was the most altered. Charlotte was a wonder with a brush, sponge and a stick of dark kohl. She'd applied a variety of dark cosmetics about his eyes and skin to make him seem older.

Weathered.

He was dressed to match his face. Tonight, he pretended to be a foreigner with a decidedly dangerous air, taking on the persona of someone Charlotte had met by chance on her travels. Winston had not recognized himself as she'd turned him toward the looking glass when she'd declared him good enough to fool any member of his family, should they happen to cross paths.

"Here we go," Charlotte whispered, throwing back the sides of her cloak to reveal the costume beneath.

The *most* changed was Charlotte.

She wore a black silken creation, something that accentuated her curves and revealed more of her pale, full breasts than he believed prudent. She'd applied cosmetics to her face, too, kohl around her eyes and rouge to redden her lips. But it wasn't just the makeup and clothes that had changed her. She moved differently tonight, as well. Confident, seductive. He found that difficult to ignore.

The wallflower he'd known for so long was gone and a mysterious seductress had taken her place. *His* secret seductress.

Men nearby noticed Charlotte as she moved through the crowd boldly ahead of him. Although he was meant to defer to her, he shifted to her side, intending to protect her from any lecherous advances that came her way. But he was almost as bad as they might be. Looking at her awoke in Winston a desire in complete opposition to the promises he kept telling himself were more important.

He tore his eyes away from Charlotte, wishing that he'd known this side of her existed before he'd set the date to wed Elizabeth.

He might not have set a date at all.

Winston suddenly imagined another life he might yet live. One where alliances and obligations could be set aside. Where he could marry to please himself.

He glanced down at Charlotte sand knew he might have courted her if he'd had leave to.

He could have been happy with her

"Remember not to react to any mention of your name," Charlotte warned him. "We don't want to draw unnecessary attention to us."

Damn it all, why should he hide the desire he felt for Charlotte? Countless other lords flaunted their love affairs openly. He slipped his hand around hers and drew her closer to his side. But right then he spotted a lady he knew well, a woman with sharp eyes and sharper tongue, and steered Charlotte away immediately.

No one could know that Charlotte was his almost-lover.

And yet that felt wrong. Why shouldn't he be with Charlotte? There was nothing about Charlotte that made her unworthy of his attentions. Nothing at all. She was lovely and soft and bold and delectable to kiss.

Charlotte, however, had other ideas concerning keeping a low profile here, and she pulled him along boldly where she wanted to go, issuing a stream of low-voiced orders as to how he should behave. She was more adept than him at identifying members of the *ton* beneath their costumes, too, and they finally found someone they were looking for in the crowd after almost ten minutes of skirting the party.

"Remember, you must not look at them directly, or address them by name. Your voice is too well known to be mistaken above a whisper."

He squared his shoulders and lowered his eyes to Charlotte. "All right. Here we go."

Charlotte laughed suddenly and fluttered her fan before her face. "Lean down to make it seem you are whispering in my ear."

He did. "What am I meant to say?"

"Anything you like. Sweet nothings or sour gripes," she replied, and then lay a hand on his chest. "But no matter what you say tonight, I'm going to act as if you are flirting with me," she said in a whisper as she stretched up.

He *wanted* to flirt with her. Her fingers brushed his clean-shaven cheek and he shivered. A whisper of a thrill rushed through Winston's entire body at the brief flirtatious contact.

He nearly groaned aloud as her finger brushed his lower lip. "What was that for?"

"Part of our performance," she whispered, lowering her eyes shyly. "Now start leading me toward that dark corner over there. Slowly."

They passed behind the back their quarry, Lord Wittle stood amongst mutual friends, and although Winston's instinct would have been to say hello, he could not. Charlotte resolutely drew him on a little farther and then stopped. "For tonight, try to remember you're on the outside looking in, or have no interest at all. Look to me instead."

Since they had reached the shadows, he was uncertain of how to stand. "What should I do?"

"Now you'd do what comes naturally for a rogue."

He gaped at her.

"I promise I won't slap your handsome face tonight, either, so you may put your arm around me. At least *pretend* an interest in seducing me."

Winston might have no experience in seduction, but of course he'd seen it done around him many times. And he didn't have to pretend the pretty woman standing loosely in his arms wasn't on his mind constantly since they'd nearly made love.

So, with the barest of hesitation, Winston crowded Charlotte and moved his free hand to rest upon her waist, then let it drift lower. For her part, Charlotte seemed pleased by his bold move and made appropriate and encouraging sounds. She pressed her body against his, her hands wedged between them on his chest, looking up at him with a coy smile as her fingers slid lower. She cocked her head a little to one side. "That's interesting."

"What is?" he asked quickly, hoping she hadn't noticed he was getting another erection, thanks to her body rubbing innocently against him.

"Someone in the group behind us just mentioned you by name. He, and I'm not sure who, can't believe you're not here."

"At least I am missed," Winston murmured, leaning closer to her. He let his fingers wander around to rest at the small of Charlotte's back and drift lower. She was so soft in all the right places…and many more he wanted to explore if he had more time and opportunity.

Her fingers suddenly rose to caress his cheek again, and then her lips, closed, pressed hard to his. He met her bright gaze, so shockingly close.

Winston pulled her in, instinctively pressing against her body and revealing his arousal. The lips under his parted, and the chaste kiss turned passionate in an instant as their tongues tangled.

But her head soon tilted away from him. "Did you hear that?" she asked of him. "Are they making plans to leave already?"

"Your hearing is obviously better than mine," he admitted. He'd heard nothing, been aware of no one else in the room but Charlotte and her luscious lips. He wanted more contact with those, and he was too distracted by her body pressed against him right now to care about anything else.

Suddenly, Charlotte pulled away completely and fluttered her fan before her face coyishly while laughing. "I'm fairly sure most have decided to head for their club including Lord Wittle, which means…Lord Wittle isn't looking for you tonight."

"I could have told you that." He turned finally and saw an empty space where his acquaintances had so recently stood. "What do we do now?"

"We continue here for as long as it takes for Lord Bain to show his face." Charlotte captured his fingers, and she laughed up at him. "Oh, you are wicked! Come with me, darling."

Darling. He could become used to hearing that endearment on his lover's lips.

She tugged and Winston tripped along after her, rather startled by how he truly wished he was about to be seduced. Though for the next half hour, they continued their little ruse, pausing near friends of his, listening to them complain and criticize society, all the while acting as lovers. He found that astonishingly easy to do with Charlotte.

Charlotte, too, had no hesitation in bestowing her affections upon him as part of a ruse. Through all their flirting, Winston suffered prolonged bouts of sustained arousal, thankfully hidden by his long robes.

Finally, Lord Bain appeared. Drunk and disorderly as he wove unsteadily from front door to library only to fall into a well-padded chair.

They positioned themselves on a single chair behind his back, Charlotte atop his lap.

He put his hand on her calf, and slowly inched it higher. Her gown, caught under his fingers, rose too.

She wore black silk slippers and white silk stockings. When he reached her knee, he found red garters. Winston pulled her lips to his and gave her a proper kiss. A kiss that meant to claim her for himself. He wanted Charlotte and only Charlotte perched on his lap, her arms snaked around his shoulders, her tongue dancing with his.

He would do anything to make Charlotte his. To make her moan and cry out again. He slipped his hand higher, sliding between her warm thighs.

But he could not reach higher. Charlotte clamped her legs together, trapping him inches from her sex.

He met her gaze and saw desire burning in hers. "No," she whispered. "Not with an audience around us."

He nodded reluctantly, chastened for his presumption that he could do anything with her, anywhere. Charlotte relaxed and put her head on his shoulder, cuddling up to him.

After loitering near Lord Bain for a good long time and

hearing nothing of value because all he did was call for more wine, Winston had heard enough. He pulled Charlotte away and into another shadowed alcove down the hall.

He was done playing investigator.

He wanted to be done with everything that might keep him apart from Charlotte, too.

He kept up the ruse of being her lover and, once they were more or less alone, pressed Charlotte against the nearest wall. He caged her with his arms and looked down into her startled eyes. "That's everyone you had doubts about."

"Yes. I'm afraid so." She put her head on his chest and heaved a frustrated sigh.

Winston cupped the back of her head, teasing his fingers into her hair. "Isn't it a good thing my acquaintances are not murderous fiends?"

"It's *not* good, because if it's not them, then I am back to my original fear that your brother wishes you ill." She looked up at him with tears in her eyes. "If he harms you again, I will be most unhappy. We need to find him. Do you have any idea of which engagement Peter planned to attend tonight?"

"Nowhere I can take you, I'm afraid." Winston caressed her cheek, moved by her tears over his safety. "My brother has made it his life's mission to avoid society events such as this. He'll be gambling or whoring with his friends again tonight."

Charlotte caught her bottom lip between her teeth for a moment. "I need to tell you something I heard…but you may not like how I came upon the information."

"My dear woman, given my current situation, I'm entirely at your mercy. I'm not about to quibble about where you get your information. Women and men gossip. That's a fact."

"It's not gossip. Not yet." She chewed her lip. "A few days ago, I had a foolish notion to renew my acquaintance with Lord Bain. What I heard—"

He frowned that she'd sought out a drunkard. "Where?"

Her gaze lowered, and her fingers fiddled with his costume. "Your brother was with Lord Bain in a carriage, in a dispute over an unpaid debt. Suffice to say, Peter owes money beyond what I believe he can repay."

Winston drew back. "Peter has not told me about any large debts."

"I'm not surprised. Lord Bain hides a vastly unpleasant nature from society. I wouldn't want anyone I love even a little to be in his debt."

Winston laughed. "The man's nothing but a drunkard. You saw him tonight. He can barely put two words together."

"Not so drunk he forgets a debt. He sounds dangerous, and I fear Peter might be pushed to do whatever it takes to repay that debt. If you were to die, he'd have your fortune at his fingertips."

"If my brother is in trouble, he's only to talk to me. We would work it out together. We always have before."

"I do hope that he does come to you," she nodded. "Unfortunately, if you remain in hiding, that will not be possible."

"I'll have to find him," he whispered, fingers flexing upon Charlotte's nicely rounded hip. He noticed they were being watched, and he twirled Charlotte from the alcove and along a dark hall.

He put an arm around her back. "We should take a turn about the party again."

"No, Winston," Charlotte disagreed. "We've been here long enough now. If we were to remain, and in character, you'd likely be expected to drag me off to a secluded corner or closet somewhere to finish seducing me."

He wanted to do that but in a soft bed and for hours not mere minutes. Winston respected her too much to take advantage of her trust. This was not the place for them to finish making love.

"I suppose we'd best slip away and secure a carriage to take us home." Winston took up her hand and wrapped it around his sleeve. Charlotte uttered a discontent sigh but cuddled up to him as they made their way toward the front door.

Winston smiled. He'd finally found a woman who attracted him. And she was attracted to him as well. She couldn't become his mistress. A fallen woman in society would be scorned.

That only left him two choices: giving her up…or breaking his engagement.

All he could have with Charlotte were stolen moments, unless he was prepared to fight for his freedom from his arranged marriage.

He wanted to be with Charlotte, and more than just a lover or a mistress. He dug his finger under his collar. He wanted Charlotte as his wife. "I'll be glad when this is over."

They made their way toward the front doors, weaving around the guests and continuing their ruse of an amorous couple.

He hurried down the front steps before they were seen, confused by the conflict within him.

A footman approached. "Your name?"

"Mrs. Fielding," Charlotte murmured in a high, breathless voice.

The man glanced at Winston.

Charlotte laughed. "I'll send it back for my husband directly."

The butler nodded curtly and rushed off down the street.

"Why are you talking like that and taking Mrs. Fielding's carriage?"

"Because she's known to leave every masquerade ball with a man not her husband," she confided. "And he's too busy pursuing some other man's wife."

"That explains why the footman wasn't surprised by my presence," he mused. "No doubt he's seen countless other occasions were a bored wife left a masquerade with a stranger." He leaned down toward Charlotte. "But how do *you* know what goes on?"

"Wallflowers see and hear everything. And we share to protect each other."

He laughed softly. "I'll have to become a wallflower, then."

"Why would you need to? It's ladies who are usually at a disadvantage. Rogues already know how to break the rules and get away with it. We women learn seduction techniques deployed by scoundrels by observation.

"This rogue hasn't yet," he promised. "I could use a few pointers understanding a certain lady, though."

Actually, two. Elizabeth and Charlotte were both on his mind right now.

A carriage arrived, and Charlotte scrambled inside quickly. He ached to remove his costume and scratch his head once inside. But he knew he couldn't yet. Not until he was safely tucked away in Charlotte's bedchamber again.

They'd learned nothing useful tonight. "Now what?"

"Now we take you where you need to be."

Home. Charlotte's bedchamber, to continue what they'd started? He certainly could be persuaded if that was what she truly wanted. Yet the carriage, however, took them in the wrong direction. "We're going the wrong way."

"No, we're not. We're going where I want you to be."

"Mrs. Fielding lives on Grosvenor Square."

"Near the Duke of Exeter's London town house. Yes, I know. Exeter will know what to do."

Winston gaped. "You're giving up on me?"

"No. I don't want to." She looked down at her hands. "But I'm not what you need anymore."

"That's not true." His feet had taken him exactly where his heart longed to be. With Charlotte, who seemed to care about him above everything else. "What more can I need than you, Charlotte?"

She looked up at him, and her smile was forced. "You need guards, allies, and you already have them in your real friends. You need to survive." She nodded. "The Duke of Exeter is still in London, and you are his heir's best friend. He'll know what to do and how best to protect you."

"I would have thought the Marquess of Wharton would have been a more appropriate savior," Winston murmured. "He'll be crushed you didn't suggest him first."

Charlotte huffed. "He was my first thought, but that may have been obvious to others, too. Whoever attacked you at Bradshaw's knows your favorite haunts."

"I wouldn't say Bradshaw's was a favorite, exactly."

She pulled a face. "You ought not go to somewhere you visit often until someone is apprehended and charged."

"Charged?"

She studied him with her head tipped to one side. "Well, how did you think this would end if Peter is involved? A slap on the wrist and to threaten to send him to his room?"

He shook his head slowly. "I suppose I hadn't thought that far ahead."

"You're too important to lose," she whispered.

Winston blushed. "You're important to me, as well."

"Then please do as I ask."

"All right. I'll speak to Exeter if he is available tonight," he agreed. "But only if you stay with me."

She stared at him a long time and then nodded. "All right. I'll come inside with you."

"Good." He opened his arm to her, and Charlotte settled against his chest. He kissed the top of her head, and when she raised her face, he rained kisses on her soft lips. He would have continued if they'd had more time together, but Exeter's home wasn't far at all. Seduction would have to wait for tomorrow.

Chapter Seventeen

It took quite a bit of fast talking to earn an audience with the Duke of Exeter. Exeter, thankfully, was at home with the duchess, but the clever disguise Winston wore was almost *too* convincing for the servant who answered the door. The man doubted his claim to be an earl, much less the Earl of Hurlston, even when he removed the yards of fabric wrapped around his head.

Charlotte had more luck when she interrupted to ask to speak with the duchess instead. She recognized Charlotte on sight, at least. "Miss Waters, what are you doing here at this late hour? Is something wrong?"

"I'm sorry to have disturbed you, but I have a great favor to ask." She gestured toward Winston. "This is the Earl of Hurlston, and he needs to speak with your husband as a matter of some urgency."

Her grace gaped at Winston.

He bowed. "A pleasure to see you again."

The duchess turned her attention back to Charlotte, a frown forming on her face. "The duke is abed and sound asleep."

"It is imperative he speak with Exeter as soon as possible. Please help him. He's in grave danger. We don't know what else to do."

"All right. I'll wake him." The duchess rushed up the main staircase while the butler directed them to wait in a nearby chamber until the duke was ready for them.

He arrived in his nightclothes and robe a few moments later.

"Exeter. Sorry to disturb," Winston said, stepping forward to offer his hand.

"Is that really you under there, Hurlston? Quite the disguise, I must say."

"I attended a masque before coming here," Winston told him.

The duke turned his gaze on Charlotte momentarily, blinked without recognition, but it was the duchess who spoke. "And this is Miss Charlotte Waters."

The duke's expression grew severe. "I was given the impression the matter was serious, not romantic in nature."

"The earl's life is in danger," Charlotte told him, fighting a blush because to her, the evening with Winston had been very romantic indeed. "Are you aware that the earl and his mother were almost run down in Hyde Park by horsemen?"

"Thaddeus did mention something about dangerous riders in the park."

"We now believe the riders were specifically looking for him."

The duke waved a hand. "A single incident is hardly—"

"I was set upon by three thugs in Green Park a few days later," Winston added.

"I heard nothing of that," Exeter said, looking between them with narrowed eyes.

"I kept to my home until the bruising faded." Winston touched his ribs. "I still have some pain."

Charlotte looked at Winston sharply. "You never told me that."

"I didn't want to worry you."

Charlotte rolled her eyes. "I'll never stopped worrying about you now, Winston."

"Ah, well. Now twice is worrying indeed," the duke agreed.

"There's more," Charlotte added. "Someone shot at him. Pursued him into the night."

The duke's gaze fell on Winston, eyes wide. "You should have come to me immediately," he chided. "You're my heir's friend, and he'll be livid that anyone dares threaten you. I am now, too. The nerve!"

"I wanted to get to the bottom of the matter myself," Winston explained. "I still find it hard to believe someone wants me dead. Even now, I cannot explain why they might."

"It happens sooner or later." The duke shook his head. "But I think it best if we discuss how we deal with this situation in my study. Come, Hurlston."

Winston held his hand out toward her. "Charlotte."

Charlotte started forward but the duchess shook her head.

"She'll stay with me," her grace murmured, putting her arm around Charlotte's shoulders and halting her departure. "I'm sure Miss Waters could use a cup of tea. I certainly could."

Charlotte nodded reluctantly. She did not know the duchess well, but she was too important a woman to refuse. All that mattered was that Winston had the help he desperately needed. "We can talk again after his grace has come up with a plan to protect you."

Winston did not look happy to leave her behind. "All right. I'll return for you soon."

She nodded, and he rushed away to consult with Exeter.

Charlotte dutifully followed the duchess into a small parlor. "I am sorry to have interrupted your sleep, your grace, but I'm sure your husband is the only one who can help him now."

The duchess turned. "It was you who persuaded Hurlston to come here finally?"

"Yes, I was afraid he would be discovered." She gathered up her courage before she continued with the unvarnished truth. "When he came to my home a few nights ago, bleeding from a wound to his head, he said men were waiting for him outside his club. They attempted to capture him and gave chase when he ran. He feared there might be others waiting outside his home, or his friends' homes. It was no random encounter. I don't believe the earlier ones were, either. I would have told the duke everything I know and suspect if you'd let me go with them."

The duchess smiled slowly and gestured Charlotte into a chair. "Exeter likes to pretend he knows what he's doing at all times. He also prefers to protect me from hearing unpleasantness. Hurlston is surely the same. It's the way of the aristocracy. So, they'll make their decisions without us, and we can point out their oversights later," the duchess assured her with a wink. "But for now, you and I shall have tea and talk some more. You have not mentioned an attack occurring tonight?"

"No. We were attempting to uncover who might be a threat to him. The two most likely lords with a questionable reputation were watched and discarded as suspects."

The duchess pulled a tasseled footstool close and propped up her feet. "Tell me how you've come to be Lord Hurlston's confidant?"

"He came to me for help, and I couldn't turn him away."

"But that was days ago, yes?"

"Yes," she admitted, gulping at how that might damage her reputation in the duchess' eyes. "He said he felt no one would look for him in a place he should not be. The first night…he was wounded and understandably upset. There's a wound on his head, the graze of pistol shot that had bled copiously all over him. We took care of him; my butler cleaned the wound and found him fresh clothes to put on from our servants, so he could go home. But he asked to stay, believing his attackers could be lurking about outside his home in wait for him. And if he went home wounded, he would have upset his mother, whose nerves were already upset by their near miss in Hyde Park."

"Not to mention his betrothed would have been worried for

him as well," the duchess added. "They must be out of their minds wondering what's become of him."

"I took care of that when I delivered a note to his home, so his mother thinks he is from Town for a few days with friends."

The duchess leaned forward. "How many days has he stayed with you?"

Charlotte gulped and didn't dare speak. The answer would not please her grace.

The duchess shook her head. "I thought better of him. Does he care nothing for your reputation?"

"He does. He's been a perfect gentleman and only asked to remain hidden. No one knows he's been with me. Not even my parents or the servants. All we have done is talk and try to decide who means him harm."

The duchess raised a brow and then looked Charlotte up and down. "You went out with him tonight, dressed like that, without a chaperone?"

Charlotte drew her clock a little closer about her chest. "It's the only costume I had. I've never had occasion to wear it before."

"If you had, you might have been married already." The duchess suddenly smiled. "It's little wonder he could not take his eyes from you just now."

Charlotte glanced down at her fingers. "We disagreed about coming here, but it's the right thing to do. The lie he told, about being away with friends, could not hold much longer."

"What friends were they?"

"Scarsdale took friends to a hunting box for a few days. Winston was originally invited, and he made it seem he'd changed his mind and followed them."

"They returned to Town tonight, I believe. Earlier than planned. They called here earlier to drink the duke's wine with Mr. Berringer. But Hurlston really should have come to the duke long before tonight."

"He's not wanted to believe he isn't universally loved, and the thought of betrayal has been hard for him to accept." She winced at that. "I fear it is his brother behind all this. There's no other suspect with a strong enough motive."

"The duke won't let anything happen to him now," the duchess promised. "But what am I going to do about *you*?"

"What about me?"

She smiled sadly. "He's to be married, Charlotte."

"I know. I swear, nothing has happened between us."

"Are you sure?"

Charlotte fidgeted. "He would never."

The older woman leaned forward and gripped her hands to squeeze them. "But you wanted him to?"

Charlotte shouldn't answer that question either. It would make her hopeless love for Hurlston all too obvious. He'd not give up his arranged marriage for her. He'd too much to lose.

The duchess gave her hands one last squeeze and stood. "I'll find a gown for you to change into before you go home."

"Home?"

"You did the right thing in sheltering him, Charlotte. You kept Hurlston safe, and for that he will always be grateful. But you must think of yourself now. We women must protect ourselves from scurrilous gossip. I can help you with that. If anyone asks, you were here with me all night. Not being swept off your feet by him."

"Thank you." Charlotte blushed, remembering the evening just past. Having Winston so close, kissing him so often, had been the stuff of dreams. But the dream was over. The reality was, she was hopelessly unnecessary to his life.

"I'll be back shortly." The duchess slipped out of the room, leaving Charlotte alone with her troubled thoughts.

She had to leave Winston tonight.

But it was hard to think of any day without Winston featuring in it. Harder now that they'd spent so much time alone together. How was she to marry another man and stay in England, watching and worrying over Winston from a distance? It would be unbearable if ever he was hurt again.

"Penny for them?"

She looked up to find the man of her dreams standing at the doorway. He'd removed his turban when they'd arrived and washed his face too since they'd parted ways. She smiled quickly. "I was thinking of your situation and hoping all would be well."

He shut the door behind him and started toward her. "Exeter has offered his personal protection and will send for Bow Street Runners at dawn."

Charlotte met him half-way. "That's a few hours away still."

Winston nodded. "He's having guest rooms prepared in the meantime. You look as tired as I feel."

"I'm not tired," she promised. Being with Winston made her feel alive and vital.

He smiled and led her to a settee on the far from the door. "Charlotte, I want you to know something important. I will be forever grateful to you for your aid. You have gone above and beyond the bounds of any friendship I have ever had. I owe you my life and there is no way I can ever hope to repay you."

That sounded like a goodbye.

"I expected no reward," she promised as she lowered her gaze to her hands. "I was happy to help, happy that you turned to me in your time of need."

Winston slipped a finger under her chin, making her look at him again. "I should not have done so. I've put your reputation at risk. Diverted your attention from your own life. Imposed upon you. That was selfish of me."

She sighed. "I knew the risks."

"You should have sent me away."

"I couldn't."

"Why?"

She winced. Did he still not understand how she felt about him? He might never know unless she told him of her feelings. She would leave this place soon and might never have opportunity to speak with him privately again. This was her one chance to be utterly honest with him, even if it would change nothing.

"You've no idea, do you? You see…you've been my ideal beau since the moment we met. You're smart and handsome and so funny. Kind to wallflowers and your mother." She lowered her eyes again. "You're everything I ever wanted in a husband. I love you, but you will marry Elizabeth, and that's the end of it."

The sound of his shock was very loud. "Oh, Charlotte."

"Don't pity me. You have a beautiful bride to look forward to marrying when you're safe again. I never stood a chance."

"Oh, I'm such a fool…" Winston began, sitting back in his chair.

She could feel his eyes upon her, and Charlotte met his gaze, finally filled with understanding. She smiled quickly to hide her embarrassment. "So you see, I can regret nothing of the time we've spent together. It was stolen and will always be cherished."

"Charlotte? Why didn't you say something sooner?"

She shrugged. "You were betrothed, of course. It never mattered what I wanted."

"Of course it matters," he promised.

Charlotte jumped to her feet as a door opened and a footman appeared. "Forgive the interruption, my lord. His grace wishes to speak with you again."

"Tell him I'll be with him in a moment."

"He said immediately, my lord," the footman said with a wince of apology.

"You had better go," she whispered to him. "Be careful, my lord, and take good care of yourself."

Winston glowered at her. "We're not done discussing this. I think—"

But they were done. In a few hours perhaps, he'd be safely back at home with his mother and future bride, and Charlotte would be with her parents, preparing to leave on another adventure. There wasn't enough time to find a husband anymore. There'd never be enough to love someone beside Winston. "You shouldn't keep the duke waiting," she interrupted

"Charlotte," he growled, sounding determined to continue their conversation. "We need to discuss this."

"Please go," she whispered, unable to meet his eyes now. "You have a difficult time ahead of you."

"We'll talk again after you've rested." Winston turned to the footman. "I was told a room would be readied for Miss Waters?"

"Yes, my lord," the servant promised. "Someone will be along for her at any moment, I expect."

"Good." Hurlston pressed something into the servant's palm. "Make sure they take good care of her," he warned. "She deserves every consideration."

Charlotte chest tightened in gratitude, but no matter how he flattered her, she knew the truth. She was a complication that would only distract him from the duty he felt. And he was on guard now and had protection. He'd be fine without her help.

"You must go," she whispered.

"I'll see you soon," he promised before he strode away.

Charlotte kept her chin up until he was gone and could no longer be heard. And then the tears came. She sat and buried her face in her hands until she had herself under control and then stood again. After checking the hall for servants, Charlotte slipped from the room and escaped Grafton House entirely. It wasn't too far from here to walk home alone if she was quick about it.

Chapter Eighteen

Finding Peter took no time at all really. Winston knew the character and habits of his brother very well. So he took great delight in discovering his brother, seated at a table in one of the worst gaming hell in London. Exactly where he thought he'd be found.

Dawn was approaching outside but the patrons inside could have no idea. The lighting in the gaming hells were kept low on purpose to ensure gambling continued well into the new day. They didn't want patrons to leave.

The darkness also concealed Winston's identity in the shadows. Peter, though, sat in a pool of candlelight surrounded by unsavory fellows. It was exactly the sort of place a desperate man might hire men for murder, too.

At his side was Thaddeus Berringer, and behind them, three of the Duke of Exeter's most loyal servants. Burly men ready to get their hands dirty if need be.

All Winston needed them to do right this moment was to drag his brother into the waiting carriage so Winston could begin to question him.

"Now?" he murmured to Berringer.

"In and out as quick as we can," Berringer confirmed, leaving his side to circle round behind Peter's back in case he tried to run for another exit.

Peter, intent on his cards, never looked up long enough to realize he was being surrounded.

Winston felt a stab of regret for his brother. It should never have come to this. He shook his head and moved toward his brother just as the game ended and his brother stood up.

Winston immediately grabbed Peter's arm and hauled him around to face him.

Peter appeared utterly shocked to see him. "Win," he gulped. "What are you doing here?"

"I could say the same for you," Winston retorted.

"I know I promised to stay out of the hells, but it was just this once!"

"Don't play the innocent with me. I could throttle you where you stand," Winston replied, shaking his head. "As it is, I'll settle for hauling your worthless hide out to the street."

Peter gaped. "But *I won.*"

"No, I won, and now you come with me and face the consequences of your recent behavior." He got a tighter grip on Peter's arm just as one of Exeter's men grabbed the other.

Peter struggled between them. "What are you doing? Unhand me."

"Outside," he barked, and together they dragged a struggling Peter toward the front door, drawing the notice of almost every patron present. The manager of the hell followed but a handful of coins from Berringer settled his feathers to let them leave without interference.

"Not as quiet as I would have preferred," Berringer lamented, as Winston and the duke's man carried their captive out the door to the street.

"Cannot be helped now." He threw Peter at the carriage door, and his brother bounced off it. But with Exeter's fellows near, he had no hope of escape. They checked him for weapons, murmuring he was safe for Winston to approach again.

"Devil take it! Get your hands off me! Don't you know who I am?"

"They know," Winston promised. "Believe me, we all know."

"What's gotten into you tonight? Has Mother been in your ear again? You dragged me away from the only decent winning streak I've ever had in my life, only to rough me up like some common criminal. I need that money!"

Winston caught hold of his brother by the cravat and held him still. He didn't know if his brother was behind the attacks against him but he'd act as if he did and see what happened next. "What the devil has gotten into you, Peter?

Peter blinked. "I know you're disappointed to find me gambling again but I have a good reason."

"I can't wait to hear it!"

"Well, I. It's just a bit of fun at first."

That did not sound good. Especially not when he'd just received his inheritance. "How much had you lost before you started winning?"

Peter gulped and then shut his eyes.

Winston rocked back on his heels. Had he gambled away all his money? "All of it?"

Peter tried to leave, but the duke's men were quicker. They shoved Peter back toward the carriage door.

"You could have come to me," Winston complained.

"I don't need you. I've got a fortune coming to me soon."

"From where?"

Peter's gaze rose to his and the calm coldness of his stare chilled Winston right through. "Where do you think?"

He took a step back from his brother, appalled to have Charlotte's fears confirmed. His brother was behind the attacks. "How could you?"

Peter scowled. "Everybody does it, you know. All my friends have tried it once or twice."

The very idea that every second son had tried to murder an older brother ahead of them in the succession was insane.

Winston clenched his hands by his side. "By my estimation,

you've done it three times here in London, but was it always this way."

Peter smirked. "How could I resist!"

"Any decent man would have," Berringer murmured with a shake of his head.

Winston turned away in disgust. His brother had no love for him at all. "Load this filth into the carriage."

Behind him, Peter struggled against his captors but was eventually subdued and convinced to get in of his own accord.

Berringer came up to stand at his side. "I feared you'd strike him."

"I came close, but I've never lifted my hand to my brother once in my life, and I'm not about to sink to his level."

"We should go."

"I'll ride on the back, if you don't mind." Winston shook his head. "I can't stand to look at him right now"

"I completely understand," Berringer murmured. "I'll keep an eye on him for you."

"Thank you." Winston displaced a groom at the back and, after a moment, Berringer climbed inside the carriage with Peter. Winston didn't envy him the view or the conversation he might have to endure.

The wind was cool in his face as they made their way along London's streets. The arrival of dawn revealing a peaceful London.

His temper settled slowly by degrees as he pondered what he had ever done to deserve such a betrayal. Was it all about the money? Hadn't he always covered his brother's losses, treated him well and turned a blind eye to his short-lived affairs with loose women? He disapproved, yes, but he'd never demanded Peter change his ways or, God forbid, marry one of his discarded and disgruntled lovers.

"I need to know why," he said out loud.

"Beg your pardon, my lord?" the groom beside him asked.

"Nothing." He looked around. The interrogation could wait a little longer. "Not a bad view from up here, is it."

"'Tis grand, my lord, except on a freezing-cold and rainy day. We see and hear all sorts of things from this vantage."

From within the carriage came a loud commotion, and Peter started yelling out Winston's name.

Winston glanced round the side into the carriage and through the window, to see Peter was attempting to climb out while the carriage was moving.

"Stop the carriage!" he yelled, clambering down quickly to get to the door to prevent Peter's exit. "And hold him still."

"Release me!" Peter yelled back.

"I should have tied you up, brat," Winston yelled back.

"Don't you dare! I've done nothing wrong," Peter claimed.

The duke's men had forced Peter back into his seat and because they were now entering the more affluent part of Town, Winston entered the carriage and sat opposite his brother. He had the carriage continue and met his brother's furious gaze. "Too late to retract your admission of guilt now, brother."

His brother tried to sit forward, leaning toward Winston, but he was held back. "I thought you would disapprove of Celeste and I," Peter hissed through clenched teeth.

He raised a brow. "Celeste?

"Lady Birch," Berringer whispered to him.

Winston blinked. "What about Lady Birch?"

"Well, yes. She's been inviting me over now and again."

"I cannot imagine what Lady Birch might ever want to talk to you about."

"Not so much talking as doing." His brother smirked suddenly. "There's good coin in it."

Winston choked while beside him, Berringer covered his mouth to muffle a sudden snort of laughter.

Peter shrugged. "I could give you a list of her intimate

requests, but I'm too much of a gentleman. Suffice to say, I earn every penny."

Winston saw nothing to laugh about in his brother's disgraceful insinuation that he was having sex for money. He was besmirching the reputation of one of the most respected and upstanding older women in society. "You slept with Lady Birch?"

"Sleeping is not what I'm there for," Peter boasted.

Berringer's laughter boomed through the carriage suddenly. He stamped his feet and pounded the side of the carriage with his fist. "I'm sorry. I'm sorry!" he managed, but clearly he was vastly diverted by this development.

"She was a close friend of Mother's once," Winston complained.

"Yes, I know. She still pats my head." Peter shrugged. "I'm not embarrassed, and I don't see how it's any of your business anyway. How I make my way in the world is none of your business. But I'm out the door the moment the fun is over, and I know to be discreet if I want to be invited back."

Berringer had by now controlled his mirth and openly grinning at Peter. "And you are?"

"Six and twenty times now," Peter admitted. "The woman has a voracious appetite for that sort of thing. Saw her earlier tonight, as a matter of fact. Seeing her again tomorrow."

Scandalous liaisons aside, Winston had a more pressing need for his brother. "The only place you're going is a very small cell."

Berringer placed a restraining hand on Winston. "You missed a bit of our conversation. Hear him out before this goes any further."

"He can explain in front of the magistrate," Winston replied, folding his arms over his chest.

"That might be embarrassing for the family, and for Lady

Birch, too. He's been her lap dog for some time, and for some other notable wives in society."

"That doesn't absolve him of his other crimes. He's not spent his every waking moment in some sordid tryst. He could have paid someone."

Berringer squinted at Peter. "Well, where have you spent your last days?"

"Sleeping at a friend's so I can avoid the guests at home." Peter shrugged. "My friends don't ask questions. They're good that way. Unlike some I could name, who think sex before marriage is wrong," Peter complained, glaring in such a way that Winston realized his brother knew of his innocence with women.

Winston sat forward and growled, "Would you stop talking about amorous activities."

"I could, but then there'd be nothing left to talk about. What's got you in a high alt all of a sudden? I haven't fiddled with a maid in your employ in years."

"This has nothing to do with your amorous pursuits."

"It's to do with you trying to commit murder," Berringer added, eyes fixed hard on Peter.

Peter blinked. "What the devil? Who would I want to kill?"

"Me." Winston shook his head and sat back, exhausted with the conversation. "Whatever did I do to make you hate me so?"

Peter blinked and stared with wide eyes. "I don't hate you. You're my brother! I love you."

"Fine way to show it by shooting at me, too," Winston said, lowing his face. He couldn't look his brother.

Peter started up again. "What is he talking about…someone shot at him, too?"

"Riders tried to run him and your mother down in Hyde Park," Berringer leaned forward. "He was set upon by thugs in Green Park. Shot at leaving Bradshaw's two nights ago."

"No!" Peter gasped, eyes going round. "Who shot at you?"

"You, I assume," Winston replied wearily.

"Two nights ago, I was tied up by Celeste's silk stockings while she ravished me all night."

Berringer choked on another laugh he quickly tried to smother when Winston scowled at him.

"Then it was by men you hired to do the job."

"Are you mad? You *are* mad," Peter decided, looking around the carriage at the otherwise stony faces of his guards. "What would I want to shoot you for?"

"I'd like to know that too, but I suppose there is a title and a healthy estate to inherit when I'm dead and buried. You said you were coming into some money."

"I don't want your title! I don't want to be Hurlston. That's *your* duty. Yours alone. You can keep all that constricting family tradition and duty for yourself, thank you very much."

Winston exchanged a long look with Berringer.

Peter was truly not this good an actor. He studied his brother again. Peter had been startled to see him at the gambling den, but not afraid to have been caught by him. At least not until he'd tried to take him away from the table, where he'd claimed to be on a winning streak at last.

Perhaps it had not been Peter, after all. However, it would be wise not to release him yet and jump to any hasty decision he might later regret. He tapped the roof of the carriage. "Grafton House."

"Not Bow Street?"

"I think my brother can answer a few more questions before I turn him over to the authorities for attempted murder."

"For the last time, it wasn't me!" Peter squinted at Winston, looking him up and down. "Were you badly injured?"

"You saw the beating those men doled out," Winston reminded him.

His brother grew pale. "You said you were shot at…?"

"Yes," he said curtly.

Peter's eyes flickered over him from head to toe again. "How'd I never hear of any of this?"

"Assuming you didn't arrange it?" He stared at his brother. "I had help evading pursuit."

Peter slumped. "Mama must be out of her mind over this. Her favorite son being shot at isn't something she'd take well."

"You are her favorite, too."

Peter shook his head. "She loves you more. Always has. Always will. Better you than me. It's way more fun being a sinner rather than a saint."

"What makes you think I'm a saint?"

"Oh, come on. Waiting so long to marry Elizabeth all these years. Honoring Father's ridiculous ambition to expand the family estate by a match with that shrill-tongued harpy. You can't tell me she was worth the wait. There were plenty of other women who would have lay down with the skirts at their waists before marriage to secure an alliance with you. Even the wallflowers pant after him," he told Berringer, utterly ignoring Winston. "There's one in particular…"

Winston grasped his brother by the cravat and shook him. "Choose your next words with care, brother."

Berringer quickly pried them apart. "Steady."

Peter smirked. "What's the matter, Win. Having doubts about tying the knot. That's my brother, indeed though. *Steady*, dependable, and above the inexcusable sin of enjoying a tumble. The perfect son and heir. Marrying a woman who cares nothing for him, but plenty for the title. And the money, let's not forget."

"You don't know the first thing about me or Elizabeth."

"I know enough to know I don't want what you have. The only good thing I can see about your upcoming marriage is that soon you'll have a son to take my place in the succession. A pity you must bed Elizabeth to get the job done, though. Again, better you than me. My God, she's a cold fish." Peter leaned forward again. "Why would I want you dead when, if you were, *I'd* have to marry Elizabeth instead?"

"You can't marry your brother's widow," Berringer murmured. "That's disgusting."

"Oh, I agree, especially in her case. Normally," Peter replied and then he tilted his head to the side, studying Winston. "Have you forgotten?"

"I forget nothing."

Peter laughed. "You have. You ought to read the marriage contract our father made with Elizabeth's parents again. If you die, the obligation falls to me to marry her."

Winston frowned. "That's…"

"Came as an unpleasant shock to me," Peter explained. "The solicitors started pointing out a few provisions in Father's will pertaining to your death, and I got very curious why they kept going on about it."

"What provision?"

"The solicitor was quite clear: Elizabeth's son must inherit Hurlston, or the Mayflower estate goes to the crown."

Winston froze. It had been some time since he'd read the marriage contract from end to end and his memory of all the many clauses and conditions was hazy now at best. But surely it was not as Peter claimed. Elizabeth should only marry him, surely. "I'll need to look into that again."

"Please do, because I certainly don't want her," Peter promised.

Neither did Winston.

He drew in a sharp breath and knew he could not go ahead with the marriage.

Not anymore.

But to break an engagement after the banns had been called would be cruel to Elizabeth after all this time she'd been promised to him. It would call into question her reputation and make it difficult for her to make a good marriage. Society would believe her at fault, and Mother would be embarrassed beyond belief by the ensuing scandal.

There'd be a heavy price to pay to win his freedom. Her father would surely demand compensation and lots of it to smooth things over, if there could ever be enough for that.

All of that, though, depended on him not being killed.

And then he could go home.

But to Charlotte first. She was at Grafton House even now, waiting for him, and it was even more important now that they speak again so he tell her what he intended.

When Grafton House loomed, he'd never been so eager to get out of a carriage in all his life. The knowledge that Charlotte was there wrapped a warm feeling around his heart. He could tell her how he felt about her. What he would do to have her always by his side.

Though wouldn't be fair to give her hope for a swift marriage until he was certain he could break the engagement.

Peter was taken into the duke's residence and led to the duke's study by Berringer to be questioned.

Winston caught the butler's eye. "I'd like to speak with Miss Waters."

"I'm sorry, my lord, but Miss Waters is no longer here."

Disappointment crushed him. "Ah, I see."

He'd have to seek her out later. And it would be soon. Today. Tonight. Their discussion was too important to put off. He could not risk losing her.

Chapter Nineteen

Charlotte had managed to slip into her parents' town house just as the sun was rising. Only the butler saw her return, and he was smart enough to remember who made sure the household wages were paid on time each quarter. He acknowledged her return with a small smile of welcome and Charlotte went about her business, trusting him to do the same.

She headed up to her room immediately, removed her costume, and took pains to wash her face free of all cosmetics. She started to brush out her long hair before strolling into her dressing closet to find a day gown to slip on.

So much had happened in the last day. So many exquisite moments when she'd let go of her doubt about herself and acted on her desires. And Winston had responded. Perhaps not as she'd hoped, but it was enough to know he found her desirable. Charlotte brushed her fingers lightly across her jaw, recalling the tenderness of being touched by the man she loved.

Charlotte had told Winston of her feelings for him, too. She wasn't a bit embarrassed by that admission. He needed to understand why she'd put his needs above her own to keep him safe. Why his good health and happiness was so important to her.

He was everything.

She studied the contents of her wardrobe, selecting and discarding each gown in turn until she pulled out the perfect dress. The dress Winston claimed suited her best. Yellow. She'd wear it today, imagining the gown were his arms wrapped around her body. Unfortunately, she might never have that happen again. Their time together was at an end.

She had just finished dressing when she heard a noise coming from her bedchamber. Charlotte didn't remember hearing a knock upon her door. Curious to know who was intruding upon her privacy at this early hour, Charlotte poked her head around the doorway. Her mother stood at the mantle, picking up and setting aside her collection of trinkets, and then she moved on to inspect the new embroidery Charlotte had recently begun.

Mother didn't believe there was much value in impractical pastimes like collecting trinkets, embroidery or dancing, either. She said they were frivolous pastimes best left to those with nothing important to do.

Charlotte liked frivolity now and then, but history was all that mattered to her mother. They bickered about that a lot.

She stepped into her room with shoulders squared for another unsatisfying conversation. "Mama, what are you doing in my chambers unannounced?"

Mother spun about, staring at her in a way that put Charlotte on her guard immediately. "I've come to see what progress you've made in packing for the voyage," Mama announced.

"I, ah…" Charlotte replied carefully. But what was the use in lying? If Mama opened any of Charlotte's trunks, she'd discover them all completely empty. "None."

Her mother sighed heavily. "We talked about this."

"No, you and Papa talked. You decided about the trip together and informed me only after the fact. My objection to leaving was completely ignored, as was my request to delay so I might marry."

Mother threw up her hands. "I can hardly believe you were serious about staying and marrying. If you were, then why have there not been gentlemen calling, or flowers delivered and cluttering up our drawing room?"

"I have been trying to find a husband," she promised through gritted teeth. But not for the last several days. She'd become so wrapped up in her concern for Winston's safety that she hadn't attended a single ball or met with anyone but him in days.

Mother narrowed her eyes. "My dear girl, it's time to face facts. Some women never marry. There's no shame in spinsterhood."

She put her hands on her hips. "And some women have the support of caring parents when they go out in society. Other unmarried women have people in their lives who want to help them make a good match. You and Father abandon me every single night we go out together. As soon as someone utters the words *new book* and *library*, you're off to spend the evening pouring over dusty pages."

"Can you not appreciate how much we trust you to mind your own reputation? I remember my parents as an obstacle to my interests until I wed your father," Mother protested, shrugging off her valid complaint as foolishness. "They were quite strict, really. When I met and married your father, we vowed we'd never interfere in our children's lives."

"You only have one daughter, and taking me away from London again is interfering."

"For heaven's sake. Do you hear yourself? Always complaining. What are we to have done? We gave you life, but you expect us to give up everything for you. Set aside your father's career while we watch you dance the night away with buffoons in overheated ballrooms. We're not getting any younger. We have this precious time to pursue our ambitions, and that's all. We are so close to a breakthrough in understanding a culture nearly forgotten by the world."

She looked at her mother in dismay. "That breakthrough has been a day away all my life. You refuse to give me a few months more of your time to pursue my dream of making a match, but you and Papa have had no hesitation to labor twenty years and more, all of my life, to understand some obscure culture time forgot."

"The dead deserve to be remembered," Mama protested.

"So do the living!" Charlotte cried out. "I needed you to help me. I've always needed both my parents, but you hardly remember I exist, do you?"

"Of course we know you exist. Children are noisy and fragrant. Your father and I know exactly when you wash your hair for the scent of rosemary that permeates the upper rooms, and when you visited a sweet shop on Bond Street, the scent of caramels is on your breath. Do you ever think to offer us some?"

It was on the tip of her tongue to suggest Mama stir herself to fetch her own damn sweets if she wanted some, but she *had* hoarded them. Treated herself. Consoled herself with the many comforts to be found in London because she couldn't have the love and support of her obtuse parents. "I'll buy some for you next week, shall I?"

Mother ignored her question and strolled about the room, stopping by Charlotte's small trinket collection. "Have we ever mentioned the increasing cost of our expenses living in London to you? You cost us far less when we travel. Perhaps you could turn your head to practical considerations now and again as you spend your father's money on nonsense like these."

She had kept within her allowance all her life, but clearly Mother was only here to find fault with her today. "I'll do my best from now on to eat only cheese and stale bread, shall I?" she said through clenched teeth.

Mother suddenly sat down and swept a hand over her silver hair. Charlotte noticed a few more strands of gray had appeared than used to be there. Father, too, had begun to stoop a little more whenever he walked about the town house. She'd put it down to the long hours spent in study, but they both were growing older, she supposed. There might be a time when travel would become difficult for them.

But Charlotte feared she would be too old for marriage by the time that happened. "I still think the expedition could be put off until next year. After the winter storms have passed, the voyage will be much gentler for us all."

"We've traveled through storms many times before," Mother chided. But then she looked at Charlotte sharply. "Have you lost your courage after spending so much time rubbing shoulders with the simpering aristocracy?"

"No. Of course not."

"You have." Mother stood again and circled Charlotte, a look of disapproval in her eyes. "Women in London behave as if they have no strength or intelligence. They live by cunning and guile alone. Anything more remarkable is considered a weakness of character and unflattering, rather than a strength. I should never have brought you back to London after your first season. You've changed."

"Everyone changes," Charlotte said, perching on the edge of her bed. "I prefer London society and balls, and dinners and picnics, too. I don't want to be like you, never keeping old friends, never putting down roots."

"So, you want to become a tree?"

Charlotte couldn't help but laugh. Mother had a dry sense of humor when she chose to employ it. "Perhaps I do. I want a home to call my own, and it is not a hut in the middle of a rain forest. Children. Daughters to proudly shepherd into society one day. A husband who adores me."

"And access to shops that sell even more impractical thimbles to add to your collection too, I suppose."

"Yes, I want to visit shops that sell any number of impractical things. I like to look my best, and I do thank you for allowing me to purchase new gowns and things whenever we're in London. They help me feel at ease here in society. This is where I long to stay, Mama. Surely you can understand that we have very different dreams for our lives?"

Mother sighed. "Your father will not entertain the idea of leaving you behind, unless you are married."

"It might not be possible to find a husband in two weeks," Charlotte admitted.

"Two days, not two weeks, Charlotte," Mother corrected. "I came to your room to tell you our departure date has changed."

Charlotte gasped. "No!"

"Yes, the day after tomorrow our carriage departs for the docks. Can you be ready?"

She looked about her chambers in dismay. "No."

"Charlotte," Mother chided. "It took you one night to be ready to leave our last lodgings before we started the journey to England."

"I hated it there."

"You'll learn to enjoy new places again, once we break you of your infatuation with the so-called delights of London."

Nothing would diminish her love of her home.

Yet, she gulped. Her parents had total control over her life until she was five and twenty, and it wouldn't be the first time her parents had laid down the law about her duty to them. She had been dragged kicking and screaming from their temporary residences to the docks once before, too. She sighed. She'd rather not embarrass herself like that leaving London. She wanted to leave a good impression behind because one day, she hoped to return to society, and perhaps catch a glimpse of Winston, too.

Charlotte looked about her current room with a feeling of hopelessness growing inside. She had liked her life here, especially recently, even knowing she couldn't keep hiding an earl in her chambers indefinitely.

She had so many things that were impractical for the life her parents wanted her to live beyond England's shores. She'd have to leave so much behind. Give her prettiest, most delicate dresses away, because Charlotte would likely never wear them again anywhere else. And if she did take them, she'd likely lose them to a thief in some distant port the first time her back was turned. She'd much rather disperse her possessions how *she* chose than have them stolen away. "I cannot be ready by tomorrow night, but perhaps the day after."

"Your father will brook no delays. We leave the day after tomorrow. Now, you have much to do before we say our good-byes to London. Get on with it. I'll send a maid up to help you pack."

"That won't be necessary," she murmured, giving in to a brief bout of tears. "I know how to pack light."

"Good. We'll all sit down to dinner tonight and plan out our visits to say farewell to friends tomorrow. No point drag-ging out the inevitable."

"Yes," she answered, numb. "It is always the same, isn't it? A swift leave-taking from friends we might never see again."

"Tears are a waste of emotion. Be excited, Charlotte. Your father is taking us away on a new ship, and soon we'll be in a place we've never dreamed existed before."

Mother sailed from the room without another word, leaving Charlotte standing in the center of her room. She had today and tomorrow, and then she'd leave everything and everyone she loved behind.

Including Winston.

But she couldn't leave London without knowing Winston would be all right. She should never had left him, or Grafton House that morning. She should have stayed to hear what happened. Winston might even be back by now with news of Peter Bell's capture.

Determined to find out what Winston's brother had to say for himself, Charlotte snatched up a shawl and bonnet. After she'd spoken with Winston one more time, she would give away her best gowns, packing her trunks lightly for the journey she couldn't avoid anymore. She would take her leave of the duchess at the same time she saw Winston, if he was still there.

Mother was issuing orders to the servants somewhere out of sight as Charlotte crept down the main staircase, clutching her reticule, shawl tight about her shoulders. There were already boxes of books being stacked in the front hall and, because of their greater height and bulk, Mother did not see her pass her by.

The front door opened silently under her hand. She stopped on the top step to check for observers. The day was sunny and no one was passing, she couldn't have picked a better time to go. Her only thought was that she ought to have brought her parasol to protect her complexion from the sun.

But it was too late to turn back now. Mother might notice her. Charlotte rushed down the stairs and headed for the Duke of Exeter's home, and once she turned off her street, she slowed her steps to a gentle stroll.

London really was her favorite place in all the world. So full of wonders and advancements every day. Mother and Father might spend their days unraveling the past, but Charlotte had always been more interested in the future and how she'd be part of it.

Because she was going about unattended by a servant or maid today, Charlotte kept her chin down and her steps unhurried so she didn't draw attention. The Duke of Exeter's residence was exactly where she'd left it, of course, and it was in sight when a glossy black traveling carriage, with most of the window blinds down, pulled up directly in front of her.

She glanced at it with annoyance and was about to step around it when a gloved hand beckoned to her from the shadowed depths. "Hurry."

She glanced at the hand, then her eyes dipped to the crest

painted upon the door. Recognition turned to excitement. "Winston?"

"Come."

Charlotte scrambled inside before anyone saw her talking with the earl. Society would be scandalized, and gossip might spread at her joining him, but she wouldn't be deterred. It had been hours since she'd seen him, and she'd missed him terribly.

Before she could even catch a glimpse of his face, he pulled her straight to his side as the door snapped shut so darkness surrounded them entirely. His arms wrapped tight around her body as the carriage took off, heading away from the Duke of Exeter's residence.

"Where are we going?" Charlotte snuggled into Winston's embrace as they left the square far behind. "I was on my way to see you just now. Did you find your brother yet?"

"I'll deal with him later, too, but you've certainly saved me the chore of finding *you*," said the man holding her.

A man she didn't recognize at all.

Charlotte struggled to turn, to escape the stranger's arms and opened her mouth to scream for help, but a scented rag was quickly pressed over her nose and mouth.

Charlotte fought harder to be free. But it was no good. The man behind her was too strong and the drug-soaked rag weakened her strength with every single breath she took until she didn't remember the next.

Chapter Twenty

Winston ran up the front stairs of Charlotte's home and knocked hard on the front door, hoping to enter swiftly before anyone passing the house recognized him. The two guards Exeter had pressed upon him followed.

It was late in the afternoon, and the butler appeared as shocked to see him at the front door as he'd been the night Winston had arrived covered in blood. "Can I help you?"

"I need a word with Miss Waters. Immediately," Winston murmured, keeping his voice low in case her parents happened to hear him asking. They might be blinkered and blind to the comings and goings of the house, but he was still an engaged man calling on their spinster daughter. They might get the wrong idea about the nature of his visit. Even if it was the right one now, he supposed.

He passed the butler—Davis, if he recalled correctly—a handful of coin. "I'm sure she'll want to hear what I have come to tell her."

At least he hoped so, because he desperately needed Charlotte's company and advice. Questioning Peter had borne no new information other than having his brother admit he was in debt and engaged in a sordid money-making scheme.

But to every question about trying to kill Winston, Peter claimed total innocence. He'd even threatened violence upon the person who was out to get him.

Winston wanted to believe his brother with all his heart, but he could not let down his guard yet. He'd always felt he could rely on his brother to be by his side through thick and thin. To tell him anything. How crushing it was to realize he might have been naïve to believe in a fantasy that a close family bond existed between them. He could hardly believe his brother could stoop so low as to engage in sexual relations for money.

After the butler ushered him inside, Davis rushed to close the door. Winston discovered a lot had changed since his last visit here. He was surrounded by packing crates and trunks of every possible size in the hall. There was barely enough room for two grown men to converse, let alone squeeze another pair in.

Charlotte's butler took a deep breath and then straightened his shoulders, moving to put the front door at his back. "I'm afraid Miss Waters isn't at home."

Winston frowned at Davis as he tucked away the coins that had gained Winston entry, and then at the locked door behind the man's back. He fought not to shiver, checking behind him for other people lurking about. But the hall only housed boxes and crates, and he relaxed slightly. "Why admit me when the person I've come to see is not here?"

The butler wet his lips and then gulped. "Miss Waters trusted you, and I fear I must do the same now. I must tell you…she is *not* to be found tonight."

Winston scoffed. "Not to be found? Likely she's visiting friends. Perhaps she's attending a musical or a ball." He glanced around him. "Or perhaps trapped behind a trunk somewhere. What is all this, by the by?"

"The family has begun packing for their departure."

He frowned. "So soon?"

"Indeed, but it now appears Miss Waters has run away from home in an attempt to delay or avoid leaving with her parents the day after tomorrow."

Winston gaped. "What?"

"Servants were sent to fetch her back from any friend or acquaintance who might have tried to harbor her, but we are now certain no one we know has her. We are all quite worried, in fact."

A shiver raced down his spine. Charlotte shouldn't be missing, and she certainly shouldn't have run away without telling anyone. She could have run to him if she wanted to hide from her parents. He owed her the return favor of sanctuary, surely. But what good could running away do? Such behavior could mean the ruin of her reputation. "When was Charlotte seen last? By whom?"

"Her mother spoke with her this morning, upstairs in her chambers, I believe. It was not a happy conversation, I'm afraid to say. Harsh words were spoken. Mrs. Waters is quite upset about that."

"Is that a fact?"

"All the servants have been questioned and their movements accounted for," the butler promised. "We are all devastated about Miss Waters being gone, and quite worried for her welfare. Her parents even offered a reward, though none have stepped forward to claim they know her whereabouts."

"At least her parents noticed she was gone," he muttered under his breath. Winston rubbed a hand over his jaws. "Are you telling me that Charlotte has been without the protection of even a servant for the last several hours?"

"It seems that way."

He glanced at the men flanking him. "One of you return to Grafton House and inform the duchess of this development. If Miss Waters is there, return immediately with the news."

The fellow nodded and squeezed out the door again.

"I'll need to speak with her parents now," Winston decided, his stomach churning with worry. "They don't know me well, but I will get to the bottom of Charlotte's so-called disappearance, I assure you."

"Very glad to have you here, sir. I'll do my best to gain you an immediate audience with them," the butler promised.

"Perhaps this will help." Winston quickly offered his card, and the butler's eyes widened.

"Forgive me, *my lord*." Davis appeared decidedly nervous now. Had he never known Winston's identity? He would have to thank Charlotte for that later. "If you'll just wait here a moment, my lord, I'll interrupt them immediately."

Winston smiled. "Thank you, Davis."

The butler slipped around a tall pile of trunks and into the drawing room on the other side. When the door opened, he heard the conversation immediately stutter to a halt as his arrival was announced.

He hadn't realized anyone else was with Charlotte's parents, but of course someone must have come to console them. Charlotte had many friends who would be concerned about her whereabouts.

The butler returned for him promptly, and he stepped into the quiet drawing room.

He was confronted by Charlotte's friends—Mrs. Berringer, and Miss Aurora Hillcrest. This was going to be a little more public than he'd care for, but his concern for Charlotte was a greater fear than any awkwardness.

All eyes fixed upon him as he made his greetings to Charlotte's parents, who looked upon him without a flicker of recognition. "I hear there's been an unpleasant development. Your daughter is missing, I believe."

Mrs. Waters clutched her hands in her lap. "Have you any news of her?"

"No, I am afraid not." Charlotte's parents seemed too distracted to make him the offer of a chair to sit in, so he chose his own place instead. He nodded to Mrs. Berringer and then turned his attention to Charlotte's parents again. The pair looked very worried, belying Charlotte's claim that they didn't care about her welfare at all. "Your butler tells me Charlotte has not been seen for hours."

Everyone looked around Winston, eyes narrowed. Winston glanced over his shoulder and found that the butler had followed him into the room, remaining behind him. The fellow was wringing his hands. Apparently, Davis was very loyal to Charlotte, and Winston thought he deserved not to be sent away for gossiping to him.

Winston shrugged. "I made him tell me everything, of course."

Some of the tension in the room disappeared, and Davis whispered his thanks. Winston put the focus back on Charlotte's parents. "I believe you were the last to see her, speak to her, Mrs. Waters?"

"Yes, we had a horrible row," Mrs. Waters admitted finally, rubbing her brow. "I left her in her room to start packing and when we went in to dinner, she was tardy joining us. I sent a servant up, only to be told she could not be accounted for."

Winston glanced at his pocket watch. It was almost seven o'clock now, and the streets were dark. "At what time did you sit down to dine?"

"At four."

"And your row occurred at?"

"About nine o'clock this morning," Mr. Waters answered, patting his wife's hand. "We'd only just risen for the day. My wife wanted to speak with Charlotte before she made any plans to go out."

So, some few hours after she'd left the Duke of Exeter's home, she'd left her parents' protection, too. "And your discussion ended in an argument. What was that about?"

"She's so stubborn," Mrs. Waters complained. "She promised to pack for the voyage, but all her trunks were empty still. We said such horrible things to each other. I'll never forgive myself if she's run away over it!"

Charlotte had a right to be angry over her parents' neglect.

Their obsession was well known and perhaps the argument was one straw too many. "Are any of her trunks missing?"

"No."

"Any of her favorite possessions gone?"

"Only her reticule, I believe."

Charlotte had some money upon her, at least, then. "Might she have gone shopping on Bond Street with friends and been lured home with them?"

"She does like pretty things. Thimbles and the like." Mrs. Waters waved her hand toward the two women sitting close together on a chaise lounge. "And there they are, her best friends sitting right in front of you, and none have seen her at all today."

Winston studied the women lined up on the other side of the room. Charlotte was very close to these ladies. But there were more. And any good friends might have hidden Charlotte from her parents and lied about it still. Coming here to wring their hands might ensure they looked believably concerned. There were a dozen ways Charlotte could remain in London if that were truly her wish. "Where is Harriet Long and Miss Draven today?"

"Bristol," Eugenia Berringer answered. "Harriet had left London before Charlotte even knew she had so little time left with us. Miss Draven had been taken to the country by her guardian around the same time."

He caught the eye of Mrs. Berringer. As a married woman, married to a man who would become a duke one day, she'd have the best resources at her fingertips that the others did not. "Are you hiding Charlotte and don't want to admit it? You are quite wrong to keep her from me, if you are."

Mrs. Berringer's brows shot up. "No. Of course I'm not hiding Charlotte. She is our dearest friend. I've openly offered her room with us, and it is her parents who have made the offer impossible to accept. They demand she marry to stay in London."

He glanced at the elder couple. "Demand?"

"She either marries or comes with us. That was our agreement," her father said, crossing his arms over his chest.

"Perhaps we were wrong to do that," Mrs. Waters whispered to her husband.

"How was I to suspect she'd run away over the matter? She'd always been entirely biddable before."

Aurora Hillcrest burst to her feet. "You gave her only weeks to find a husband, and then announced an intention to leave a week earlier just this morning. Unfair and unkind, making it impossible for her to succeed! I would have run away under the same circumstances."

Winston sat back, appalled by Charlotte's parents' lack of feeling. He could easily believe that she might have panicked about an early departure and done something rash, but surely, she would have gone to a friend to tell them what happened *before* disappearing entirely.

He would have liked to know what was going on himself. He would like to know where he might find her again. They had important matters to discuss. She claimed to love him, and he felt the same about her. Something had to be done about his wedding to Elizabeth, too, before the day got any closer. But now he was committed to finding where Charlotte had gone. "This is odd indeed."

He looked up as a throat cleared loudly and found Aurora Hillcrest staring at him. "Why are you so interested in Charlotte's whereabouts?"

A fair question, and one he couldn't answer honestly just yet. He smiled quickly. "She's a friend of my friends, and I don't like when you're all upset."

Aurora squinted at him. "Yes, but why *you* when no other gentleman has come to show any concern."

"He's here on his mother's behalf most likely to set her mind at ease," Eugenia Berringer soothed. "It doesn't matter why he's come, only that he's willing to help with the search. Yes?"

"Indeed I am." He turned to her parents, who were now huddled together, a lost look in their eyes. "What has been done so far to recover her?"

Mr. Waters heaved a heavy sigh. "We sent out our servants and they looked up and down the streets nearby. She knows the dangers out there and how to defend herself."

"Quite," he answered, fearing he might throttle Mr. Waters if given half the chance. Charlotte should never have *had* to protect herself. He was proud that she could, but her father was lax in protecting his only daughter from danger. She needed someone in her life to put her first.

Winston's heart started to beat very fast. He could be that for her, and would be one day. He looked over his shoulder. "If Miss Water's had gone out in the morning and fallen or been injured, someone should have stumbled over her. Send a servant to any local physician, apothecary or physician that lives nearby and make inquiries."

"Yes, my lord," Davis promised without waiting for the Waters' agreement. "It will be done immediately."

"You can go with him, too, and help with the inquiries," he told the duke's man.

"But I was told…"

"Do it. I'm quite safe here I assure you."

The fellow did not look very happy about the order but eventually nodded. "Very well, my lord. I'll return as soon as I can."

Winston nodded and turned back to Charlotte's parents. "Did she happen take her parasol with her?"

Mrs. Waters frowned. "I don't know."

"She usually carries one," Aurora murmured.

When the butler returned saying servants had been dispatched, Winston asked to view Charlotte's bedchamber.

Mrs. Waters opened her mouth to protest, but Mrs. Berringer nodded. "Perhaps you'll see something we all missed."

Aware he was watched closely, he strode from the room. Halfway up the stairs, he heard footsteps rushing to follow behind him. He glanced over his shoulder to find Aurora Hillcrest climbing the stairs. "Is there something wrong?"

"Not yet, but I'll let you know in a moment," she replied.

He strode ahead of her, straight into Charlotte's room, and looked around. Everything was more or less as Winston remembered seeing it last. Her thimble collection had been shuffled about but there were still thirteen of the original collection on display.

"Where is it," Winston murmured, checking around the room.

"Perhaps she's taken it with her," Aurora suggested.

But he found it a moment later, propped against a wall in her dressing closet behind the door.

He glanced out upon the street from her window. If Charlotte had decided to run away forever, she might have left some belongings behind, but he didn't think it likely she'd forget her parasol. She carried that item everywhere. She would have taken something else from her room, too. Gowns, coat, etc. One small trunk at least. A thimble. Thanks to his extended stay in her dressing closet and bedchamber, Winston was well acquainted with everything Charlotte possessed.

Although it was a futile thing to do, he checked behind her trunks in case she was hiding there. When he didn't find her, he flicked through the contents of her wardrobe one gown at a time. The yellow gown he'd favored was missing. His favorite out of all she owned. In the corner was her carefully folded costume that she'd worn the prior night.

He turned around slowly, trying to imagine her going about her daily routine.

She came home, dropped her reticule on the bed, kicked her slippers under it, and then went into the dressing room to change.

That's where the yellow day gown had been the last time he'd been here, too. So, it was possible she was wearing it now. And once dressed, she'd sit down at her dressing table and comb out her long dark hair.

He strode to her dressing table and found the combs she'd worn the prior night, and then he saw a damp cloth smudged with kohl balled up in the wash basin. God, he'd felt more alive with her last night than around any other woman he'd ever known. More himself and not the Earl of Hurlston.

Just Winston.

The man she loved, and he wanted to be that man forever.

"It seems to me that you've been in this room before," Aurora murmured.

Winston ignored that. "She's wearing a yellow day gown. Not an easy color to forget or overlook."

"Yellow? How can you be sure?"

"If you love your friend, don't ask me that."

Aurora left the door and came closer. "Are you hiding Charlotte? Preventing her being taken away from London by her parents?"

"Don't be ridiculous. I'd never be so underhanded." Winston stalked up to the woman and looked down at her. She suspected him of being involved now with Charlotte for certain, given the defiant glint in her eye. "If I knew where Charlotte was, I'd be there right now."

A flicker of a smile touched Aurora's lips but quickly vanished. "Where could she have gone?"

"I don't know, but I'll tear London apart to find her."

Aurora smiled fully then. "Now *that's* the sound of a man who truly knows my friend's worth at last."

Priceless. He scowled though. If Charlotte had been harmed, someone would pay dearly. "Excuse me."

"By all means, go find her. Send word back that's she's safe and well. She means the world to us."

And to him, too. He wouldn't rest until Charlotte was in his arms again.

He rushed downstairs and out to the street without saying goodbye to anyone else. He raised his hand to stop an approaching hack but saw his own carriage coming down the road. He waved off the hack and waited for his own conveyance to come to a stop. As it halted, he spoke to the coachman. "I could have sworn I sent you home without me."

"Change of plans, milord."

He glanced up at hearing an unfamiliar voice from the box, only to see a stranger wearing his coachman's livery. "Who the devil are you?"

"Better to ask who *they* are," said the man, pointing behind Winston. "I wouldn't resist if I were you."

Winston attempted to turn and look about, but all he saw was the descent of a pistol butt toward his head.

Chapter Twenty-One

Charlotte sat up and immediately pressed a hand to her aching head where it pounded with the rhythm of her own heart. "Oh, stars!"

The sound of her voice bounced around her and echoed horribly. She took a moment to look around carefully. How she'd come to be here, and for how long she'd lain upon the rough wood floor, she'd no idea. Last thing she remembered, she'd been on the street on her way to Grafton House again in broad daylight, and Winston's carriage had stopped in front of her, a hand beckoning to her from within.

At the time, she'd believed it was Winston inside the carriage. A man she trusted. A man who would never hurt her.

Foolish. Foolish, Charlotte.

She'd been so consumed by her desire to be close to Winston again that it had not occurred to her it could be someone else. Someone who had meant to trick her into joining him in that dark carriage, though for what purpose she couldn't imagine right now.

Nothing good, no doubt.

Gingerly, she climbed to her feet, reaching for a wall for support as her senses swam until she was steady. She'd been drugged and a bitter taste of it lingered in her mouth and nose. She quickly swept her hands over herself to check for pain or any damage made to her gown during her abduction. She had fought hard for her freedom but had lost the battle.

Charlotte suddenly remembered she'd carried her reticule

and a shawl with her when she'd left home. A quick search of the ground around her revealed they were both missing. "Drat!"

She'd had a tiny pair of embroidery scissors in her reticule. It wasn't much, but she might have used them as a weapon when her abductor come back.

If they hadn't already.

She listened carefully but heard nothing. It was chilly wherever she was being held, and as she looked about again, she concluded she was very likely in the bowels of a large house. A basement or unused storeroom, perhaps.

There seemed to be no one nearby at the moment though. Charlotte could hear nothing but the beat of her heart and rush of her breath, both racing too fast. She worked to calm herself. She was still alive and that was promising. Whoever had taken her could have easily murdered her instead of imprisoning.

Her stomach growled loudly, but here were no scents coming from any kitchen to have caused that reaction. But time might have. Had she been asleep all day? Given the darkness around her now, she suspected it was some hours deep into the night.

She put her hand over her mouth to hold in a gasp. Did anyone even realize she was missing? How would anyone possibly find her here? Wherever *here* might be.

No one at home had seen her leave. She'd made sure of that herself.

Would her parents have noticed?

Of course, they wouldn't.

Charlotte flung herself at the door and when it wouldn't budge easily, she put her back into it. It finally moved, hinges creaking in protest under her weight. She squeezed out through the narrow gap into a hallway just as dark as the room she'd recently left, and as empty, too.

Had someone brought her here and not even bothered to lock her in? How strange. And why would they have done so?

She looked up and down the hall, trying to get her bearings and see anything to identify her location. There was no light, no sounds but the rush of her own breathing. Why bring her to somewhere like this, only to desert her?

Maybe they hadn't yet.

Charlotte crept down the hall with one hand extended, fingers skimming the wall to guide her past other empty chambers. Her eyes were adjusting to the gloom now, and she could make out a space that must have at one time been home to servants.

The place was not derelict, but it was utterly abandoned. No one must have lived here for some time, given the dust covering the floor, which meant when and if someone came back, she'd be entirely at their mercy unless she was better prepared to defend herself.

She was relieved to find the kitchen, with a solid-looking range set apart at one end of the room, neat and moderately clean—even if no fire burned in the grate to lend any warmth. The high windows in the room seemed to be boarded up from the outside. Only a little bit of moonlight crept around the edges, confirming that it was night outside, but that weak light allowed her a better view than she'd had since first waking.

She looked about the chamber, hoping to find something to use as a weapon in case her abductors returned. In one corner, there was a shadowy shape.

Charlotte rushed toward it but only found a filthy potato sack covering a single length of smooth timber, possibly a chair or low table leg. "Well, at least I can whack someone with this if they come back for me," she muttered, feeling better to have a solid weight in her hand again.

What she wouldn't give for her parasol, though that item had been forgotten when she'd set out to see Winston again in a rush.

She leaned against the wall to think a moment. She could

scream, but that might only invite her abductors to check on her. And if they didn't, who would hear her? The walls seemed quite thick.

She looked at the stick in her hand and swung it around a few times, getting a feel for it. She put the point of the stick against the rougher stones around the hearth and dragged it back and forth a few times, attempting to sharpen it to a point as she'd seen the natives do on countless occasions during her travels.

Someone coughed.

The sound scared Charlotte witless and she spun about, stick raised, only to find herself still alone in the abandoned kitchen.

But the cough happened again, and it echoed round and round the chamber, giving her no sense of the direction it came from. No matter how hard she listened and peered, she couldn't tell where it had come from or see anyone sneaking up behind her.

Waiting to be attacked would not do.

Charlotte brandished her weapon and slowly left the kitchen, one silent step at a time, in search of the source of the cough. But whoever they were, they were making no attempt to be quiet at all. In fact, between coughs, they—a man— appeared to be cursing in a steady stream.

Charlotte reached the chamber she'd woken up in, certain whoever it was lay ahead of her still. By the sound, it was a man who was rather unhappy.

She risked peeking around a corner into a room she hadn't noticed before and could just make out a shape crouched across the room. He stumbled and groaned, and then straightened completely. He was tall, well above her own height, with long arms and hands that clutched his head. But Charlotte sensed no threat from him. None at all.

He suddenly walked into a wall and blistered her ears with another coarse curse.

"What are you doing?" she whispered.

The fellow nearly fell over his own feet in his haste to get turned around. His fists rose before him, and he took up a boxing stance. "What do you want from me?" he demanded, looking every which way but at where Charlotte stood. "Show yourself!"

She gaped, finally recognizing the voice and the form. "Winston?"

"Charlotte?" came his incredulous reply as his hands fell to his sides.

"Oh, you found me!" she cried and rushed at him, relieved beyond measure to not be alone anymore. "I'm so glad you're here."

Winston's hands fumbled awkwardly over her body, then she was nearly crushed by his embrace. "Believe me, *I'm* not happy to have found you."

She drew back from him. "You're not?"

Even in the dark, she could sense all was not right with him. He pushed his fingers through his hair. "Well, no. Actually, I appear to have been imprisoned alongside you."

She shouldn't laugh at his disappointment, but she couldn't help herself. She had been so afraid that she'd never be found. But if Winston was here, she felt better about her imprisonment. If she was to be trapped, she was glad it was with him and not someone else. She hugged him tightly, wishing she never had to let him go. "Oh, Winston. What is going on? Why am I here? Why are *you*?"

"I don't know. But I'm just glad to know where you are. You have no idea how worried I was when Davis confessed you were gone from home and no one could find you." His lips pressed to her brow. "There doesn't seem anyone to fight right now."

"No. There's no one here but us," she told him, resting her cheek over his heart.

His fingers teased the back of her neck. "As pleasant as that development seems, we'd best get out of here."

She looked up at him quickly. "I haven't found a way out. Have you?"

"No. But I don't remember even arriving either. How are we going to escape this disaster, Charlotte dear?"

"I haven't the faintest idea, Winston. I don't even have my parasol."

"I'll buy you a dozen if we make it out of here in one piece," he promised. He laughed suddenly and rocked her in his arms. "Oh, it's good to be able to talk to you again."

She liked talking to him, too, but they had both been imprisoned. With Winston here now, the situation couldn't be good for either of them. "Do you think they'll come back soon?"

"I hope so, and I hope not."

"Winston, I'm scared."

"I am, too, I assure you," he replied, kissing her brow again. "But we'll be all right now we're together. Gods, I missed you today."

She looked up at him in surprise, astonished that he'd repeat the sentiment. "You really missed me?"

"Of course. I had just started out looking for you when I was tricked into taking my own carriage. It was being driven by my abductors, you see, and I was forced inside after being clubbed over the head. I don't remember much after that because they drugged me."

She reached up to gently smooth her fingers over his skull. She found a lump but since it was dark, she couldn't tell if he was bleeding or not. "That happened to me, too, but not the being hit over the head part. I thought you were inside the carriage I entered, but it was someone pretending to be you instead. Winston, I think it was Peter."

"Impossible," he insisted, bringing her fingers to his lips to kiss them.

"You can't ignore my suspicions forever," she warned, placing her fingers firmly over his lips so he wouldn't interrupt. "It's a bitter pill to swallow, I know."

He dislodged her fingers. "The truth is, my brother is an unwilling guest of the Duke of Exeter right now. I found him in a gaming hell early this morning, not long after leaving you. I have questioned him the entire day. He could not have been in that carriage and staged your abduction. Do you know what time you were taken?"

"A little before ten, I believe it must have been," she answered, frowning at an unpleasant thought. "I wasn't very far from home. It must be someone who works for him, then. A paid thug."

"A possibility, but he's given nothing away today."

"If not Peter, then who can it be, and why? They said I had saved them the trouble of waiting for me to come out. They intended my abduction. Knew where I lived."

"That is not a difficulty. Your address is widely known in society." He heaved a sigh. "They must suspect my involvement with you, and perhaps realized the extent of the help you'd given me in avoiding them before. Damn." Winston eased her back from him but quickly took hold of her hand. "Where do you think we are?"

"A vacant house. I don't know where. There's no furniture, no possessions in any of the rooms I've looked into. Nothing to identify the owners."

"We're still in London, I suspect, but I want to be sure." He began to lead her from the chamber, only to come to a halt in the hall. "Is there no light at all in this damn place?"

"There's a little moonlight in the kitchens. All the windows are boarded up there, though. Why?"

"I want to know the time to judge how far we've been taken from home."

Charlotte led him directly into the kitchen, where there was at least some light. He quickly pulled out his pocket watch, turning and twisting it this way and that, then announced it was only eight o'clock in the evening. "It's only been an hour since I was taken."

"I think I've been here all day. My stomach is empty."

He took hold of her hands. "Did they hurt you?"

"No. I'm well."

"Good." Winston pulled her to his side again. "They surprised me."

"At least you were not shot at again." Charlotte shivered as a thought occurred to her. "Was I the bait meant to lure you out, Winston?"

"I don't know," he said before kissing the top of her head. "Irresistible bait, though. We have to get out of here. Now, before…"

"Before they come back to finish us," she finished. "I'd only just started a search for a way out when I heard you sneeze."

"Damn dust." Winston laced their fingers together tighter. "Let's continue looking for a way out. Your parents believe you ran away from them."

She snorted a laugh and then covered her face as her nose twitched. "I'm surprised they noticed I was even gone."

"They noticed." He sighed. "You didn't show up for dinner."

She shook her head. "It took them over six hours to miss me, then?"

"Well, I missed you the moment we went our separate ways," he promised, and that made her feel infinitely better. "I gather you snuck out of the house while their backs were turned. Were you really running away?"

"No, I was running to *you*. To find out if Peter had been caught and to know you were safe. But you're not. Winston, you must know that Mother and Father have changed their plans about leaving."

"I am aware. Your friends complained all about the surprise your parents announced this morning when I found out about your disappearance. Quite unfair of them. I don't doubt you're angry."

"I am, but what can I do? I made a promise, and I won't go back on my word. It was either marriage or go with them. I don't want to leave, but…"

"You think you've no choice."

They reached the part of the house where they'd found each other again, and ahead in the gloom she saw an archway. An archway led to somewhere. Perhaps to stairs. "This way," she murmured, taking the lead.

Winston tugged on her hand. "Charlotte, when we get out of here, we'd better talk about the future."

She pulled him onward. "What's left to talk about, Winston? We must go."

He pulled her against him. "There's quite a lot. I've never actually talked so much to a woman I like before. I'm not done talking to you, either." He leaned down and gave her a smacking kiss. "There."

"There what?"

He stole three more kisses, whispering between each, "There, and there, and there."

She put a hand on his chest. "Winston. Stop."

"What's wrong?"

"I'm leaving."

"Ah," he complained, sliding his arm around her waist. "What if I knew a way that you could pack your trunks but stay here in London?"

"I don't want to be a companion or someone's charity case,"

she said slowly, squinting up at him in the dark. "Or your mistress."

"I assure you I wouldn't want that for you, either. But as I recall, it was only last night that we pretended to be lovers… and our performance was very convincing. I'll not give up on us so easily. But it would have to be our secret."

Chapter Twenty-Two

Charlotte shoved Winston away from her.

"Charlotte? Did I misunderstand. Do you not love me after all?"

"Of course, I love you. Nothing will ever change that."

Winston's heart leapt with undeniable joy. If Charlotte loved him, and he loved her, Winston couldn't marry Elizabeth.

He could have this—companionship, friendship, with Charlotte.

Forever.

And love.

He'd make Charlotte his wife, of course, but it likely couldn't be soon enough.

Winston would not like Charlotte to be gossiped about as *the other woman* in his life. She deserved to be the only one, so they'd have to keep what they felt for each other a secret for a while. Breaking his engagement was going to be a devilishly complicated business. But worth it.

He cupped her face. "That is all I need to hear," he whispered, before crushing his lips to hers."

Winston was not about to deny himself the pleasure of Charlotte's kisses.

He put his arms around her. "I love you," he whispered in the dark. "I love you, Charlotte, with all my heart. No matter what happens next, you're the one."

Charlotte sobbed. "I would have waited my whole life to hear that."

"Me too," he promised. "But there's something I have to tell you. I've been keeping a secret from you."

She shivered. "You can tell me anything."

"I've never made love to a woman before," he admitted slowly. Embarrassed but oddly glad she'd know the truth about his hesitations.

"Few men love their lovers, I suppose."

"That's not what I meant." He leaned close to her ear to whisper, "I'm an innocent. Just as innocent as you."

There was a long pause, during which Charlotte seemed frozen. But before the silence could become embarrassing for him, she finally whispered, "*Never?*"

"Never. I suppose that's why we blush around each other so often. We both are curious, yet unsure of our welcome."

"You are welcome," she whispered. "I've always wondered what sort of women you were attracted to."

"To Charlotte." He reached for her face. "Only to you."

She drew back. "What about Elizabeth? Surely—"

"Never. We've only kissed a few times, and never with a tenth of the passion of my first with you."

"Then why marry her?"

"It was my father's dying wish," he admitted. "I intended to honor his arrangement, but now I cannot. It will be expensive and likely cause a scandal society will gossip about for years, but given enough time, I hope to be free to marry you one day."

"But you haven't asked me."

"I will, as soon as I know I can honor my promise to you," he said. "But I will need to engage lawyers and likely repay funds the estate received from Elizabeth's father on the signing of the agreement when I was a boy. I'd best break the news to my mother first, and deal with my brother second. It will be complicated. But I'm sure with patience, I'll win through. That's why we must keep us a secret. I'll of course tell my mother about you."

"She'll blame me. She *likes* Elizabeth!"

"Mother will understand, I'm quite sure."

"Displacing a woman your mother considers a daughter already, and for so many years, will not endear me to anyone," Charlotte warned.

He drew her close. "I'll take care of everything."

"What you ought to be taking care of is finding out for certain who wants you dead, and me so humiliated and embarrassed that I might never show my face in society again. What will your future wife think when she finds out we were abducted more or less together? She'll think I did it solely to steal you away from her or cause a scandal to embarrass her."

"Consider me stolen," he said with a spluttering laugh.

"This is not funny, my lord." Charlotte suddenly marched off into the dark until he could no longer see her back.

"Charlotte," he cried out, fearful of being left behind. "Where are you going? I didn't mean it badly. You know what happened between us was unplanned, and wonderful, too."

There was a long pause and then an equally long sigh before, "Follow the sound of my voice, my lord. I've found a staircase going up."

"You've much better night vision than I," Winston marveled as he hurried toward Charlotte's voice in the dark, only to discover her partway up a narrow staircase, skirts lifted above her ankles to avoid tripping over them on the treads. Winston rushed up and quickly put his hand at the small of her back to steady her and they continued up a dusty staircase together.

Charlotte came to an abrupt stop, dropped her skirts, and thumped her fists upon the wall. "It just goes up but there's no door or handle where there should be one by now. What kind of house is this?"

Winston reached past her and ran his hands over the wall ahead of them. He discerned a sliver of a gap that, when shoved, slid pocket door away, into the wall itself. Unfortunately, that didn't grant them freedom. "One that's been renovated since its original construction." The staircase had been blocked off from the rest of the house some time in the past and the doorway plastered over on the other side. "That's unfortunate."

"Only unfortunate?"

"I'm going to have to make some noise to get us out," he muttered. "Stand back."

Winston backed up a few steps, and then took a run at the door, throwing his body into the newer renovation, shoulder first. He bounced off the first time. On the second attempt, a board cracked, and on the third, he burst though into another space.

Winston blinked as he looked around his new surroundings. But he was standing in a moonlit chamber. Enough light came in through the front windows to show him his surroundings very clearly. Charlotte picked her way through the rubble to join him, waving away the dust he'd stirred up.

They were now standing in a furnished house, though everything was hidden under protective dust cloths right now. He moved away from Charlotte, taking everything in, listening hard for persons that should not be there…

In the house he'd recently purchased for his brother to live in.

"Dear God."

"No one seems to live here at the moment," Charlotte murmured, peeking under the nearest dust cloth to the upholstered chair beneath. "I wonder whose house this is?"

"No need to wonder." He gulped. "It's mine, or I should say, it's Peter's."

"Peter lives with you," she reminded him.

"I bought him a town house, remember? I'd planned to present it to him on his birthday, so he would have a place to call his own. He and Elizabeth do not get along, so…"

"So, he knows about this place."

"About the house? Yes, he saw the papers on my desk once before I put them away. He didn't know then that it would be his one day soon." Winston looked around. "I wanted to arrange a few repairs first and to have a thorough clean and stocking of the kitchen carried out before he saw it for the first time. He thought it was meant for my mistress, until I disabused him of that absurd notion."

"So, knowing the house was empty, Peter or someone else might have ordered his henchmen to bring us both here. Were they trying to embroil you in a scandal now, too?"

"You as well." Winston shook his head. "The only reason to do that would be to cause trouble for my family and between Elizabeth and me. You know, Peter nearly had me fooled, you know. He's always claimed not to like Elizabeth but what if that was a lie all along. What if he wants her instead?"

"She is very beautiful," Charlotte murmured.

"Not the way you are," Winston promised, meaning every word. Charlotte was beautiful inside and out. "I considered letting him go this afternoon, but I wanted to talk to you first. I think we should have another talk about Elizabeth."

"We're all fools when we trust someone we love completely." Charlotte rubbed her hand up and down his arm and then she walked deeper into one of the rooms, brushing dust from her gown. "It's a pretty place."

Winston battered his arms and legs, sending up plumes of the wretched dust around him. "And not somewhere we should remain in case our abductors return. Come, Charlotte. It's a short walk to my home from here."

But Charlotte didn't move. "I'm not going to your home with you. I'm going to speak with Peter, perhaps crack something hard over his head, and then I'll go home to pack for the voyage."

"No."

"Someone had me abducted, Winston! I intend to find out who. If you love me at all, you won't stop me. If he's at all involved, I want to hear it with my own ears."

As much as Winston wanted to shield Charlotte from unpleasantness, he'd no right to deny her.

Winston took Charlotte's hand in his, then wrapped it about his arm firmly. It was dark enough outside that they might pass unnoticed leaving this house, and if he were swift in walking with her, she might yet get through this ordeal with her reputation untarnished.

To his surprise, the front door was not locked and the key rested in the mechanism. The last place he'd seen that key was locked away in his desk drawer in his study at home. Peter, of course, knew where he kept any important papers and keys… but so did a few others he could think of at home. He kept his suspicions to himself as he relocked the town house upon their exit and pocketed the key.

Mindful of not drawing attention, he rushed Charlotte down the street as gently as he could.

Still, it felt like they nearly ran all the way to the Duke of Exeter's residence. It was as exhilarating as it was frightening, thinking that someone might be watching them. Following them.

"Keep your face lowered," he whispered.

"Any lower and I'll kiss the ground," she complained.

He couldn't help but smile. Charlotte's wit under pressure was priceless and reassured him. All would be well eventually. Not easily, perhaps, but right in the end.

He had fallen in love with Charlotte—the wrong woman—and every moment spent in her company felt easy and right. He was glad he had gotten to know her better before it was too late, because being with her every day was what he wanted to do for the rest of his life.

Elizabeth had never cared about him the way Charlotte did.

She never fussed over him or confided in him. She never questioned what he was thinking just because his expression subtly changed.

He could imagine marriage to Charlotte and no one else now. Mother would simply have to accept his change of allegiance if he explained how much Charlotte had done for him already. Mother talked of love and hope.

That could only be found with Charlotte now.

He would make that happen or die trying.

Chapter Twenty-Three

Charlotte lifted her chin high as she walked ahead of Winston into the chamber Peter Bell had been kept in for the last day. Although the duke did not appear happy with her request to speak with Peter in private, but being informed of her abduction by Winston he'd agreed very smartly.

Lord Peter Bell looked decidedly unkempt as he lay upon a bed, tied to it, too. She was glad to know he suffered a little after all Winston had been through.

Unfortunately, despite needing fresh clothes and a shave, he seemed oddly merry. He glanced at her only briefly before addressing Winston with a grin. "I hope you've returned to set me free, brother."

Winston stopped and just stared at the brother he claimed to love with such sadness in his expression that it hurt to witness. Charlotte stepped between them. Like Winston had done, she too intended to speak to him as if he were guilty of wanting his brother dead. "He cannot set you free. Not after today."

The smile on Peter's face vanished in an instant as he glared at his brother. "Did you know that today I was given no choice but to piss into a chamber pot a servant held?" he bit out. "What is it you want me to say to prove my innocence? I'll say it! I'll give up drinking and gambling. Give up those women."

Charlotte ignored the offers and pressed on with her own questioning. "Why did you do it?"

"Do what? And who are you to talk to me? Get on with your chores and get out."

She studied Peter, puzzled by his words. "I'm Charlotte."

"Wonderful. I'm happy for you. Whoever you are can be of no consequence to me. Hurry up and get on your way. My brother and I have unfinished business."

Winston moved forward but Charlotte held him back. "Not so fast." She stared down at Peter. "Imprisonment in an empty house was an odd choice after your other attempts on Winston's life. But what did you intend for *me*?"

Shouldn't Peter be at least annoyed to see his plans foiled and Charlotte walking free after all he'd done to abduct her? "It was clever of you to take me to a place no one knew your brother owned. My family and friends would never look for me there and I'll be ruined for sure if society ever learned I was alone with Winston."

"What are you still blathering on about? My brother would never seduce a mere maid. And where is the duchess to take this maid to task for questioning her betters? Send her away, Winston, or heaven help me, she'll feel the lash of my tongue."

Charlotte glanced over her shoulder at Winston. "He doesn't know me."

Winston's eyes narrowed. "He's proven to be a good actor."

"No, he's not acting at all…but then again, scoundrels and rogues really don't pay much attention to a wallflower's face or name, do they?" she murmured.

"I do," Winston promised.

That made her smile.

Charlotte perched on the edge of the bed, facing Peter Bell. Now when she looked at him, she saw a different sort of character to Winston. A rogue and a scoundrel to watch out for. A man who knew women well. A man a woman couldn't trust with her reputation, let alone her virtue. But could she trust Peter with his brother's life? She was inclined to believe he'd played no part in her abduction. But that didn't absolve him of having deadly ambition. "Tell me about your older brother."

"Why? He's right there."

Winston stepped closer to Charlotte's side. "Humor her."

"What is there to say," Peter began. "Win's the apple of my mother's eye, a favorite of society."

"You resent that," she murmured. "Tell me something true. Something only you and he would know about each other."

Peter glanced at his brother and away again, lips pursing. Finally, he looked back at her. "The day our father died, he pretended not to be upset but he was devastated. He went riding to hide his tears, I think…and when he came back, he wasn't my brother anymore, but the earl."

Winston sighed. "I had to take charge of the family."

"I could have done something to help you. But you sent me away a month after we buried him. He didn't want me around, you see."

Charlotte clucked her tongue. "That's likely not why he did it."

"No, it's not. I sent you away to spare you Mother's tears," Winston murmured. "She cried night and day from when we buried Papa."

Peter looked away. "Did you think I would not be of help to her, either?"

"I knew you could be, but then both of us would have continued to grieve with her for too long. You were Papa's favorite. I wanted you to have a chance to remember how to be happy again. You and Father loved visiting the sea together. That's why I sent you there."

Charlotte smiled and glanced down at her hands. "Admit it. You love each other very much. Anyone can see it when you speak of that trying time. Your instincts were right, Winston. It's not him trying to harm you. But it must be someone from your household who has the key to your new property."

"Perhaps it's your mistress got it in for you?"

"There never was, nor will there ever be, a mistress kept by me," Winston said as he set his brother free. "Unless *you* put one there."

Peter rubbed his wrists and then his gaze locked on Charlotte. "Who are you again?"

"Just a wallflower."

Winston gestured to her. "This is the woman I am going to marry one day, brother."

Peter looked as surprised as Charlotte was at that bold announcement. Hadn't Winston said she was to be a secret?

Peter smirked. "Well, well, well. One wife is not enough, so you're going to complicate your life with two? Bad form, brother."

"There'll only be one. Brother, I'd like to introduce you to Miss Charlotte Waters."

"Waters? Waters? Where do I know that name?"

Charlotte winced. "I have eccentric parents who prefer the silence of other people's libraries better than dining as their guests."

"Oh, right. Now I remember." Peter stood up and stretched. "Once tried to talk to your father, and he told me I needed to broaden my horizons. See the world before there was nothing new to discover in it. I must admit, I've considered that a lot lately."

"That does sound like something my father would say to a young man, but why only lately?"

"I suspect I need a better profession. One that doesn't scandalize my poor older brother." Peter looked between them again. "Should I offer congratulations to you both now or later?"

"You didn't last time."

Peter pulled a face. "Offering my sympathies would be more apt there, I think. I'd be very grateful to not have Elizabeth become part of the family. Too bossy for my taste. Do marry him, Miss Waters, although I'm afraid you'll wed the lesser Bell."

Winston hugged his brother. "Don't ever change."

Charlotte cleared her throat to draw their attention. "Lord Peter, I feel I must ask your opinion. Your brother was almost run down by a pair of horses, beaten by several men, shot at and pursued by even more men, and yesterday, he was abducted and left in a house meant for *you* to live in. Can you imagine anyone with a reason to show him so much violent contempt in recent weeks?"

"Not me, nor any of the family. Uncle Percy is peculiar, but he's not left his estate in years. I certainly haven't seen him lurking about. Cousin Albert might want the job but he's too dim to commit murder for it. The only real reason I can think to do away with Winston would be to stop his wedding taking place, which he's about to do for you, I believe. I'm too young to be leg-shackled to that shrew. Promise me you'll stay alive long enough so I don't have to marry her."

"Why would Winston's death mean you had to marry Elizabeth?"

"Yes, well. I'd be Hurlston then, wouldn't I. It's always been the Earl of Hurlston's fate to marry Elizabeth."

She looked quickly at Winston. "Is that true?"

Winston rubbed his jaw. "I suppose it might, in a manner of speaking."

"I don't understand. It's Winston's marriage contract."

"Now there, I'm afraid to say, you're wrong, Miss Waters. Our father was shrewd when he wanted to expand his holdings though marriage. He pledged his heir to marry his neighbor's female relation."

"That is common knowledge."

"His *heir*—not Winston by name. If Winston dies, it's my neck on the chopping block."

Charlotte frowned. "So, you would have to marry Elizabeth in his place. After a period of mourning, I hope."

"Exactly. I really have nothing to gain if my brother were suddenly to fall down dead. I'd inherit the estate and Elizabeth, too. And that would mean Hunt as well, since he's forever hanging about like a bad smell."

"Leave our friend out of it. He's taken himself back to the country, so you can have no reason to complain about him anymore."

Peter shook his head. "Oh no he hasn't. He's still in London."

"Nonsense. He accepted the use of a carriage rather than take the mail coach, home."

Charlotte turned to Winston. "I got into your carriage. It had your crest upon the door."

"Yes, I had two in Town with crests. Hunt took the older one."

"I never knew you had more than one here. That's why I joined you, or I mean, *him*."

Winston stared down at her a moment, but she was sure he didn't see her. He turned slightly to address his brother. "Where did you see Lucien Hunt and when?"

"Before you imprisoned me, of course. I'm sure he didn't see *me*, though. He was leaving the hell with friends at the time, and since I didn't want to talk to him I kept my distance."

"Hunt doesn't have any friends but us in London."

"He does now. Three hard looking fellows, they were. I didn't get the usual wave from the coachman, come to think of it."

"Or he's a new man employed by Hunt," Charlotte whispered to Winston. "I don't know your coachman but did any groom try to prevent your abduction?"

Winston's jaw clenched. "No."

"No." Charlotte put her hand on Winston's arm. "Do you think…"

"…my oldest friend is trying to stop my marriage?"

"Yes. Hunt might want Elizabeth," Peter murmured, joining them in whispering. "And good luck to him if he does."

Winston walked away from them both, his hand over his mouth. Charlotte, who had never met Hunt, looked up at Peter. "What does he look like?"

"Who, Hunt? I don't know that I can describe him well enough. As tall as Winston. Not so handsome. He's a bachelor and has always fancied himself Elizabeth's friend, too. Always wears a smile when she's about now I think about it further." Peter glanced down at his chest and plucked at his wrinkled shirt. "I don't suppose my brother abducted me a fresh set of clothes?"

"I doubt it," she warned.

"Oh well, I guess I'll just have to risk giving offense to my mother again when I go home. She's got a thing about keeping up appearances."

"She's not wrong. You stink of gin and cigar," she whispered. "Excuse me."

Charlotte moved to Winston's side, and when he didn't acknowledge her immediately, she took hold of his hand. His skin was icy cold. "Winston?"

"It's true. All of it." He rocked back on his heels. "Hunt is out to get me. But I can hardly believe he'd go so far."

"People will do anything to get what they want."

"That's why he came to London. Not to attend the wedding but put a stop to it."

He put his hands over his face, and Charlotte's heart hurt for him. "You couldn't have known? You had no reason to suspect him?"

Winston's head shot up. "No."

"What about Elizabeth?"

"Elizabeth doesn't know about the threats against my life. I didn't want her upset, or Mother upset, either."

"She'll have Hunt to comfort her if he succeeds in sending you off," Peter murmured, buttoning up his coat. "She'd never suspect him."

"I didn't suspect him!"

"Where should we start looking for Mr. Hunt?" Charlotte asked.

"We go home first. Warn mother and Elizabeth to be on their guard. You're in danger now, too, Peter, so you will come with us," Winston told his brother.

"I wasn't planning to stay behind. I'll be right by your side."

"Do you think he'd harm your mother or Elizabeth? They're alone in that house."

"Dear God, if he hurts either one…" He might not want to marry Elizabeth anymore but he cared about her. He only hoped her father was home to protect her from Hunt. "The servants know Hunt is welcome. They'd let him in."

"We'll need weapons," Charlotte suggested to Peter, sending him toward the door so she could talk to Winston alone for a moment. "You must promise me to be very careful when we arrive at your home. Keep the wall at your back at all times."

Winston smiled grimly. "I take it you're coming home with me?"

"Yes, of course, I'll come. I'm worried about your mother."

Winston strode straight for the door, calling out, "Peter, tell Exeter we're going to need a parasol, too!"

Chapter Twenty-Four

Winston's butler stared stony-faced at him over the top of Winston's hat and gloves. "I'm happy to see you've returned, my lord."

"Are you? Why?"

Damned if he now didn't doubt the sincerity of every word spoken to him today.

The butler blinked in surprise at the odd question from him. "I, ah… It will please Lady Hurlston to have you back at home. She's been asking if you'd returned every hour since she rose."

"I said you were her favorite," Peter muttered, nudging Winston in the ribs. "Bet she didn't ask about me?"

"She did not, Lord Peter, because I always inform her if I know your whereabouts first thing every morning."

Charlotte was next in line for attention and offered the butler a warm smile. "It's good to see you again, sir."

"May I take your parasol?" the fellow queried.

"If you don't mind, I shall keep it with me," She tapped the tip of her borrowed parasol lightly upon the parquetry. "You never know when it will come in handy."

"And Mr. Berringer, too." The butler looked his friend over. "May I take your hat and great coat?"

Berringer patted his side where he'd concealed a pistol—just in case one was needed before they reached Winston's study, where he kept his own. "I'll keep the coat if you don't mind. Definitely a chill in the air today."

"You may take mine," Exeter offered, passing over his hat and gloves and great coat.

The duke's decision to join them had come as a surprise.

"We'll find Mother and then go to my study second," Winston announced, striding into the nearest room.

Winston made it as far as two steps in before he spotted Elizabeth. She was seated, a piece of embroidery in her hands. She smiled. "There you are."

He rushed to her. "Are you alright?"

"Of course. Whatever could be wrong?"

He caught her by the elbow and drew her to her feet. "There's a situation. I'm sure you're not in any danger but you'll need to stay close."

"My lord, you're scaring me."

"There's nothing for you to be afraid of, I'm sure. Just stay close and do as I say. Where's your father?"

"Upstairs."

"Right. And mother?"

"Sleeping, I should think." She glanced past him to his companions. "What's going on?"

Charlotte moved forward. "I'll check on you mother."

"She's resting." Elizabeth warned. But then eyes narrowed on Charlotte and he saw anger reflected there. "My lord, what is she doing here?"

"She's ah…" Winston floundered. He hadn't thought of the consequences of bringing Charlotte home with him. "We'll talk later. I trust you remember Mr. Berringer and the Duke of Exeter."

The duke jostled to the front. "Miss Mayflower, a pleasure to see you again."

Elizabeth dipped him a deep curtsy. "Your grace. We are honored by your visit."

"I'll find Lady Hurlston and bring her to you," Charlotte whispered, slipping away before he could stop her. Both of them had been abducted, and he still didn't know what purpose that had served anyone.

Winston wanted to call her back. But the first thing he needed to do was talk to his mother and explain the situation to her. The danger. His suspicions about Hunt. His falling in love with Charlotte instead of Elizabeth and his plans to call off the wedding today.

The latter could wait though.

"We'll join you in my study shortly."

He grasped Elizabeth by the elbow and steered her along at his side. "Have you seen Lucien Hunt?"

"He returned home."

"Do you know if he could have reason to come back? Do you know of any new friends he might have made during his recent visit to town? Where he might stay?"

"I'm not sure why you're asking me."

"I have it on good authority Hunt has returned to Town. Has he called here in the past few days?"

"I'm sure I don't."

Winston found Charlotte leaning over his mother, shaking her. "Winston, I cannot rouse her."

Winston raced forward to see. Mother was quite still, and no matter how Charlotte called or shook her, not an eyelash fluttered. Charlotte turned to him and whispered, "Is she known to take laudanum during the day?"

"No, never."

Charlotte suddenly sniffed the air around his mother. "It's the same scent as when I was taken."

Winston inhaled sharply, catching a whiff of the same scent he remembered, too. "Hunt has been here already."

"Hunt never left you arrogant bastard," Lucien Hunt replied, emerging from behind the curtains hanging behind Winston's insensible mother. He was also holding a pistol loosely in his hand. The pistol that should have been in

Winston's study desk drawer, if he was not mistaken. Elizabeth gasped and backed away to a safer distance.

Peter nudged Winston in the ribs. "I told you this was a bad idea."

"I don't remember you saying that," Winston murmured.

"'Course, I did. Miss Waters heard me, I'm sure."

"I only remember you asking if you had time to change your clothes," Charlotte murmured, moving forward a step. Her eyes were locked on Hunt, her grip on the parasol tight. "Good morning, sir. I don't believe we've been introduced, but we've met, haven't we?"

Hunt ignored Charlotte completely.

"That was you I saw riding in Hyde Park with a companion," she said, attempting to get a rise out of Winston's adversary. "Surely you remember the occasion, sir. Your first attempt to dispose of your rival, wasn't it?"

Hunt's lips twitched.

"Not the first, then, nor the last was it?" Charlotte noted with a dip of her head. "It's hard to be committed to your cause when you're trying to hide your identity like that."

Hunt glanced at Charlotte then. "He never saw me coming until you spoiled my fun, slut."

Charlotte's lips twitched into a dangerous smile. "I could call you names, too…or is your wish an unfulfilled dream still like mine?"

Winston took a pace forward as Hunt's jaw clenched. But then the next moment, he calmly placed the point of the pistol at the base of Mother's skull. "She's mine."

Charlotte's smile grew wider. "Do you want Lady Hurlston?"

"No."

"Ah, you mean Miss Mayflower then," Charlotte murmured, then she smiled again. "Your lover. Where is she now, then?"

Hunt glanced around and a worried expression crossed his face briefly when it was clear Elizabeth had fled the scene. "She'll be back. She always comes back to me."

Charlotte clucked her tongue. "Are you sure she will this time? Attempted murder of an earl carries a harsh penalty. Hanging I think if you're convicted."

"Then I'd better make sure I end you all while I can," Hunt said as he turned the weapon on Charlotte.

It all happened so fast.

Charlotte unfurled her parasol and threw it up in front of herself even as she dove sideways to land on the floor by Mother's feet, pulling her down onto the carpeted floor.

Winston lunged for Lucien Hunt but was knocked aside by another body flying through the air as a shot rang out.

Peter landed on top of Winston, winding him momentarily. He shoved his brother off and scrambled after Hunt, catching him attempting to reach a second pistol hidden behind his back.

Winston lunged and bore his old friend to the ground, sending the pistol flying from Hunt's hand, landing across the room. Winston got Hunt under him, pinned him down, and hit him—then hit him a few more times for good measure, until he stopped fighting back.

He glanced around quickly to see how everyone fared.

The duke and Berringer burst into the room, both holding a variety of weapons. "The damn door was stuck. Had to break the glass. What did we miss?"

Winston laughed. "A feat of heroics never before enacted, and I hope never to again."

Peter groaned. "Hit him again but for me, brother."

Winston considered it and then shrugged. "I have the answers I needed. Hunt was behind it all."

Yet Hunt started to grin maliciously. "You think you know it all? You know nothing of the truth. If you have anything important to say to your brother, I wouldn't waste any time."

"Winston!" Charlotte gasped, then scrambled on all fours across the room to Peter's side. "Peter's wounded!"

Winston pulled back his arm and knocked the grin off Hunt's face once and for all.

Berringer pried him away, promising he and the duke would tie Hunt securely and send for the watch—and a physician—while he saw to his brother.

Winston hurried across the room, removing his cravat along the way. "Idiot! What were you thinking, jumping in front of me like that?"

"It was a leap, brother."

"Keep him distracted," Charlotte murmured as she snatched Winston's cravat out of his hands and peeked under Peter's waistcoat.

Winston shook his head. "Why did you have to go and do this?"

"I thought of you and the happy marriage you're going to have with her," Peter whispered, gesturing to Charlotte. "Have lots of sex when I'm gone."

Winston scowled. "Don't talk like that. I'm never letting you out of my sight again."

Charlotte clucked her tongue, pushing the cravat under the shirt and against Peter's side. "It's no use."

"Don't say that," Winston begged. "The physician is on his way even now!"

"It won't matter. He'll still live—and have a scar to flaunt for the ladies, too," she whispered, winking at him. She put her hand on Winston's shoulder. "He's bleeding less than you did. Put your hand against his side and hold the cravat in place for a minute or two. I want to look at your mother again."

She stood and left them on the floor.

Peter tried to peer at his injured side, then glanced at Charlotte as she sat his mother back up in a more comfortable position. "She seems to be taking your little drama in her stride. No hartshorn needed at all for her. I couldn't even shock her."

"She's one in a million, *my Charlotte*."

Peter grinned. "That's better. You mean it now."

Winston stood and helped his brother up to sit in a chair. He left him there, holding his side, and went to Charlotte and his mother.

"She's just starting to come around," she whispered. "What do we tell her?"

"Everything when she's alert enough to understand." Winston glanced around the chamber, finding Elizabeth had returned. But she stood frozen against the far wall. Her gaze was fixed on Lucien Hunt, an arrested look on her face.

Charlotte noticed the direction of his gaze. "You should explain what's been going on to Elizabeth, though. She trusted Hunt and he betrayed you both."

Winston tugged down his waistcoat. "I shall indeed explain everything to her right now."

He stalked across the room, passing Hunt along the way. Berringer had him tied up in a chair and he wasn't a danger to anyone right now. Winston scooped up the discarded pistol and approached Elizabeth. "Are you all right?"

Her eyes were huge. Frightened and scared. "Yes."

"Do you understand that Hunt tried to kill me today?"

"Yes.

"It's not the first time."

"Yes," she answered in the same flat tone as all her previous replies.

Concerned she was about to faint, Winston reached for her elbow. Elizabeth flinched away from him.

"It's all right, my dear. You are perfectly safe now." He set the pistol aside on top of the pianoforte beside her. "Hunt will be removed from the house soon and the magistrate and courts will deal with him. There's no need for you to be afraid anymore. You'll never see him again."

Mr. Mayflower appeared at the door then, wig askew, shirt untucked, hair sticking up at all angles. "What the devil is going on down here? I won't be woken by rabble rousing at this hour on any day!"

Winston turned to him. "There's been an incident. Nothing to worry about now. Hunt tried to kill me."

Mayflower stuck his finger in his ear and wiggled it about. "Now what was that you said?"

"Hunt tried to kill me," he repeated more slowly.

Mayflower gaped. "You're serious?"

"Never more so."

He left Mayflower reeling and turned back to Elizabeth. While he'd been speaking to her father, she'd moved toward Hunt. "Elizabeth, come away from him."

"No."

"Winston," Charlotte said urgently, rising to her feet. "Be careful."

Winston headed for Elizabeth, intending to drag her away. "He's bound, what more harm can he do to me?"

"Elizabeth holds a pistol now," she whispered.

Winston froze, and glanced behind him. The second pistol he'd left on the pianoforte was no longer there. "Don't hurt him," he cried, fearful of what she might intend.

"I have already hurt him." Elizabeth reached out and caressed Hunt's face. "I'm so sorry."

"I broke my promise."

"No, you didn't. Together?"

"Forever," Hunt promised her, with a look of love that could not be mistaken for anything but complete devotion.

"Oh my God. They planned this together," Charlotte whispered, horror written all over her face.

Elizabeth turned her gaze on Charlotte then. "You've no idea what it's like to have no say in who you marry."

"But you have a choice now," Charlotte began, taking a step toward Elizabeth.

Elizabeth pointed the pistol at Charlotte, then let the muzzle drop to where his mother slept on, unaware of the danger. "Don't come any closer."

"Please don't hurt her," Charlotte begged. "She loves you as the daughter she never had."

"She's as bad as everyone else!" Elizabeth complained. "Always telling me what I want, as if she ever knew the real me. *Hunt* knows what I want."

"Freedom," Hunt murmured. "Do it now, my love. I'll see you soon."

Elizabeth smiled down on him and the smile chilled him through to the bone.

Then Elizabeth moved the pistol, aiming not at anyone in the room, but at her own head. Winston rushed her then, catching her wrist and forcing the point of the weapon toward the ceiling.

The pistol barked and plaster rained down upon them both. Elizabeth shrieked, a high and insane sound that she'd been thwarted. Winston wrapped his arms tight about her as she fought to gain her freedom. "Lucien," she screamed.

Winston dragged her away from Hunt, who'd done nothing to stop her from attempting to kill herself. In fact, he'd encouraged it. Even now, as he gazed upon Elizabeth, an insanely happy light shone bright in his eyes whispering, *my love, my love forever*.

Winston shuddered, sickened. Hunt had wanted to watch her take her own life. That wasn't a love he understood.

With help of footmen, Elizabeth was taken to another room, kicking and screaming for Hunt and wishing Winston to hell. Eventually she was subdued, drugged with laudanum by her father so she couldn't hurt herself or anyone else.

"She's mad," Mayflower muttered, over and over.

"Yes, perhaps," Winston agreed, feeling he'd played an unwitting part in that, perhaps. He'd pressured her to say yay or nay to marriage, then immediately announced their wedding date. But if he'd known of her and Hunt, he never would have. "Sir, I cannot marry Elizabeth now, given everything that has happened today. And even before knowing this about her, I was going to speak to you about ending the engagement."

Mayflower looked at him with surprise.

"I'm in love, and I thought it wouldn't have been fair to marry Elizabeth under those circumstances. I wish she'd thought the same and told me…because I would have let her go easily."

Mayflower shook his head and looked away. "I understand. You always wanted to do right by her. This will ruin me when everyone learns what she tried to do."

Mayflower had been part of his life just as long as Elizabeth had. His reputation would be shattered if word spread that she'd been part of a plot to kill Winston to escape the marriage neither of them wanted, and then had tried to kill herself. He wouldn't like for his own family to be embroiled in such a scandal, either.

"We can try to keep her part in the affair quiet," he offered.

Mayflower looked at him with such gratitude that Winston felt embarrassed. "How can I ever apologize for—"

"Don't. Just see that she's made comfortable and safe from herself. Take her to Bath. It's where she wanted to be, and I promise to never go there again. I'll make arrangements for you both to leave London today with an armed escort for your protection and servants to help in case she becomes distressed on the journey. What becomes of her after that is no one's business but yours. Take care of her. I may not have loved her, but I cared about her."

"What of Hunt?"

Winston pursed his lips. His friend had betrayed him and meant him and Charlotte harm. He could never be forgiven for that. "That is out of my hands now, I'm afraid. The duke has sent for the magistrate. It all could have been avoided if either one had just told me the truth about their feelings for each other."

"Hunt spoke to me last year. Tried to talk me into giving up the alliance with your family so he could have Elizabeth and her dowry instead. I said no, of course. I'd given my word, and that was that."

"It might have been wise to inform me I had a rival for her hand," Winston chided, then sighed. What did that matter now? He'd lost a best friend and a bride today. He had a gentleman's agreement to call off the wedding to Elizabeth. And he'd have it in writing before Mayflower took Elizabeth away with him, too.

He was lucky to still have his health.

And Charlotte.

He turned on his heel when he heard voices in the hall and left Mayflower to wring his hands over his daughter. Hunt was just being dragged out, still tied to a chair, to the front hall.

"Elizabeth!" he called.

But of course, Elizabeth, in her current condition, couldn't hear him anymore.

Exeter intercepted him. "I'll handle this to begin, but you'll be called to stand as a witness to my almost-murder."

"*Your* murder?"

"Well, I was in the house too, wasn't I?" Exeter set his hat at a jaunty angle on his head. "I'll make sure he's convicted and punished to the limits of the law. I'll leave you to follow as soon as you've tidied up here. Until later, Hurlston."

When he left, Berringer followed but paused in front of Winston, grinning, "There's no stopping him once he decides to take over. This way, if he's involved in the trial, he thinks you'll not become distracted from marrying Charlotte."

Winston grinned as well. "Nothing could ever distract me from that."

Berringer nodded. "I'll let my wife know what's happened here today, and she'll tell anyone who needs to hear the truth about all this. I recommend Gretna Green for an expedient wedding, and do it soon. I hear the roads only get worse at this time of the year."

"I'll keep that in mind," he promised, seeing the fellow off.

Winston let out a long shuddering breath. He was safe and he was free of a wedding that should never have been.

Only now he had to arrange another, and nothing would stop him from having his way.

He rushed back into the drawing room, only to find it empty of everyone. But he could hear voices coming from farther along the hall. He followed the sound, finding Mama, Peter and Charlotte taking tea together. He quickly joined them.

Mother held out her hand to him immediately. "Hurlston, I had the most unpleasant dream, and your brother promises it was all true," she murmured. "You were there, Peter and Miss Waters. Elizabeth, of course, and the Duke of Exeter was there as well. But Hunt... Someone screamed, and a pistol shot rang out through the house. I was quite frightened until Charlotte promised everything was all right again now."

He crouched down beside his mother's chair, smiling at his confused mother, and took up her tiny hand. He noticed that she had at last called him by his title, too. He'd feared she never would. "Mama I've so much to tell you and some of it is unpleasant, and some incredibly good. I'm afraid I'm going to need your patience and understanding in the coming year.

There will likely be a scandal. But the most important detail, for now, is that you understand I will not be marrying Elizabeth anymore."

Mother gulped and her hands fluttered about, revealing her distress. "But why?"

Winston took a seat and began his long story, beginning with that day in the park until the most recent events. Everything he'd kept from her, the dangers, the delights, and the altercation she'd missed while drugged. She cried when she heard of Elizabeth's love for Hunt and what she'd conspired to have come about. "She would have loved you if not for Hunt."

"We will never know if that is true or not. Given her behavior today, it is likely we will never see her again. I would like you to promise not to seek her out. She's more devious than you know."

"But I thought she *wanted* to marry you," she gasped out finally. "I was so blind."

"As was I, but no more," he promised.

Mother suddenly glanced at Charlotte who seemed decidedly nervous as she sat across from them.

Charlotte was the best part of his story. He hoped mother would accept that they would wed eventually.

"Now I am afraid I must go. I want to ensure Elizabeth's removal from the house and then I must play my part in dealing with Hunt." Winston smiled down on his mother. "Can I leave you and Peter to escort Charlotte home for me now? Her parents will be beside themselves with worry."

"Yes, yes of course," Mother promised but then she frowned. "Do you really love her?"

"More than life itself." He kissed the top of mother's head and reached for Charlotte's hand. He drew her aside. "I'll call on you as soon as I can tomorrow."

Charlotte nodded. "I'll be waiting."

"That's all I ask," he murmured before he hurried away.

Chapter Twenty-Five

The last thing Charlotte had ever expected was for her mother to welcome a chance to entertain a countess. But here they all were the next day, Mother and Lady Hurlston, and Lord Peter sipping tea and chatting as if it were something they did every day. "Can I offer you more tea, Sophia?"

"Yes, I would be very glad of it, Olivia. It's been a most distressing time," Lady Hurlston confessed.

"Such a shocking betrayal." Mother glanced at Charlotte. "The young do make a mess of things."

Charlotte sank a little lower in her chair. She also noticed that Lord Peter did the same.

Mother had not asked her to explain very much upon her return last night. Mother and Father too had met her at the door, asked if Charlotte was well, and whether father needed to dust off his dueling pistols. Charlotte had promised that further violence was the last thing she needed.

And then this morning she had sat them down and explained what she'd been up to for the past week. She thought it prudent to leave key details that might incriminate herself and cause father to fetch his dueling pistols though. She could not have Winston shot at again.

"Imagine the foolishness of my son almost letting this clever girl slip through his fingers," Lady Hurlston chided. "He knew I had a fondness for sensible young ladies."

Mother's brow rose. "Not always so sensible."

Lady Hurlston leaned forward and lightly touched Mother's

hand. "Forgive her, Olivia, she acted out of love for my son. We cannot fault her for that."

Mama smiled at Lady Hurlston over her teacup. "The young are always so impulsive and headstrong."

"Indeed, they are. Take my younger son here. If he'd ever stuck to his studies, he could have done anything at all with his life."

Charlotte hid a smile as Peter squirmed even lower in his chair. He was here at Winston's request, not because he wanted to be. Winston was meeting with the magistrate still. "At least my eldest son has a sensible head on his shoulders. He's sure to join us soon."

Mama started to tell the countess of their upcoming adventure just as the front knocker rang through the house.

Charlotte waited on pins and needles until the door opened. It was Eugenia Berringer and Aurora Hillcrest come to see her. They embraced and exchanged greetings before sitting again for even yet more tea.

"Don't worry, he'll be here soon," Peter whispered to her.

"I don't doubt him."

"That's why I like you so much. You're practically jumping out of your skin in your eagerness to see him," he whispered again. "She never did."

Charlotte winced. It was true she could hardly keep still today. She'd been glancing out the window from when she'd woken until the countess' arrival. Hoping to see Winston striding along the street toward her door.

"Would anyone care for more tea?"

Aurora caught her eye. "I wonder if you have the time now to return that book, the one I lent to you last month."

"Oh, yes," Charlotte promised, thankful for any excuse to leave the room. "Yes, of course. I'll get it for you now."

Aurora and Eugenia stood. "We'll come with you, if you don't mind."

"Not at all," Charlotte agreed as they hurried from the room like naughty children. Once outside, Charlotte grinned and hurried them all upstairs. After they reached her room, she shut the door. Charlotte rushed for the window to look out but there was still no sign of Winston.

Aurora's gaze was alight with excitement. "We know what's been going on between the two of you," Aurora whispered. "Do you love him very much, Charlotte?"

"Yes. I love him all the way," she admitted to her friends. She loved Winston, but there was a chance she'd never see him again after tomorrow if he didn't come today. Mother and Father were still leaving on their voyage.

"I'm so happy for you both. We never thought he'd be happy with an arranged match," Eugenia promised.

"Yes, and I completely agreed with you at the time for entirely personal reasons."

Aurora laughed. "What a happy surprise this will be for everyone that loves you."

Surprise or a shock.

Charlotte moved toward her trunks and started opening them. There was no point putting off the inevitable. No matter what happened next, she had to pack away her belongings. "Mother and Father leave tomorrow morning, at first light. It's bound to be a bit brisk setting sail at this time of year."

She put her first piece of clothing into a trunk. She rushed back into her dressing closet and brought forth all the gowns she might never need again. "If he doesn't come in time, these are for you to pick through to share with others. I hope you can find a new friend my height who can wear them."

Aurora's hands closed over hers. "He'll come."

"I hope so."

"If he doesn't, I've got a nice sized closet to hide you in," Aurora offered.

Charlotte laughed. "I really hope he comes then. Your closet is so bursting with gowns that there'd be hardly enough room for me, too."

"He'll come and we will all dance at your wedding and spend every Christmas together," Eugenia promised.

Charlotte teared up, too, then and hugged the women who'd befriended a hopeless wallflower. Christmas was her favorite season. "I'm sure it will be the best Christmas ever."

Eugenia cleared her throat and pulled Charlotte down to sit by her side. "There's something I need to tell you."

"What is it? What's wrong?"

"I'm with child," Eugenia admitted.

"No!"

"Indeed, it is true, and we wanted you to know before you left."

Charlotte gaped and then hugged her friend. This was so exciting! "Who else knows?"

"Shh, not so loud. Just the three of us, and Teddy, of course. We want you to be Godmother."

Her eyes filled with tears again. "Oh. I should like that very much, but what if I'm not here when the child arrives."

"You will be, and Hurlston will be asked to be godfather." She murmured. "But remember, you must keep this quiet."

"Do they know? The duke and duchess, I mean?

Eugenia shook her head. "Thaddeus says Exeter wouldn't be able to keep it a secret, so telling him is the last thing we plan to do."

That made Charlotte feel so honored. She turned to Aurora. "Have you some deep dark secret you want to confess to me before I go?"

"Yes." She sat forward. "I hate to be the one to tell you this, but I'm in love with…that last bit of cake downstairs."

Charlotte laughed. She'd never had better friends in her whole life. They were always trying to cheer her up with silliness. She'd been part of something so special. She didn't want to give that up.

She took a glance around the chamber and continued packing until all her essentials were done. All in all, she wouldn't be taking very much with her on a voyage, really. "Well, that's it for me for now. I can tell my parents I've made a start."

Aurora stood. "We want to stay with you today."

"I'll probably cry."

And then she was crying. She couldn't seem to help it. It had been the most exhilarating, worrying, frightful week.

"We won't leave you alone."

"She won't be alone—and she's not leaving," Winston announced, stepping into the room. "She's going to marry me by special license before the week is out."

"Perhaps we ought to make ourselves scarce," Eugenia Berringer murmured as she caught her cousin's arm and towed her to the door.

Charlotte watched Winston's face as he advanced. When he reached her, he wiped away her tears with his thumb. "You saved me, and now I'm saving you."

Her brow furrowed, but he wrapped his arms around her and squeezed her tight. "Your Father has agreed to stay until the wedding if it is done by special license. Mother has offered to help your mother with anything you need so she can continue packing without interruption. They'll stay for the wedding and then they will go off in one of my carriages. Without you, as you wanted."

"Winston?"

"I know I am rushing things by accelerating the wedding, but I'm not about to let the love of my life slip through my fingers. The thought of never seeing you again for two long years is utterly unbearable."

Charlotte looked up at him, unable to contain her happiness. He'd done everything he'd promised and more than he ever needed to. "Can this be this easy to have my dream come true?"

"My dream too, remember." He pulled her back into his arms and heaved a heavy sigh.

"We could wait. Wait for everything to settle."

"And where might you be then? Far out of my reach, threatening elephants with only a parasol. You act brave, but I know they scare you witless."

"What about Miss Mayflower?"

"Elizabeth and her father are gone. My betrothal is at an end at last. I have it all in writing. There's nothing to stop us now."

"Will it seem cold and calculated to wed so quickly."

"Charlotte...Elizabeth wanted me dead. I would have let her go if she'd revealed a partiality for someone else. I cannot forgive her for that."

"How is your mother taking the news? I haven't really had a chance to speak to her alone yet."

"Surprisingly well. I spoke to her briefly before coming up. She loves me, and prefers I not be married to a would-be murderess but rather the one who did all she could to save me. Repeatedly. There will not be a way to avoid having the family scandal aired in public through Hunt's trial, though."

She smoothed her hands over his chest. "But you will be free of it all one day, and alive, and that is all that really matters to me."

He grinned. "I was hoping you'd see the bright side."

"I am truly astonished by everything that has happened. Why on earth couldn't Elizabeth love you?"

"*You* love me, and that is enough." Winston took up her hand. "I wouldn't be here now, alive today, if not for you."

She blushed. "You would have managed to survive without me."

"No, I really don't think so." He kissed the back of her hand. "You are the best thing that has happened to me in all my life. I cannot bear for us to be apart."

Charlotte glanced at the door and back at him. "Do my parents know you came upstairs?"

"Since I'm proposing, they were easily convinced to let the proprieties lapse just this once. I promised to return with good news."

Charlotte stared at him, and then one brow rose high. "Well? Get on with it."

Winston chuckled and then sank to his knees. Charlotte nearly danced on the spot as he caressed her hand, and he looked up to her face. She belonged to him, even before he spoke the words that she had waited all her life to hear him speak.

He swallowed and stared at her a long time.

"I have so much to say, and I want our marriage to start off the right way. With total honesty, commitment, and hope for a brighter future. I want to say just the right words to convey how much I've come to care about you. I have been in agony, thinking how narrowly I avoided a miserable life without you by my side."

His words brought a flush of heat to her cheeks.

"I fell in love with you by degrees since that day in Green Park, and perhaps even before that. Seduced in secret by a woman I trust with my life. You are the woman who seduced me without me realizing it could ever happen. I love your bravery, your kindness, your patience, and…"

She reached out and put her fingers over his lips to silence him. Anymore and her face would burst into flame from embarrassment. "It's all right, Winston. I don't need to hear anymore. Yes, I would be the happiest of women to become your wife."

She kissed him and it was like they'd always been meant for each other.

Epilogue

Winston turned his face up to the clear blue sky, noticing that the seagulls whirling over the ships in dock had increased in number. It was a perfect day for a homecoming, but it was a tedious business waiting for the ship's passengers to disembark.

He brought his gaze back to earth and the woman nestled in his arms. "Can you see them yet?"

"Not from here. There are too many people waiting ahead of us. And I'm still too short," Charlotte complained.

"The perfect height for me," he promised. Winston rested his chin on the top of Charlotte's head, little caring that they were making a spectacle of themselves by their embrace. He cared not who saw them standing together like this and gossiped later. The worst they could say now was far less damning than had been thrown about during the trial for his would-be murderer and former best friend—Lucien Hunt. A man who'd hung for his crimes against two peers.

It had been an ugly business indeed, and Charlotte had unfortunately been drawn into that nightmare of allegations when Elizabeth's involvement had come out. Hunt had accused Winston of keeping Charlotte as a mistress and driving him to act on Elizabeth's behalf.

The whispers and gossip had become frenzied then, and hurtful. Charlotte had once been a wallflower, and many thought she'd unfairly benefited somehow.

But Charlotte had been his true love all along. Eventually people had packed away their prejudices, but he'd lost respect for a few members of society along the way.

They'd been married two blissful years now, and Winston never stopped showering her with his love and affection and constant attention.

He fixed his gaze on the quarterdeck of the ship before him and heaved an exasperated sigh that disembarking took so long. A week after their marriage, Charlotte's parents had taken off on their voyage. Peter had been invited to join the Waters on their travels, and he'd actually jumped at the chance to go. That had relieved Charlotte, but worried Winston a great deal. He'd never gone so long without seeing his younger brother.

He looked down at Charlotte's pinched face. She was incredibly anxious to see her parents again. She had missed them, despite her initial claims that she wouldn't. "We can move closer if you want."

Charlotte clutched his arm tighter about her body. "No. This is as close as I need to be to any ship."

He chuckled softly. "I'd not let you board her."

"I'll not allow you to, either, no matter how innocent the offer made."

He chuckled softly. "Your parents are unlikely to want my company. They've suffered Peter's for two long years now."

"Hopefully they did not leave him behind in their last port of call like they did me once."

"They left you behind?"

"They boarded the wrong ship. I had to wait a month before they realized their mistake and returned for their books."

"I'm sure they returned for you, too."

Charlotte huffed, and Winston drew her tighter to him. Two years married and the time together had flown by. Not even the arrival of their children had come between them.

He glanced over his shoulder at the carriage and smiled at the pair of young faces pressed against the glass, and the older one hovering immediately behind. Charlotte would never hear of leaving their children behind. Or his mother, for that matter either. Winston didn't mind the extra baggage. The children made Mama happier than she'd ever been since his father had passed away.

"There!" Charlotte cried out.

There was Peter, who looked to be a whole head taller than the gathered crowd. Winston shot up his hand to wave and received an answering wave in return. It took an eternity for Peter to shuffle the older couple through the crowd toward them, though. He looked harried indeed when he finally reached their spot.

Winston embraced his brother, who he'd not seen since his marriage to Charlotte. "Brother."

"Brother!" Peter exclaimed, then drew back and grinned as he looked him up and down. "Have you always been this short?"

Winston had to admit, it did seem he needed to look up to his brother now. "Yes, I suppose I must have been. Is that all you have to say for yourself then?"

"You look happier, too." He turned to Charlotte, who'd turned to first greet her parents. "Sister."

She curtsied to Peter. "Welcome home."

Peter glanced around and then down to his feet. He stamped them. "It's good to be back on solid ground at last." And then his gaze fixed upon the carriage behind Winston, and his eyes slowly grew wide. "Twins? You might have warned me," Peter complained, placing a hand over his heart. "If they're both male, that's me out of the succession at last."

"You've a pair of nephews," Winston laughed. "And why should you have been spared the shock of discovering it was a pair at once? Imagine *my* shock. No one prepared me for that."

"Congratulations, old man."

"Enough of that 'old man' nonsense," Charlotte chided Peter. "Your brother is exactly the right age to have a wife and children."

"If you say so," Peter grudgingly agreed. "I'd better greet Mama, since she's clearly not coming out to meet me."

"It's the children," Winston murmured. "They've changed her life for the better."

Peter left them to say hello to his mother and be introduced to his nephews—James and Peter. He seemed quite overcome to hear the younger twin had been given his first name.

Mr. and Mrs. Waters nodded to Winston. "Well, we'll be getting along now, I suppose."

"But I thought you'd come home with us," Charlotte wailed in an exasperated tone.

"My dear girl, what need could you possibly have for a pair of crusty historians underfoot?"

"You're my parents," she reminded them. "You have grand-children now to tell your histories to."

The pair exchanged a long look. "There is that."

Winston leaned forward. "I have a library of rare books at home you haven't seen yet, and more at the town house in London, too. Charlotte has added to the collection in prepara-tion for your return, buying up anything she thought you hadn't read yet."

The pairs eyes lit up with excitement. "Well, why didn't you say you had such a perfect homecoming? Indeed, we should be happy to take a peek at your collection."

"Indeed yes," his mama-in-law enthused. "Lead the way to your library, my lord."

Winston shrugged at Charlotte and led them toward the traveling carriage, where Mother, a maid and the children waited to greet them. He helped them inside and shut the door firmly on them all. He moved back to Charlotte's side and put an arm about her waist. "Well, that was relatively easy to get them into the carriage."

"The books definitely swayed them." She looked up at him. "Has he seen it yet?"

"I don't believe so. Oh, Peter!" Winston called out. "Your carriage is over there."

Peter looked, turned a stunned face toward them, and then returned his gaze to the high-perch phaeton being held by a Hurlston servant. "You didn't!"

"Happy birthday, brother." He took his brother aside. "I sold the London town house and made a tidy profit. You'll stay with us now you're back, until it becomes inconvenient for you and you want a place of your own."

"I wouldn't have it any other way." Peter strode across the cobblestones and circled the conveyance, greeting the horses attached, and said hello to the young tiger waiting on the seat at the back. "Now this is a proper homecoming." He vaulted up to the seat and took up the reins, the servants wasted no time in scrambling out of the way. "Farewell!"

"I want to see you at home this month. Charlotte has a dinner planned."

"I'll be there, perhaps sooner than you when I'm driving this," he warned. "But first…"

He slapped the reins and took off as fast as the swirling crowd allowed.

Charlotte slipped her arm through his. "We will see him again, won't we?"

"I'm certain of it. He'll run out of money sooner or later," Winston warned.

"Let's hope not."

Winston sent the family carriage on its way and led Charlotte back to the smaller one he'd had follow them from the estate.

Charlotte settled in his arms as soon as they were underway. "I'm glad everyone is safely home in England again."

He kissed her brow. "Within a month, we might be wishing them far away."

"Mother and Father will take over the library, and likely eat all their meals there. Your mother will supervise the children's care as she usually does. Peter will come and go."

"What does that leave us to do with ourselves?"

Her fingers slipped across his thigh. "Plenty of time to explore each other...and perhaps make a daughter for us to spoil."

"I'll do my best to oblige," Winston promised as he drew down the carriage blinds and wasted no time following where their love for each other always led them.

Distinguished Rogues Series

Book 1: Chills (FREE READ)
The rogue she can't have is the only one she wants.

Book 2: Broken
His wicked ways could be the best hope for her future.

Book 3: Charity
Reclaiming the love of his life is bound to break a few rules.

Book 4: An Accidental Affair
Being good was a damned nuisance!

Book 5: Keepsake
The runaway bride is back to cause trouble!

Book 6: An Improper Proposal
Educating the innocent might have been a mistake.

Book 7: Reason to Wed
Duty is the last thing on his mind once they kiss.

Book 8: The Trouble with Love
Keeping a promise has never been harder!

Book 9: Married by Moonlight
The marriage mart is murder!

Book 10: Lord of Sin
In the battle between love and duty, the heart has the most to lose…

Book 11: The Duke's Heart
He's looking for love…just not for himself!

Book 12: Romancing the Earl
Can a broken heart be won?

Book 13: One Enchanted Christmas
He's betting on love…

Book 14: Desire by Design
It's the quiet ones that bear watching…

Book 15: His Perfect Bride
Accept no substitute when it comes to love…

Book 16: Pleasures of the Night
Friends with benefits has never been so tempting…

Book 17: Silver Bells
She didn't trust him in her youth, so how can she depend on him now?

Book 18: Seduced in Secret
Falling in love with the wrong woman has never felt so right…

More Regency Romance...

Wild Randalls Series
Book 1: Engaging the Enemy
Book 2: Forsaking the Prize
Book 3: Guarding the Spoils
Book 4: Hunting the Hero

Saints and Sinners Series
Book 1: The Duke and I
Book 2: A Gentleman's Vow
Book 3: An Earl of Her Own
Book 4: The Lady Tamed

Rebel Hearts Series
Book 1: The Wedding Affair
Book 2: An Affair of Honor
Book 3: The Christmas Affair
Book 4: An Affair so Right

Miss Mayhem Series
Book 1: Miss Watson's First Scandal
Book 2: Miss George's Second Chance
Book 3: Miss Radley's Third Dare
Book 4: Miss Merton's Last Hope

...and many more